Sugar and Ice

ALSO BY KATE MESSNER
The Brilliant Fall of Gianna Z.

Sugar and Ice

Kate Messner

Walker & Company
New York

First published in the United States of America in December 2010
by Walker Publishing Company, Inc., a division of Bloomsbury Publishing, Inc.
www.bloomsburykids.com

For information about permission to reproduce selections from this book, write to
Permissions, Walker BFYR, 175 Fifth Avenue, New York, New York 10010

Library of Congress Cataloging-in-Publication Data
Messner, Kate.
Sugar and ice / Kate Messner.
p.   cm.
Summary: When Russian skating coach Andrei Groshev offers farm girl
Claire a scholarship to train with the elite in Lake Placid, she
encounters a world of mean girls on ice, where competition is
everything.
ISBN 978-0-8027-2081-8 (hardcover)
I. Title.
PZ7.M5615Su 2010   [Fic]—dc22   2009054217

Book design by Nicole Gastonguay
Typeset by Westchester Book Composition
Printed in the U.S.A. by Quad/Graphics, Fairfield, Pennsylvania
2 4 6 8 10 9 7 5 3

For Ella, with love

Sugar and Ice

CHAPTER 1

Claire Marie Boucher!" Mom shouted extra loud across the sugarhouse, but the maple steam was so thick it just about swallowed up her voice anyhow. "Make sure you come straight home from the rink after the show's over. We don't have Holly and Camille to run pancakes this year, nor Austin to cook. And I've got Jake and Christopher running wild under my feet." Claire's brothers were fighting again instead of bringing in wood. A snowball flew in through the open screen door and sizzled into the bubbling sap.

"I'll be back by noon." Claire tossed her skating bag over her shoulder and stepped out of the steam into the cold March air. Even with the sun shining, spring wasn't ready to climb out of the snowdrifts and shake itself off just yet.

She already knew there wasn't enough help for sugaring weekend this year. Holly and Camille from the Ladue Farm left for college last August and hadn't even come back to visit. Austin Gonyea from the next hill over had traded in pancakes for a job tossing pizzas in Plattsburgh, half an hour away.

Even her cousin Charlotte, who used to spend every spare minute with Claire skating on the cow pond, was off skating on some fancy college rink in Pennsylvania. Claire's boots crunched through iced-over puddles all down the driveway. Who could blame them for leaving? Mojimuk Falls didn't have much to offer unless your life revolved around maple trees, like hers did. You could farm or work at the border, and that was about it. The very name of the place—Mojimuk—was the Abenaki word for "going away." Maybe that's why they all did.

Claire leaned against the mailbox to wait for Natalie. At least Natalie couldn't go anywhere for a while. They both had more than five years until graduation, and that was just fine. Five more years of skating on the cow pond as soon as it froze solid enough. Five years of milk-shake nights, talking about classes and skating and Nat's honeybees in their hives out by the orchard. Five years of boiling maple sap and serving up pancakes every March, fighting over who got to wait on the cute boys.

Tires crunched in the gravel at the end of the road, and Natalie's brother, Keene, pulled up in his rusty green truck. Claire climbed over his hockey bag to join Natalie on the duct-taped vinyl seat and waved a hand in front of her nose.

"Jeezum crow, Keene. How long you been driving that smelly hockey bag around?"

He reached over, pulled out a sock, and dangled it in front of her. "I'll have you know this sock is extremely valuable. I'm gonna set a world record—most times worn without washing."

Claire swatted the sock away and laughed as Keene pulled onto the main road.

"Yep," he said. "My name's gonna be up in lights."

"There are no lights in Mojimuk Falls, dork," Natalie said. She pulled off her knit hat, and her black hair fizzed out with static electricity. "You'll have to carve your name on a tree trunk or something."

"Go ahead. Laugh. But when I get outta here, I'm playing with the Rangers."

"When I get outta here, I'm living someplace with music and theater and art museums." Natalie reached for the radio as they drove past their dad's store, Rabideau Hardware. An award from Sticky-Do Incorporated hung in the window, honoring Rabideau Hardware for selling more Sticky-Do Duct Tape than any other store in the nation that year. Natalie sighed, pulled down the visor mirror, and rolled a layer of sparkly gloss over her chapped lips. "I want to live in a town known for something other than duct tape and sap."

"But you're still coming today, right?" Claire asked as the pickup pulled into the rink parking lot. "It's been so warm the sap's running like crazy. We could use the help."

"Of course I'm coming." Natalie unbuckled her seat belt. "But I'm going home to check on my bees first. It's getting warm, and I need to put in some sugar water for them."

"Oh come on, Nat. Today?" But Claire knew she wouldn't win an argument about Natalie's honeybees. No matter how much Nat talked about getting away from the farm when she got older, the hives she tended out by the orchards were her pride and joy. The bees made Claire nervous—there were just so many of them—so she kept her distance. "Isn't it early for them to be active? There aren't any flowers yet."

"They won't actually leave the hives for another month or so." Natalie jumped down from the truck. "They haven't been out since that one really warm weekend in February when they had their cleansing flight."

"Cleansing flight?"

"To go to the bathroom. They wait like two months for it to get warm enough, and then they all fly out and go at once and then go back in. Can you imagine holding it that long?"

"Gross, Nat." Claire grimaced as she slid toward the door. "Thanks for the ride, Keene!" She always remembered to thank him, and not just because he was cute with his black hair and blue eyes. Without Keene, she'd never make it to half her skating sessions, between Dad's schedule at the border and Mom's work on the farm.

When Mojimuk Falls moved the annual figure skating exposition to Maple Weekend, it messed everything up. Once the sap started to run, it had to be collected and put through the evaporator the same day, so it was round-the-clock busy at the Boucher farm. By the morning of the show, her parents had been boiling sap for three nights running and couldn't even think of leaving to watch her skate.

Claire followed Natalie up the steps and into the arena. They passed the soda machine in the heated hallway, pulled open the second door, and were met with a blast of air even colder than outside. Claire ran her hand along the curved wall of Plexiglas that enclosed the rink and plopped down on the bench where she and Nat always put on their skates.

"Is Keene coming to watch later?" Claire rummaged through her skating bag for her gloves.

"Probably." Natalie grinned. "How come, Claire? Gonna land a double for him?"

"No. I was just wondering." Claire felt her cheeks flush hot and pulled the flaps of her knit hat down to cover them. "Besides, I haven't hit that jump right all week."

"Today would be a great day to pull it off." Natalie stood and pointed to the box, where a lanky man dressed all in black was talking with the coaches. He had dark hair and eyes, and a perfectly pointed triangle of a nose that made him look like one of the ravens that circled over the orchard sometimes. "Andrei Groshev's here from Lake Placid, scouting."

Claire stepped onto the ice and pushed off. "Scouting for what?"

"Skating talent. Lucy's mom told my mom they've set up scholarships for kids to train in Lake Placid, so they're coming around to the regional competitions to look for candidates."

Claire turned to skate backward, facing Natalie. "The Maple Show isn't a competition." She didn't do competitions. Last year Claire's cousin Charlotte had convinced her and Natalie to sign up for the Champlain Valley Open, a Vermont competition with official US Figure Skating judges and everything. Claire was a bundle of nerves all day and ended up running back to the locker room right before she was supposed to skate. She never made it onto the ice.

"No, but Lucy's mom says they know some kids can't afford to travel for competitions and they want to"—she used her fingers to make quote marks in the air—"see what's out there."

"Lake Placid, huh?" Claire stretched her leg up behind her in a backward spiral.

Natalie grabbed her hand and twirled her around. "Hey— you're good, Claire. It could happen."

No it couldn't. Just the thought of training with a Russian skating star who looked like some mean bird gave her major butterflies in her stomach.

"No way." Claire started skating faster, but Natalie kept up with her.

"Seriously, Claire. Focus today—you never know."

A whistle blew from the hockey boxes, announcing it was time to clear the ice for the show.

"I have to help the kids get ready," Claire said. "I'll see you right before our act."

As the youngest junior coach for Northern Lights Skating Club, Claire was in charge of the littlest skaters and had to make sure they were in costume, ready to skate—or at least wiggle their way out onto the ice when it was time.

"Hey there! Are you guys ready for the show?" Claire squatted down to smile at her five little skaters, still holding their mothers' hands in the lobby.

The twins, Bethany and Jenna, were already in their skates. They held hands the whole time they were skating, whether the program called for it or not, and Bethany was a strong skater, so she just dragged Jenna around behind her, even if Jenna fell. Kianna, a tiny four-year-old who would try anything, was ready, too.

So was Rory. At three, he was the youngest skater and the loudest. Rory liked to run halfway across the rink, then drop to the ice, curl up, and skid the rest of the way as a human bowling ball. Whenever he crashed into somebody he'd yell, "Ka-PLOW!"

"No bowling today, Rory," Claire told him.

"I know." He looked deflated. "My mom said so, too."

Ivy was the only one not wearing skates. She stood with one hand in her jacket pocket and the other clutching a stuffed cow with white spots showing through the worn patches in its brown fur.

Claire reached out to pat the cow on the head. "Is your cow skating, too?"

Ivy shook her head so her strawberry blond pigtails flopped back and forth. "Roger and I are going home. We don't feel good."

Claire knelt down. "Maybe you and Roger need a snack. I have Pop-Tarts in my skating bag."

Ivy's eyes got big. "Roger *loves* Pop-Tarts. Especially with frosting." She took Claire's hand and headed for locker room three, where the costume moms were waiting with five maple leaf costumes. There were shiny gold bodysuits for stems and shoulder harness contraptions with giant red maple leaves, fashioned out of bent coat hangers and stretchy fabric, sticking out the back. After Ivy and Roger shared a Pop-Tart, Claire helped the kids into their costumes and lined them up.

"Ready?" Claire opened the door and heard the music starting. "It's time to get on the ice."

The little skaters shuffled out onto the rink, with Ivy still clutching Roger in one hand, and Claire leaned back to watch. She laughed her way through the whole two-minute routine. Rory didn't knock anybody over, but he did do a wild sit-and-spin trick in the middle of the show. It got a terrific round of applause.

When they finished, Claire hustled her skaters back to the locker room, gave them hugs and Goldfish crackers, and hurried to get into her own costume. She only had two numbers in between to get ready.

She changed into her dress; it was a velvety, crystal blue. Charlotte had loaned it to her for today's Maple Princess solo—the two-minute break in the group routine when the rest of the girls would skate behind the curtain and leave Claire in the spotlight alone.

Claire had been stunned when she got the part. The parents on the skating club's board of directors took into account all kinds of things when they cast the show—skill level, attitude, junior coaching work—but she still couldn't believe they'd chosen her.

Claire tied her skates, lifted her brown curls, and reached behind her neck to fasten the dress with trembling hands. She shouldn't be nervous. She'd been skating with Natalie and Lucy and the other girls here since third grade. And besides, this wasn't a competition. No one was judging her. The audience was just a bunch of her neighbors, watching for fun. They were the people whose kids she taught to skate every Saturday, the people she'd be serving pancakes to in a few hours. And she knew her routine cold. She'd worked on it with her coach, Mary Kate, for nearly two months and landed the double toe loop almost every time until this week. She'd even landed a double axel in practice once, but she couldn't master it in time for the show, so they'd backed off that one. The toe loop was enough.

Claire shook out her hands, took a deep breath, and opened the locker room door. The last notes of Lucy's solo music drifted in.

Claire hurried out and stepped into place next to Natalie just as she heard her cue, the beginning notes of Vivaldi's "Autumn."

The first minute of the routine went by too quickly. Claire skated in formation, following the line to shape swirling figure eights on the ice. Skating in a group like this, all together, filled her with an energy like the buzz of the farm at sugaring time. Claire turned on her blades to skate backward in a flowing circle, then lunged at the same time as seven other skaters, all in a perfect line. When the line swirled off to the left and looped back behind the black curtain, Claire swirled off to the right.

The pace of the music picked up as she gathered speed, and everything left her except the feel of the cold air on her face, her blades on the ice, her movements in time to the music.

When the violin notes grew playful, like leaves dancing and flipping in the October wind, her feet grew playful, too, switching back, crossing over, in the moves she'd spent hours choreographing with Mary Kate. There was applause when she finished the footwork sequence, applause when she landed the series of waltz jumps, when she crouched into her sit spin, then stood and spun faster still. The music was spinning, the world was spinning, and she was at the center. And there was applause—the loudest of the morning—when she leaped into the air, made two revolutions, and landed the double toe loop. Perfectly.

One last sequence of dance moves, one last twirl, and she struck her final pose—a lunge with her head tipped back, her hands in the air.

She stood and curtsied, and, for the first time, noticed the huge crowd. The Maple Show must have been a sellout. Claire hoped they were all going to come for pancakes later.

"Great show!" Natalie skated over and hugged Claire so hard she almost knocked her right over.

"Thanks, you too." They skated off the ice, and Claire reached for her guards. As she was sliding the second one onto her blade, she felt a hand on her shoulder.

"You nailed that double," said Mary Kate, grinning.

"Finally," Claire said. "Thanks." She started for the locker room, but Mary Kate stopped her.

"Hold up a minute, Claire. I need to make an introduction." The man from the box, with the dark hair and sharp nose, stepped forward, and Mary Kate nodded toward him. "This is Andrei Groshev. He saw your solo today and would like to have a conversation with you."

CHAPTER 2

It wasn't a conversation, exactly. In a conversation, both people talk. In the front lobby of the Northern Lights Rink, only Andrei Groshev talked. Claire sat with her hot chocolate gripped in her hands and tried to listen, but her stomach was turning flips.

"You are familiar with the Silver Blades Scholarship program, no?" he said.

"No," Claire said. "I mean yes, I've heard of it."

"So you know why it is I wish to speak with you. We have one slot left for this summer, and we wish to offer it to you."

He said more after that, but Claire's head was spinning faster than her skates ever had. A scholarship to skate in Lake Placid three days a week? The Olympic Center was an hour and a half away. How would she even get there?

She finally squeaked out a word. "Why?"

"You must know that the double toe loop is a difficult jump for someone your age to have mastered. That shows me that you have . . . ah . . . what is it . . . the promise to do well. And your program as a whole, it was lovely. You move with the music, feel the music. You do not just go through the motions; you skate. You will do well in Lake Placid."

But Claire couldn't imagine herself there. Having a world-class skater for a coach? Training for competitions? She took a sip of the hot chocolate and burned her tongue. This was way, way, way out of her league. She'd have to tell him no thanks, if she could ever find her voice.

Claire stole a glance at her watch. Terrific. She was going to be late for the pancake breakfast now, too.

"You are looking at your wristwatch," Andrei Groshev said. "Are you needing to be someplace?"

Claire nodded. "My . . . uh . . . family is expecting me."

"Very well," he said. "We begin in two weeks with orientation."

She took a deep breath to say her no-thank-you, but he was already handing her a thick folder of information. "Here are the papers you'll need to fill out."

"I . . . uh. . . . I'll have to talk with my parents."

He nodded. "We will see you on the ice in two weeks."

⁊

"There's just no way. No way." Claire grabbed for the dashboard to keep from sliding into Natalie as the pickup took a sharp turn. "I can't even go through with a stupid competition in Vermont without getting all queasy. There's no way I can compete with the Lake Placid girls."

"You *have* to!" Natalie's blue eyes were huge. "Claire, do you have any idea what those training sessions cost? My mom looked into it last year; it's insane. And they're offering you a free ride. You *can't* say no."

Keene stopped at a red light and turned to Claire. "Seriously, Chipmunk, she's right."

Claire scowled. She'd hated that nickname even back in kindergarten when he tagged her with it, thanks to her squeaky voice and chubby cheeks. She preferred the new nickname Keene gave her after she let it slip that she was going to a special after-school math club party for National Pi Day a couple weeks ago. It wasn't romantic, but at least "Pi Face" was more respectable than Chipmunk.

"Well, maybe *you* ought to go train in Lake Placid if you think it's such a good idea." Claire jerked her head at the light. "Go. It's green. And I'm already late."

⤷

"Heavens to Betsy, where on earth have you been?" Aunt Maureen lifted a ladle and made eight perfect circles of batter on the griddle. "Get on over and wash your hands. There's an apron on the hook. You can run coffee, and these'll be ready by the time you're back."

Claire took off her watch and scrubbed her hands as guitar notes drifted in the window. Uncle Bruce and his friend Jennifer were already warming up to play for the crowd outside. They called their duo Crossing North and played at the local coffeehouse mostly. Maple Weekend was their big show of the year.

Soapsuds swirled down the drain, and Claire's thoughts swirled with them. There was no way she could train in Lake Placid. Even if she wanted to, there was nobody who could drive her there after school.

Jake and Christopher came running into the sugarhouse.

"Shut that door behind you!" Mom hollered.

"Claire, will you hide the holy grail for us in the woods?" Jake bounced on his heels.

"Maybe later, if there's time." Their favorite game was playing *Raiders of the Lost Ark*, acting out scenes from that Indiana Jones movie. Claire would hide "artifacts" in hollow trees and set up obstacles the boys would have to cross to find them. She loved coming up with complicated maps and math puzzles for them to decipher. And of course, they'd pretend to be bitten by venomous snakes and dodge bullets from bad guys the whole time.

"Come on, let's start now. I'll be Indiana Jones, okay?"

"Okay, but just for a minute." She whirled around to face him and said in her best bad-guy voice, "Dr. Jones, we've heard a lot about you."

Jake crossed his arms and stuck out his chest. "Have you?"

"Professor of archaeology. Expert on the occult. Obtainer of rare antiquities. And what will we be seeking on today's quest?"

"Claire!" Mom's voice broke the movie spell. "Get moving!"

"Curses! The evil supreme ruler of the sugarhouse calls." She went back to her regular voice. "Maybe we can play later."

"Fine," Jake said, and tore out the door after Christopher, leaving it open again.

Claire closed the door and glanced up at the white dry-erase board where the sugaring calendar was posted. The season only lasted six weeks—that's if they were lucky—and with so many of the cousins gone at school, she was on the list for collecting tonight after the festivities were over. And the next night. And the next one after that. She didn't have to be a math genius to figure out there weren't enough hours to add trips to Lake Placid into the mix.

Claire picked up the regular coffee in one hand and the decaf in the other, pushed open the screen door with her hip, and headed out to the tent.

"There's my butterfly girl!" Grandpa Leo held out a rough hand and leaned back so far in his folding chair she thought he'd tip right over. She put down the coffee and took his hand so he could pull her in for a hug. Grandpa Leo had taken her to her first ice show eight years ago when a bunch of Olympic stars came to Lake Placid for an exhibition. She sat with her chubby four-year-old hands wrapped around a box of buttery popcorn and stared at the way the skaters' iridescent skirts flipped and fluttered when they twirled.

They looked like the butterflies Grandpa had taught her to name when he took her out for walks in the fields. Grandpa Leo knew the name of every single insect that might be a problem for the trees or in the garden, and he knew the friendly bugs, too. Claire liked the butterflies best. She'd memorized their names. Monarch. Painted Lady. Red Admiral.

The skaters were just like them, with their bright colors, dancing and leaping, flying across the ice on the invisible wings Claire was sure they must have. Otherwise, how could they move like that?

She still remembered telling Grandpa, "I want to be a butterfly, too!"

And now she was. A butterfly with an invitation to skate on that same rink, to train with the best.

"Hey!" Christopher skidded up to them, sliding in the

half-frozen mud. "Who's that guy?" He pointed to a tall, skinny man with blond hair and glasses, sitting two tables over and smiling like crazy.

"Let's see . . . ," Grandpa said. Who's That Guy? was a game they'd played since forever, where you point to a stranger and everybody has to make up a story about him.

"An undercover spy from . . . ah . . . Sweden," Grandpa said, "searching for Maureen's secret batter recipe."

"Nah . . . he's probably just an undercover spy from the Ladue Farm," Claire said.

"Actually, he's not really a *guy*." Christopher's eyes narrowed. "He's an *alien* from another galaxy posing as a geeky TV weatherman who really likes pancakes. And when he finishes eating and wipes that syrup off his chin, he's going to go back to Planet Zorko and then they're going to take over the world, and—"

"Christopher, get in here and get this tray, NOW!"

He ran off.

"Guess we'll never find out when the aliens are coming." Grandpa slid his empty coffee mug across the picnic table to Claire.

"Regular or decaf?"

"Better make it regular." He lifted his mug. "Weatherman—the real one, not that alien one—says it's going down to twenty tonight and back up to fifty tomorrow. The sap's gonna be runnin' hard."

Claire poured his coffee, then took a quick peek back at the kitchen to make sure she could sit for a minute without Mom or Aunt Maureen going all sugar-crazy on her.

"You're not going to believe what happened at the rink." She pulled a folding chair from the next table and squeezed it in next to him.

"I don't have to believe it. I was there, darlin'! I saw you land that double sure as I can see the dill pickle on my plate."

"No, I mean after that. When I was done."

Grandpa Leo took a big bite of his pickle. "Maureen did a good job with these this year." He took a swig of coffee. "Well, what else happened?"

Claire told him all about Andrei Groshev and his offer. "And I mean, it's great that he noticed me and everything, but don't you think that's, like, the craziest thing you've ever heard?"

Grandpa Leo dipped his pickle in the last of the syrup left over from his pancakes and took another bite, chewing thoughtfully. "Well, no, it's not crazy," he said finally.

"But Mom and Dad will never say yes. I can't go to Lake Placid every day."

Grandpa Leo raised his eyebrows and picked up his coffee mug. "Seems to me that kind of training could lead to some darn good opportunities. You never know."

"Claire Boucher!" Mom came swooping out the door of the sugarhouse with fingers of steam drifting after her. She tucked a wisp of brown hair back into her bun. "Get a move on! We got another batch ready and they're gonna get cold if you don't hurry."

Claire picked up the coffee pot and stood.

"Think about it, at least," Grandpa Leo said.

Claire nodded.

The whole time she ran syrup and poured coffee that afternoon, she had a tough time thinking of anything else.

∽

"Show go well this morning?"

"Yep." Claire took her father's arm and balanced against the fender of the old red farm truck to buckle her snowshoes. By the time the pancake folks finally left, the maple shadows stretched long and thin on the melting snow. There was a lot of work to do and not much daylight left.

Claire stomped her foot to make sure the snowshoe was secure, then looked up at her dad. "I landed my double toe loop."

"S'good." He turned and crunched off into the trees, and Claire followed. She loved walking through the maples on snowshoes, loved the way her smaller tracks fit right inside her father's big ones. She felt like a baby rabbit, following him along the trail.

"Pancake day went well, too," she said.

He nodded. "Big crowd." And kept walking.

Nobody could accuse Claire's dad of talking too much, and usually she didn't mind. Today, though, she wished he'd ask more about the skating show.

"I . . . uh . . . talked to a coach from Lake Placid."

Her father stepped up to one of the big maples—her arms barely fit around this one if she hugged it—and lifted the lid on the bucket. "Nice one." He lifted the bucket from the tap and nodded toward the tailgate. Claire stepped around him on her snowshoes and unlatched it so he could climb up to the big tank in the pickup bed. She climbed up, too, and opened the lid so he could tip the weathered gray bucket. Sap poured out in a clear, cold stream, sloshed over the edge of the bucket a little, and splashed onto Claire's boot.

Her father jumped down and hung the bucket back on the tap. "Lake Placid, eh?"

Claire nodded. She shuffled around the tree to check the second bucket—you could put two or three taps on a big one like this—and found it almost full, too.

"He's one of the coaches they brought in from Russia. He competed in the Olympics, and he was . . . scouting." She said the word quietly, not sure if her father would want her being scouted.

"Scouting who?" He raised his eyebrows and reached to steady her hand as she tipped the bucket to pour the sap into the tank. "You?"

Claire emptied the bucket and jumped down from the truck bed. "Well . . . yeah. Kind of. I got invited to train in Lake Placid." It came out in a whoosh.

"Lake Placid? Wow." Dad took the second bucket from her and hung it back on the tree. "Quite an honor." He paused. "But I bet it's pretty expensive, Claire. That's going to be out of our league, I'm afraid."

She took a deep breath. "They offered me a scholarship."

"For how much of the cost?"

"All of it."

"No kidding." He paused. "Well, how about that news." He pointed to the next group of trees. "Let's keep going or we're not going to be back in time for corn chowder."

She crunched and sloshed her way through the melting

snow to a new stand of maples—skinnier trees with just one tap each.

"So." Her father lifted a bucket, half-full of sap, and climbed up to empty it into the tank. "When you going to start with that fancy new coach?"

"What?" Claire wasn't ready for that. She had expected Grandpa to be excited, because he was her grandpa and loved everything that had to do with her, even the lumpy clay ladybug she'd made for him in third grade.

She had expected Charlotte to be excited, too. Claire had stolen a minute to fire off a quick e-mail to her after the pancake breakfast. But Charlotte hadn't answered yet.

And she had expected her father to be happy for her, sure, just for getting the invitation. But actually accepting it? She had played out the conversation in her head a dozen times; it always ended with them laughing at what a silly idea it was, her going off to train in Lake Placid.

"Well?" Dad shook the empty bucket at her. How long had he been holding it out?

"Oh, sorry!" She took it and hung it back on the tap.

He shook his head. "I mean when do you start?"

"Start training?" She kept her hand on the top of the sap bucket, tracing the rim with her finger. "I didn't figure I could—I mean—it's so far away. . . ."

He moved on to the next maple, a bigger one. The sinking sun turned the trees into long blue shadows on the snow.

Claire took quick steps to catch up. "I just . . . didn't think it would work out, is all. So I'm saying no."

"Listen, Miss Claire." He turned and took off one leather glove to cup her chin in his hand. The callus on his thumb scratched her cheek. "I've seen you out there on the pond. I may not have been there today, but I know what this face of yours looks like when you're on skates. I know how much you love it. And if some fancy coach from Yugoslavia or—"

"Russia."

"Or Russia . . . if some fancy coach sees that, too, and wants to help you get better at doing what you love, we're going to make it happen." He tipped her chin up, just a little. "You understand that?"

His words—all those words—would have been enough to change her mind by themselves. But when she looked into his eyes, she saw something there that she usually only saw when one of the boys scored a hat trick or one of the big trees gave up twenty gallons of sap in a day. Pride. She nodded. "How am I going to get there, though?"

"I'll see about working the earlier shift so I can drive you."

Claire couldn't remember the last time she'd had an hour in the car with her father all to herself. The idea made Lake Placid feel warmer.

"So when do you start?" he asked, lifting another sap bucket lid. It tapped against the tree with a soft thud. This one was full, too.

"Two weeks. Orientation's the Saturday before Easter." She climbed into the truck and took the bucket from him. The deep sound of sap pouring into the tank was sweet and big and full. Almost like a promise.

By the time they finished and parked the truck, the sun was long gone over the hill. Yellow orange rectangles of light from the sugarhouse windows lit billowy clouds of steam pouring out the top.

Claire pointed. "Mom's still cooking."

Dad put his hand out to help her jump down from the truck. "I hope she's cooking something other than sap in there. I'm starving."

Smells of fresh-baked biscuits and thick corn chowder swallowed them up when the door opened, and Claire's mouth watered. They'd drizzle the biscuits with honey harvested from Nat's hives last summer.

"We were getting ready to send out a search party. Where have you two been?" Mom wiped flour off her hands onto her khaki pants.

"Collecting." Dad leaned in to kiss her on the cheek and sniff the chowder all at once. "Lot of sap tonight. And Claire's got some big news to share at dinner."

"Well, good. Wash up then, Claire. I can't wait to hear your big news."

Claire nodded and headed to the back room, where there was a bathroom and more important, a computer. She wanted to fire off a new e-mail to Charlotte, to let her know she was going to accept the scholarship.

Claire pecked at the keyboard to log in—

Username: cbskater
Password: sugaronsnow

—and thought about how she'd tell her cousin the news. Charlotte would be more excited than anybody.

Ding. The little envelope on Claire's home page lit up. She already had mail from cboucher@pennsu.edu.

Claire,

Holy Moses! They offered you the Silver Blades
Scholarship!

Claire smiled. Charlotte was already happy for her, even
when she thought she'd be turning down the offer. Just wait
until she found out Claire was going to say yes.

I have to say I'm not surprised, though. That scholarship
is always heavy on artistry, and you're awesome, even if you
do keep flubbing your double toe loop (did you land it
yet??).

Anyway, major congrats, even if you're not going to
take it. I don't blame you. I'd never be brave enough to walk
into the Olympic Center. A couple girls from my synchro
team used to train there in the summertime, and they say
it's the most cutthroat place you've ever seen.

Very cool that they chose you, though. Congrats!

Tell Aunt Becky and Uncle Paul I said hey.

Love, Charlotte

Claire read the e-mail again. Charlotte, who wasn't afraid
of spiders or big snakes and who even touched a scorpion at a
museum once, said she wouldn't be brave enough to train at
the Olympic Center.

How could Claire be brave enough if Charlotte wasn't?

But then she remembered that shoot-SCORE look in her
father's eyes. She hit the reply button.

Char,

I landed the double toe loop at the Maple Show today.
And as for the scholarship . . . I've decided to go for it.
Orientation is in two weeks.

Love, Claire

She sent it.

There.

She actually told someone she was going to do it.

Her fingers tapped the edge of the keyboard.

She clicked over to the local weather page. Grandpa was right; with a low of twenty tonight and a high of fifty the next day, the sap would be running like crazy. She ought to get some dinner and some rest.

But as she was logging out, there was another *ding*. New mail from cboucher@pennsu.edu. It was a short one.

Claire,

Wow! That's great!! Be sure to let me know how
orientation goes. And be aware . . . Lake Placid may be
only an hour-and-a-half drive, but it might as well be
another planet, compared to Mojimuk Falls. The girls there
are from all over the country, and they're competitive.

I'm excited for you. Just make sure you toughen up
before you go, kiddo. Otherwise, they'll eat you alive.

Hugs,
—C

CHAPTER 3

Quit it, dork!"

"You quit it!"

Claire felt a thump against the back of her seat. Jake and Christopher were at it again in the tiny backseat of the pickup, shoving and tugging and thumping on each other like they were in one of those wrestling shows on TV.

"All right, boys." Dad looked relieved when they pulled into the rink parking lot. "Mom'll pick you up at noon. We'll color Easter eggs when Claire gets home later."

" 'Kay . . . bye, Dad!" Jake tugged his hockey bag out of the back and took off. Christopher ran to catch up. At nine, he was only a year younger than Jake, but Jake was at least six inches taller. Claire watched them disappear inside.

It was only two weeks ago that she'd shared her Pop-Tarts with Ivy and Roger here. Two weeks ago she'd landed that double. Two weeks ago she'd burned her mouth on her hot chocolate listening to Andrei Groshev offer her a life-changing opportunity.

Her father pulled the truck away from the curb and looked at his watch. "We're doing good on time. Should be in Lake

Placid by a little after ten, so you'll have plenty of time to get ready."

"If I can find the right rink." Claire hugged her knees to her chest. It was mud season, so her boots left brown smudges on the edge of the seat.

"You're going to do just fine." Her father reached over and tugged her ponytail. "It's just orientation. They're going to understand if you have questions."

She hoped so. Because she sure had a lot.

Driving into Lake Placid, Claire counted the family-run motels along the road. The vacancy signs were all lit; it was too late for skiing and too cold, wet, and muddy for anything else.

Dad slowed to a stop so a Pepsi delivery truck could pull out of the pizza-place parking lot.

"How did they fit everyone in this town for the Olympics?" Claire asked. "And how did they ever pull that off twice?"

"Well, the Olympics haven't always been as huge as they are now." He waved to the Pepsi guy and pulled through the intersection. "Back in 1932, I'm sure it was no problem at all. Traffic was something in 1980, though. Lots of delays." He flicked on his blinker to pull into the Olympic Center parking lot, right next to Lake Placid High School. Claire wondered what it would be like to go to a school with an Olympic speed-skating oval in its front yard.

"Where do we go?" Claire asked. The Olympic Center was huge. There was the old part from the 1932 games, a traditional-looking light brown stone building with the Olympic rings above the front doors and flags from different countries lined up along the front. Built onto it was an enormous white-domed building. That was where the 1980 rink was—where the "Miracle on Ice" happened when the United States hockey team beat the Soviets. Jake and Christopher were insanely jealous that she got to skate on that same rink. "Should we go in the front door, or where?"

"Your letter said the athletes' entrance." He glanced down to a pile of papers between the seats and nodded. "Double-check it."

Sure enough, it said she should report to the athletes' entrance. The whole idea of that made her feel half-pleased and half-squirmy. She wasn't an athlete. Not really. She was a girl who liked twirling on the cow pond. She imagined an alarm going off when she stepped through the doors, *Athlete imposter alert! Athlete imposter alert!*

"Here we are." Her father pointed to a set of glass doors with a sign for the athletes' entrance above them. Even if the sign hadn't been there, Claire would have known. The tall blond guys with the hockey sticks were a giveaway. She lifted her skating bag off the floor as her dad backed into a parking spot. Then she followed him to the entrance.

"After you." Her father held the door, and she stepped through.

There was no alarm. Inside, a young woman with a blond ponytail sat at a folding table full of red and blue folders. She wore a black fleece jacket with LAKE PLACID SKATING embroidered on it in silver.

"I bet you're one of our new girls." The ponytail lady reached out to shake Claire's hand.

"Today's my first day. Well, not really my first day. I'm not training yet, just here for orientation."

"And you are?" The woman smiled.

"Oh, sorry. I'm Claire Boucher."

"Ah, the Maple Princess girl, right?"

Claire felt her face flush. Was everybody going to call her that here?

"And I'm Paul Boucher." Her father shook the woman's hand, too.

"I'm Marianne Preston, figure skating director for the Olympic Center." She shuffled through folders and pulled out a blue one with Claire's name on it. "Here you go. This has your schedule for orientation. Just head down that hallway." She pointed to a metal door with the words NO ADMITTANCE written on it. "Go all the way to the end and take a left. Then go through the double doors and you'll see the Hall of Fame Room on the left. That's where orientation starts."

"Thank you." Claire's voice came out in a whisper as she took the folder and headed for the doors with her father behind her.

"Oh, just a minute!" Marianne called. "The orientation's just for new skaters. But if you'd like, some of the moms are getting together at that cute little coffee shop across the street."

Her father's brown gray eyebrows knitted together. Claire couldn't picture him sitting in some designer coffee shop. He always made fun of Charlotte when she wanted to go to the Starbucks in Plattsburgh for her "fancy-pants mocha swirly-do drink."

But he smiled and gave Claire's skating bag a tap. "Go on. I'll meet you right outside this door at . . ." He looked at Marianne.

"Five o'clock," she said.

Claire watched him leave and head down the hill to Main Street. Was he really going to drink lattes with the moms?

"All set?" Marianne chirped, and Claire remembered she was supposed to be on her way to the Hall of Fame Room.

"Yep. Thanks." She pulled open the heavy gray door, started down the hall, and only jumped a little when the door clanged behind her. The whole hallway smelled like Keene's hockey bag, and pretty soon she saw why.

"Vat time is ze ice?" A voice drifted out of one of the locker rooms, and after it came a half-dressed hockey player with dark eyes and sharp features. He looked like a younger Andrei Groshev.

Claire walked past him, to a table in the hallway where a trainer was kneading another player's calf.

"Hut! Hut! Hut!" She had to flatten herself against the wall to avoid getting run over by what appeared to be a full hockey team, jogging along on their skate guards. Finland, their helmets said. Could they have come all that way across the ocean just to train here?

When she reached the Hall of Fame Room, another girl was hurrying down the hall from the other direction. She had that popular vampire book tucked under her arm and pulled a green skating bag on wheels behind her.

"Could you hold that door a sec?" The girl tossed her shiny black ponytail. She had warm, smooth skin, ears that stuck out just a tiny bit, and a broad face that glowed when she smiled. If Aunt Maureen ever met this girl, she'd be pinching her cheeks in half a second.

"Thanks," the girl said as they stepped into a room full of hockey posters, wall plaques, trophies, and brown tweed couches that looked like they'd been around since the 1980 Olympics. Still smiling, the girl plopped down on a couch and opened her book. Claire sat next to her and held her skating bag in her lap like a security blanket while she looked around.

The room buzzed with chatter as the girls laced skates, pulled hair into ponytails, and fastened clasps on their dresses. They all looked ready to perform. The only boy in the room, dressed in black skating pants and a jacket like Marianne's, sat next to a girl who looked like she might be his sister. Three of the other girls wore matching royal blue skating dresses. Claire pulled at the neck of her sweatshirt. Her fleece sweatpants felt thick and itchy.

"Excuse me," Claire whispered to the girl with the ponytail. "Was I supposed to wear something . . . more formal?"

The girl looked up, using her finger as a bookmark. "Don't worry." She glanced around the room. "Some of them dress for competition even when it's just practice, but you're fine in that." She unzipped her jacket, and Claire was relieved to see an ordinary gray hoodie underneath.

"Well, that's good. I was worried I messed up on my very first day." She nodded at the novel in the girl's hands. "Good book?"

"Really good. I love anything with magic or the supernatural," she said, "though the main character in this one just swoons over her vampire all the time."

Claire laughed. Natalie had started reading that one and said the same thing.

The girl put down her book. "I'm Tasanee Luang."

"That's pretty. I'm Claire Boucher. Do you live here in Lake Placid?"

Tasanee nodded. "We do now. We moved here from Washington DC. My parents are from Thailand, originally. They run the restaurant Lemongrass Thai up the street. How about you?"

"My parents run the maple farm way, way, way up the street. In Mojimuk Falls."

Tasanee raised her eyebrows. "Up by Canada?"

Claire nodded. "My dad works at U.S. Customs."

"At least he doesn't come home smelling like shrimp and curry every night."

"No, he just smells like maple syrup. We run a sugarhouse, too."

"Do you have to help out a lot?" Tasanee asked. "The restaurant's crazy, and my parents don't understand that I can't always be . . ." She trailed off. The room had suddenly grown quiet.

Claire looked over at the door, where Andrei Groshev stood, arms folded across his chest.

"Finally, I have your attention." He clapped his hands twice and took long strides to the front of the room. His eyes were so dark they felt like darts every time they landed on Claire. She wanted to crawl behind the sofa.

"Welcome to orientation. The fact that you are training here means you are some of the best skaters of your age in the country." His eyes widened when he saw two of the blue-dress girls whispering. He glared until they stopped.

"The fact that I did not have your attention immediately means that you are perhaps not ready for this level of commitment. If you are here to visit or fluff your dresses or fix your—how do you say it—making up the face . . . if you are here for those things, leave now." He lifted his chin toward

the door, just as it opened. A girl with two dark brown pigtails and a round face stepped through. She froze when she
saw everyone in the room staring at her.

She was shorter than Claire and looked miserable standing there in her red velvet dress and skate guards. "I'm sorry
I'm late," she finally squeaked out.

"And if you are not able to arrive on time and give your full
attention to the ice, you do not belong here." The pigtail girl
wobbled on her feet, like she wasn't sure if she should stay.

"Here," Claire whispered, and pointed to the empty space
beside her on the couch. The girl wobbled over on her guards,
mouthed the word "Thanks," and leaned back to listen.

"Some of you have trained here before, and you know
what is expected. Give that and give more." The blue dresses
sat huddled together. One of them, a blond girl with a perfect
French braid, fingered the buttons on her dress frantically.
Claire thought she'd probably pull them all off before Andrei
Groshev was done talking.

"And some of you are new." He looked right at Claire, and
her breath caught in her chest. "We will be finding out soon
if you belong or if you do not. We work hard here and we get
results." He gazed out over the roomful of skaters, as if he
could tell just by looking who might not work hard enough.

The girl with the blond braid twisted the top button on
her dress until her friend, a tall girl with brown hair pulled
into a long ponytail, swatted her hand. A bored-looking girl
leaning up against the wall next to them twirled a lock of her
curly brown hair. Claire didn't know how she could look so
relaxed listening to Groshev.

"You have ten minutes to get dressed," he barked. "Then

meet me on the ice." He clapped his hands twice, took four long strides to the door, and disappeared.

The room looked like it had been frozen in time—then magically unfrozen by a magician's wand. Tasanee shoved her book into her skating bag and bent to untie her shoes. The three blue-dress girls huddled together talking and tightening the laces on their skates.

Tasanee nodded toward their tight circle. "The Ice Queens are back for another season."

"Ice Queens?" Claire watched the button-twister pass her lip balm to the one with the curly hair.

"Better learn their names. They're Coach's favorites. That's Meghan James passing the ChapStick," Tasanee said. "She's the only one of those three who might give you the time of day. She's actually pretty nice."

"Is she from here?"

"No, she's from the city."

"Plattsburgh?"

Tasanee laughed. "No. *The* city. Her dad's an on-air sports guy with NBC in New York. Her mom used to be on TV there, too, but she moved up here with Meghan."

"Are her parents split up?" Claire couldn't imagine living away from her dad.

"She says no, but . . ." Tasanee dug in her skating bag. "Shoot. Where are my gloves?" She pulled out a black pair and stretched them onto her hands.

Across the room, Meghan leaned in closer to the other girls and whispered something. They all turned to look at Claire. Her eyes met the tall girl's steely gaze, and she felt her heart jump. She rummaged in her bag for her own gloves and tried to calm herself down. It was natural that they'd talk about her; she was the new girl. She looked up again. Meghan was putting something away in her bag, but the other two were still staring. Still not smiling.

Claire tried to keep her voice steady. "So what about those other girls with Meghan? They look like maybe they're . . . not so friendly?"

"That," Tasanee said, "is an understatement. See the one standing up right now, with the curly hair?"

Claire nodded.

"That's Stevie Van Syke. Her father's Claude Van Syke."

"The speed skater from the cornflakes box?"

"Yep. Her family's huge in Lake Placid and boy, does she ever know it. Her dad was the Olympic speed skating gold medalist from 1988. He got tons of endorsements after that, so they've got this huge house on Mirror Lake. He's the chairman of the Silver Blades Scholarship committee, too."

"Bet she's not here on scholarship," Claire said.

"Nope. Half the time, she wasn't even here last session; she kept skipping and got into huge trouble with her dad. But he wanted her back skating this spring, so she's back. Now, Alexis—she's the tall one with the ponytail—she's here on scholarship. She's the only one. Well, besides you now. Her dad's a guard at the federal prison in Ray Brook. Groshev saw her skating here on a school field trip and could see she had potential, so he scooped her up for Silver Blades."

Claire watched Alexis adjusting her skate guards while the other girls waited. "Have those three been friends for a long time?" They reminded Claire of her and Natalie, the way they stuck together.

"Kind of. Stevie and Meghan have skated together since they were in fourth grade, so it was just the two of them for a while. Alexis just started two years ago, but she's done great. She's been Groshev's star since she took second place in regionals last year. That's when Stevie and Meghan decided to cozy up to her."

"She did all that in two years? Wow. She must be serious about skating, to get that good so fast."

Tasanee raised her eyebrows. "Oh, she is. Serious enough that you want to make sure you stay out of her way. On the ice and off." Tasanee lowered her voice and pulled her skates under the bench as Alexis clunked past on her skate guards, leading the other two.

"What about those two?" Claire nodded toward the boy and girl with the skating jackets. The girl was pulling her light brown hair into a ponytail. The boy had headphones in his ears. He was nodding his head and tapping his skate in time to whatever was on his iPod. He had brown hair like his sister's; it flopped into his eyes when he tipped his head. Claire wondered what he was listening to.

"That's Luke and Abby Collins," Tasanee said. "They train with us, but they only do the pairs competition and ice dancing; they don't skate individually."

That must be nice, Claire thought, *to never have to go out there alone.*

"Come on." Tasanee tugged the sleeve of Claire's fleece. "We better get moving."

Claire stood and turned so quickly she almost tripped over the feet of the girl with the pigtails who'd come in late.

"Oh, sorry!"

"S'okay," the girl said, tugging her second skate onto her foot. Her cheeks were red and blotchy. *Probably still upset about coming in late*, Claire thought.

"And I'm sorry he gave you such a hard time when you came in. I'm Claire."

The girl nodded gratefully. "Thanks. I'm Hannah. And I'm not usually late for things." She shook her head. "I can't believe he just stared at me like that. I wanted to crawl under a chair. I've heard he's intense, but . . . geez. . . ."

"You're new here too?" Claire asked.

Hannah nodded. "It's my first day. I've been skating since I was five, back home in New Hampshire, but we moved to Au Sable Forks a few weeks ago. My mom asked around about lessons and got Groshev's name. He seems pretty tough, though."

"You think that was tough?" Tasanee tugged on a skate, checking her watch. "We better get moving, or you'll see what tough really looks like."

CHAPTER 4

Let's go! Push off! Push!"

Claire pushed off from her left foot, then her right, stroking her way around the rink for the twenty-fifth time.

"I thought today was just orientation," she whispered as Tasanee glided up beside her.

"It is," Tasanee huffed. "But he's always tough the first session on the ice after a break. Wants to know who's in shape. Sometimes we lose people by the end of the day."

"All right!" Andrei Groshev clapped his hands. "Let us see what you have done since our last session. We will run your routines now."

"We're supposed to skate a routine today?" Claire whispered to Tasanee. "I didn't even bring music."

Tasanee nodded. "It said so in the paperwork."

The paperwork that Claire had been too nervous to read with much attention. She felt like her whole body was tightening around her heart and it was pounding to get out. What was she going to do when it was her turn to skate?

Tasanee put a hand on her shoulder. "It's okay. It's your first day. Maybe he'll let you skate your program without the music."

Groshev clapped his hands again. "First up?"

Meghan glided forward into a T-stop. "I'll go first." Her voice was calm, but when she stopped in front of Groshev, one hand crept up to the blond braid that hung over her shoulder, twisting it like crazy.

"Very well." He nodded at Meghan with the closest thing Claire had ever seen to a smile on his face. It was gone before she could be sure it had ever been there.

"I have my new routine, the one with the double salchow." Meghan let go of her hair and did a quick twirl.

Groshev nodded. "Watch your edges now. And concentrate. Do not disappoint me."

Meghan skated quickly to center ice, struck a pose with both arms raised in graceful curves above her head, and gazed down at her shoulder to wait for her cue. Claire and the others skated to the penalty box to watch.

Groshev gave a sharp gesture, signaling to someone Claire couldn't see up in the press box. After a few seconds of silence, Claire heard the familiar, brisk strings of Vivaldi's "Autumn." She and Meghan had something in common.

But their skating styles were different. While Claire always liked a slow buildup to her routines, there was no warming up for Meghan James. The second the music started, her skates moved like fingers flying on a typewriter with each staccato note. When the first long chords echoed through the empty seats of the 1980 rink, Meghan's strokes across the ice lengthened, too, until she spun into a camel, her leg extended in a straight line with her back and head, a perfect, twirling letter *T* at center ice.

"Arms! The arms!" Groshev called out to the ice, and Meghan stretched her arms out longer.

Claire was impressed with the girl's focus. Meghan skated past the penalty box, close enough so Claire could hear her blades scraping the ice and see the expression of complete concentration in her eyes. She wasn't smiling, though. Her mouth was tight, and her eyebrows were furrowed enough to leave nervous wiggly lines on her forehead.

Claire clapped along with the other skaters when Meghan took off from her left foot, threw herself spinning high in the air, and landed on her right foot. A perfect double salchow.

But just when the music slowed into a gentler, quieter melody—the part that should have let Meghan relax and maybe finally smile—her toe pick caught on the ice, and she stumbled.

Claire heard a collective gasp. Were the skaters here so perfect that no one ever fumbled? Meghan had recovered and was skating again; she wasn't hurt or anything. It was the kind of mistake Claire and Natalie made—and laughed about—at practice all the time. Claire stole a glance at Tasaneo, whose eyes were fixed on Groshev.

Meghan finished her program, but not with the same heart. Her spins were slower, her jumps lower than that first gorgeous salchow. Finally, the music slowed, and Meghan struck her final pose.

Claire clapped—but her hands only met twice before she realized she was clapping alone and stopped.

The scrape of Meghan's blades echoed through the rink as she made her way to the boards. She stopped in front of Groshev and stared at her skates.

"I'm sorry," she whispered.

Groshev folded his arms and stared at her.

Claire wished he would let her try again. Wished the next routine would start and fill the awful, cold quiet. She heard Tasanee's breathing next to her and wondered how long the silence could go on.

Finally, Groshev said quietly, "We'll work later. You have time before the first competition."

Meghan glanced up at him but looked away within a split second, as if his eyes had burned her, and skated off the ice. She sat in the far end of the box, next to no one.

Groshev turned to the rest of them. "Let us continue. Next?"

Stevie Van Syke, the one with the curly hair and the speed skater dad, skated a fun routine to some sixties song—the Grateful Dead, maybe. Stevie didn't trip or fall, but she didn't try anything too hard either. Every jump was a single.

Groshev raised an eyebrow at her when she finished. "Where are your doubles?"

She shrugged. "My ankle's been bothering me."

Alexis Rock went next, and when she moved across the ice on her long legs, Claire could see why Groshev had noticed her on her field trip. She skated to a classical song Claire didn't know—a beautiful, swooshing, swishing song that seemed to lift her right off the ice.

"Very good," Groshev said as she left the ice, and Alexis paused, breathing in his compliment like oxygen before she found a spot in the stands behind Claire.

"I hear you're a Silver Blades skater, too," Alexis whispered, leaning forward.

"Yep—just started today." Claire turned to face Alexis. Maybe she was friendlier than Tasanee had said. "I heard you started a couple years ago. You looked great out there." She smiled, but Alexis narrowed her eyes.

"I don't need compliments. I know I can skate," Alexis hissed as Groshev talked with Hannah at the edge of the ice. "I already placed at regionals once, and I'm going to do it again." The determination in her voice felt solid enough to touch. Solid enough to knock a person right over.

Why was she telling Claire all this? "Well, that's great. I—"

"Look, I don't know if they've added funding for a second scholarship or if they're waiting to see which one of us turns out to be a stronger skater, but I can tell you this. If there's only one Silver Blades spot on this ice, it's going to be mine. I *will* skate at nationals this year, and nothing is getting in my way."

"Alexis!" Groshev called from the ice. "I understand that you wish to get to know our new skater, but do not do your getting-to-know on my time. We continue now."

Claire turned to the ice, and Alexis moved up a few rows to sit with Stevie, but Claire could still feel those cold whispered words in her ear. She shivered as Hannah skated out onto the ice. Charlotte said it would be competitive; Claire just needed to worry about her own skating and try to toughen up. She forced herself to focus on Hannah's routine.

Hannah was one of those people who surprised you; she looked a little clumsy and awkward in real life, but something magical happened when she stepped onto the ice. She skated to a song Claire recognized from her mother's music collection, "Crazy Little Thing Called Love" by that old group Queen.

It was a bouncy, fun song to begin with, but somehow, Hannah made it even livelier, wiggling her shoulders in time to the beat, gradually letting more and more of her body take on the bounce of the song. Then she took off, skating way faster than any of the Ice Queens. She used every last inch of the ice, twirling and dancing, sidestepping and grapevining. Hannah's smile said it all; she loved every second of the routine, and when the song ended and left her at the center of the ice, holding her imaginary guitar, a huge smile on her face, even Groshev was grinning.

The two kids from Plattsburgh went next, skating together in an ice dance routine to an Elton John song, "Written in the Stars," that was part of a musical Claire saw at the college once. Abby and Luke skated beautifully. Every coordinated movement, every unison spin, every leap and every turn, felt right for the music. It was hard for Claire to imagine skating with someone like that, so close and so in tune. She tried to picture herself ice dancing with Keene and laughed. He'd dance her right down toward the goal and then shove her aside to look for a hockey puck.

When Abby and Luke's number ended, Tasanee leaned over to Claire. "Wish me luck."

Tasanee skated to the center of the rink, dropped to one knee, and folded herself over it, her head bowed. When her program song started, clear, warm alto saxophone notes melted out over the ice, and Tasanee unfolded like a flower reaching for the sun. Her whole routine was like that, fluid and beautiful. Like warm maple syrup. Tasanee's spins weren't the fastest and her jumps weren't the highest, but she landed every one, came out of every spin gracefully, as if she'd been spinning her whole life.

When the saxophone notes drifted away and Tasanee folded back into her first pose on the ice, Claire could only sigh.

"Beautiful," she whispered.

"Indeed." Andrei Groshev was standing over her, his eyes piercing. "And I believe you are the last skater. Let us see what you can do on a real rink." He opened the door of the penalty box, and Claire took a step toward the ice on wobbly knees.

"I . . . didn't bring music," she said.

He stared at her. Did this man not understand what that kind of look did to a girl's insides? Or did he understand perfectly?

"I know I was supposed to bring a CD, but I was wondering . . . well, I've skated to 'Autumn,' the song that Meghan had? I was thinking . . . I wondered if . . ."

Andrei Groshev snapped his fingers at the penalty box. "Meghan. Your music is still with Bella, yes?"

Meghan nodded. "Why?"

"Go tell her that Claire will skate to the same song today."

Meghan's eyes widened. "Is that your music for competitions? I still use it sometimes even though I'm working on a new routine."

"Oh, no, I don't do competitions. I mean, I haven't much," Claire said. "It was just my music for the Maple Show."

Alexis stepped forward and snorted out a laugh. "The *Maple Show*?" She turned to Meghan. "I don't think you need to worry. Let's go tell Bella to cue up the music for Mrs.

Butterworth here." She clattered up the stairs with Meghan behind her.

Claire's throat went dry. She looked at Groshev, waiting for him to say something. But he either didn't hear or didn't care. He just looked down at Claire. "Should you not be on the ice?"

She skated out and struck her opening pose, her heart pounding, until Vivaldi's first notes filled the rink for the second time.

Claire started slowly. What if she fell in front of Groshev her first day here? Maybe they'd take back her scholarship. Could they do that already? There was no way she could skate like Alexis.

Stop, she thought. *Stop. Just skate.* And she did, into the second turn—the one with the tough footwork pattern. And she did it.

Just skate. As the song picked up its pace, Claire's heart finally slowed down so she could hear the music over its pounding. She loved this song, the way the notes seemed to hold the memory of every step of the routine and give them all back to her just in time. She felt her movements grow quicker, lighter, like Tasanee's. Like a butterfly. She turned away from the penalty box and smiled.

She pushed harder than usual, gearing up for the big jump. Groshev would expect her to land it; he'd already seen it. But she forced that thought from her mind, forced it from her muscles, and instead let the music fill her like helium in a balloon.

She jumped, higher than she had at the Maple Show, even, she could tell. She turned above the ice and landed firmly, arms out, leg stretched behind her, and a smile that met Andrei Groshev straight on. She twirled away for the final sequence. But not before she saw him smiling back. And this time, she was sure.

∽

It was 4:50, but before they went back to the locker room, Andrei Groshev called them to stand around the circle at center ice. He stood in the middle and rotated slowly, meeting all of their eyes as he spoke.

"You have put in a full day. That is good, for a start. But make no mistake: you have a long, long way to go if you are even to think about competing nationally. You will not make it if you are not giving everything that you have." Claire saw his eyes rest on Stevie for a second.

"Skating here is not a right. It is not something that you are entitled to." He paused. "It is a privilege that some of you may not have much longer if I am not seeing you grow. If I am not seeing the commitment. The passion." Across the circle from Claire, Meghan twisted her braid and looked at the floor.

"But some of you"—Groshev pivoted until he was facing Claire, and she felt everyone's eyes on her—"some of you have impressed me today." She should have felt proud; she should have been absolutely bursting. He liked her! He liked her skating! But her knees shook.

Groshev held up a stack of papers. "Take a schedule, and then you are dismissed. We begin real training on Wednesday." Claire's hand shook as she reached for the paper.

Groshev held on to it for a moment and looked down at her. "Very nice work today." Claire squeaked out a "thank you" and skated toward the boards but sensed someone too close behind her. When she turned, she saw what she had already felt—Alexis's eyes burning into her, cold as ice.

CHAPTER 5

So what was it like?" Natalie leaned toward Claire as Mr. Duckster dropped worksheets on their desks and moved down the row. After Claire's skating session on Saturday, the long Easter weekend had been swallowed up with family dinners and more sugaring, so fourth-period science was the first chance she and Natalie had to catch up. Nat had apparently been saving up her questions. "Was it totally intense? How many skaters were there? What are they like? Tell me, tell me, tell me stuff!"

"Slow down!" Claire laughed and stretched her legs under the table. Her first-period gym class had just about killed her; she was so sore from that first session with Groshev. And that was supposed to have been an easy one? She took a deep breath and turned to Natalie. "Okay . . . yes, it was intense. There were seven other kids there. And they're . . . intense, too."

"Are they all girls?" Natalie picked up her pencil and made a point of looking busy while Mr. Duckster shuffled to his desk. Claire glanced down at her worksheet. Fill in the blanks, straight out of the textbook again. At least it was easy, but sometimes when she heard the clinking of test tubes and Bunsen burners in Mr. Cho's lab next door, Claire wished she hadn't ended up with "The Duck" for science. Claire looked around. Fern LaValley seemed to be the only one actually doing the worksheet. Maya Sullivan and Riley Cooper sat next to each other wearing their maroon team jerseys, passing a notebook back and forth with some kind of diagrams in it. Probably making a lineup for their softball game later. Brady Bentley was trying to find someone to loan him a pencil because Mason Short, who always loaned pencils to everyone, was absent. And Henry Noogan was folding his worksheet into an origami animal of some sort.

"Sooo?" Natalie scooted closer to Claire once The Duck had pushed up his glasses and settled back at his desk with his newspaper.

"It's mostly girls. One boy who skates pairs with his sister."

"Is he cute?"

"Well . . ." Claire had been too stressed out to notice much at orientation, but thinking back, she realized Luke Collins *was* cute. Really cute, actually. The kind of boy she and Nat would probably fight over if he came for pancakes.

"Is he as cute as Denver Moon?" Natalie batted her eyelashes, and Claire laughed. Nat and Denver Moon were in drama club together. She'd been in love with him ever since the third-grade class play, when she was Snow White and he was Sneezy. Their teacher had to keep reminding Natalie that she was supposed to like the prince better than the dwarves.

"He *is* cute, isn't he?"

"Ladies?" The Duck was peering over his newspaper.

"Sorry," Natalie said. "I was asking her about number

five." She studied her worksheet for a minute, then tore off a corner, wrote on it, and slid it over to Claire.

IS HE AS CUTE AS KEENE???

Claire laughed. She didn't write back, but she thought about it as she started her worksheet. She used to think Keene was the cutest guy in the world. And he *was* cute. But maybe the world was a little bigger than she thought.

The next period at lunch, Claire plunked down at the usual table by the window with her lunch box. Natalie was already unwrapping her peanut butter-and-honey sandwich. "So you have training after school this week?"

"Yep. Today, Wednesday, and Friday. And we have the end-of-the-season skate for the club tomorrow night, don't forget."

"And sugar on snow at your house after. I didn't forget." Natalie licked some honey off her thumb. "Your week is pretty much booked. When are you supposed to get homework done?"

"Good question." Claire had been trying to figure that out. She could do some on the ride to Lake Placid and maybe some during downtime in the locker room. "I'll have to figure something out. Today's not bad. I just have a few pages to read and summarize for social studies. So far, the homework gods have been with me."

The homework gods hung in there until advanced math class eighth period, when Claire got hit with a big research project—Math Out-of-Bounds, Mrs. Cosgro called it. She said the idea was to break out of the textbook and explore "the wild side of math." Claire had to smile. The project was *so*

Mrs. Cosgro, with her gray ponytail and long skirts with jingly beads at the bottom. Mrs. Cosgro loved sharing real-world math stories, and she brought in all kinds of stuff to help them with math concepts—cereal boxes and video clips, sculptures and toy airplanes. She even brought in a ramp and skateboard one day when they were learning about angles.

Claire had always been good at math, able to figure out problems in her head, but it had never been her favorite subject until this year. Mrs. Cosgro had persuaded her to sign up to try the September math league test and put her name on the announcements when she'd gotten the highest score. Normally, Claire would have loved the idea of Math Out-of-Bounds, but today, all she could think about was when she'd possibly be able to get to the library. She had to choose a topic by Wednesday and make a list of questions for research by the following Monday. Claire thought about raising her hand to ask about the deadline, but Riley beat her to it.

"Mrs. Cosgro, I don't know if you know this, but Maya and I have a crazy-important softball game tonight. It's against Ticonderoga, and if we win, we go on to the tournament this weekend, so we're really not going to have time for much research. Monday's like a really bad day for this to be due."

"I see." Mrs. Cosgro tipped her head. "Riley, there's a reason they call you a student athlete—and not an athlete student. The student needs to come first." She smiled, but her voice was firm.

"Fine," Riley mumbled.

Claire was glad she hadn't been the one to raise her hand.

"Mrs. Cosgro?" Henry Noogan called from the back of the room, where he had assembled a row of origami frogs on his desk. They looked like a big frog family—two big ones and five little ones. "What if we don't believe that what we're learning in math class actually has real-world applications?"

"You're telling me that you don't have an appreciation for geometry?" She raised an eyebrow at his folded frog family. "I think an exploration of the patterns of paper craft might be an interesting topic." The bell rang, but Mrs. Cosgro held up her hand. "Hold on! Don't forget the homework! I need topics by Wednesday, then a project plan with a list of questions you hope to answer through your research for Monday!"

∞

"Hurry up, Nat. Let's get out." Claire slipped off her skate guards. "You can read that later. This is the last ice of the year."

They'd gone straight from school to the Northern Lights Rink for the end-of-season free skate, but Natalie was more interested in talking about Lake Placid than getting on the ice. "Holy guacamole, this is intense." She waved Claire's new training schedule in the air. "Three *school* nights a week for three hours a night? How'd you ever get your parents to go for this?"

Claire shrugged. There hadn't been much discussion, really. When her father had picked her up at the Olympic Center after Saturday's orientation, she'd simply handed him the schedule. He'd raised his eyebrows, and that was it. Later, after Claire went to bed, she heard her parents talking, their voices drifting up through the heating vent. She'd leaned over the edge of her down comforter to listen.

". . . *have* to make it work for her. She'll never have another opportunity like this."

"I know, Paul, but it's just so far. She won't be home until after nine."

"I'll see about working different hours at the border. If I can get on the shift that goes in at six, I'd be finished in time to take her. It's the opportunity of a lifetime, Becky. We'll make it work."

Claire couldn't sleep after that. She slipped out of bed and turned on her computer. There was mail from Charlotte.

> Claire,
> Don't have much time b/c I'm going to dinner with roommates but wanted to see how it went today. Still in one piece?
>
> —C

Claire thought about it. She felt tired but whole, she guessed. She hit the reply button.

> Hi, Charlotte!
> I'm still in one piece. Coach is intense. Made friends with a girl named Tasanee, and the other skaters are mostly okay. Except for Alexis. She's . . .

Claire hit the delete key. She didn't want to talk about Alexis just yet.

> There's one guy skating with us, Luke. He's kind of cute.

She hit the delete key again. Charlotte would ask too many questions if she mentioned that he was cute.

He skates pairs with his sister and they're really good.
All in all, I survived. I'll keep you posted!

—Claire

She hit the send button and climbed back into bed, but stayed awake for hours.

∽

Now, skating around the ice, Claire was feeling that lack of sleep.

"So your dad's going to drive you down every day?" Natalie handed the schedule back to Claire, who folded it, tucked it into the pocket of her fleece, and nodded.

"Mondays, Wednesdays, and Fridays. And some weekends, I guess, too, when we get close to competitions, especially over the summer." She held open the door to the rink and waited for Natalie to step through.

"You're skating all summer? Right up until school starts? And what about your birthday?"

Claire shrugged. She'd been so overwhelmed with the whole idea of her skating schedule she hadn't even thought about her thirteenth birthday at the beginning of September. "Pretty much. We're doing a couple competitions this summer. Regionals are in October, but my scholarship's only through August, so I won't have to worry about that."

"Well, what if you do really well at the other competitions?"

"Nah . . ." Claire waved the thought away. When she'd finally gotten around to reading the paperwork, she had discovered that the scholarship could be extended for "exceptional skaters" with "potential to compete at the national level," but that wasn't an issue for her. "I can't even believe I'm going to try competing again."

"You'll be fine." Natalie waited for a break in the circling skaters and merged into the crowd.

"Maybe," Claire said. She'd been pushing the whole competition idea out of her mind, trying not to think about where all this training was going. But she knew.

Claire picked up her pace and stuck her hands into her pockets to warm them. Her finger slid across the edge of the schedule and made her shiver. In spite of everything, the skating scholarship still felt unreal—like a movie she was watching that was going to end with the credits rolling any minute. She kept expecting someone to announce that it had all been a mistake, or her parents to tell her that they were sorry but there was no way they could keep traveling to Lake Placid.

Instead, they'd whispered words like *proud* and *opportunity*. They said she'd never have another one like this, and they'd make it work. That meant she had to make it work, too. Claire sighed, louder than she meant to.

"What?" Natalie asked, skating to a stop at the boards.

"I guess I'm just feeling overwhelmed. Like this happened so fast. And I don't know how I'm going to do everything. Like that project for math? Did you guys get that?"

"Nope." Claire wasn't surprised. Natalie had math with Mrs. Kramer, who wore a gray or black suit every day, loved her math textbook, and didn't believe in doing anything out of bounds.

"It's a cool project—we have to research something that's

not in the textbook. Real-world stuff. Fun stuff. But I just don't know when I'm going to do it. I don't even have a topic."

Natalie flung a leg up onto the boards to stretch. "Hmm . . . What about that Fibo-Rama guy you were talking about this fall. The one who wrote about that series of numbers that are like all over the place?"

"Fibonacci?" Claire stretched alongside Natalie.

"Yeah, him. All I remember is that pinecone you kept shoving in my face."

Claire laughed. She had loved Mrs. Cosgro's lesson on the Italian mathematician who called himself Fibonacci. She tried so hard to show Natalie how the numbers in the sequence he wrote about repeated themselves over and over in nature— like with petals on flowers, leaves on some trees, patterns on a pinecone. Apparently she'd gone overboard on that one. But Natalie was right—it was a great project idea. If she could just find some time for research.

"Moo!" Claire felt a tap on her elbow and looked down to see Roger the cow in Ivy's hand.

"Well, hello, Roger!" She started skating slowly, so Ivy could keep up. "And hello, Ivy. All set for the party?"

Ivy nodded. "Roger and I were excited about skating, but we're even more excited to go to your house after."

"I'm glad you're coming," Claire said. Ivy reached up with the hand that wasn't holding Roger, and Claire took it to spin her around. "My dad's home right now, boiling the sap for sugar on snow."

"Ooh! Roger loves sugar on snow! I'm going to go tell Jenna. Bye!"

Claire watched her skate off. Ivy had come a long way this season.

"I bet you're going to miss working with them." Natalie skated up alongside Claire.

"What?"

"Ka-PLOW!" Rory slid across the ice on his knees, and Claire had to jump over him so she wouldn't trip. She turned back to Natalie. "What do you mean?"

"Junior coaching." Natalie reached down to help Rory up, and he skated off. "It must have been hard to give it up."

Claire watched Rory go. It hadn't occurred to her she was giving it up, but of course she couldn't junior coach in Mojimuk Falls over the summer. Not if she was training an hour and a half away every weekend.

That meant no more rides to the rink with Keene. No more sleepy Saturday-morning conversations with Natalie in the truck. No more "red light, green light" games to teach Rory and Ivy how to stop and start on the ice.

"Come on." Natalie tugged her arm. "There's Lucy. Let's see if she's coming out for the party."

☙

Lucy came out to the farm. And so did half of Mojimuk Falls. Uncle George was going to need more hot dogs for the grill. It was just starting to get dark, and Claire's dad had a big bonfire sending up sparks next to the cow pond. The smoke drifted over to Claire and Natalie, on dessert duty outside the sugarhouse.

"Isn't it something how kids who never show up for skating

lessons manage to make it to the party?" Natalie whispered as she smoothed the trough of snow with her metal trowel. It looked like a snow cone for a giant.

"They figure you get credit just for having attended the Maple Show," Claire whispered back as she poured a steaming line of boiled sap from the pitcher in her hand onto the smooth snow.

"I love how it's the exact color of honey. Just as sweet and less painful." Natalie rubbed the welt on her cheek. One of her bees had gotten inside her veil and stung her while she was putting in the sugar water. "That whole hive's just mean. I don't know what I'm going to do with them." She stuck a Popsicle stick at the end of each wavy brown line, and one by one, kids came up to twirl the hardening sweet syrup around and around until it made a sort of frozen taffy lollipop on the stick.

"Can I have another one?" Ivy asked. She'd polished hers off in two chewy, gooey bites.

"Better just have one for now," Claire told her. "They're pretty sweet."

Ivy looked around, leaned closer to Claire, and lowered her voice. "Well, I know that, but Roger really wants his own. He only got a tiny bite of the last one."

Claire grinned, but she felt tears tug at the corner of her eyes as she twirled a second serving of sugar on snow for Ivy and Roger. She was going to miss junior coaching. Would she still have time for things like sugar parties?

After Groshev had passed out the schedules at the end of Saturday's orientation session, Tasanee had been so excited. "Oh, it's good to be back. And I'm psyched you're skating with us now," she told Claire as they'd wiped down their blades in the locker room. "You'll love training here. Before you know it, Lake Placid's going to feel like your second home."

Maybe it would, Claire thought, pouring six more lines of hot syrup onto the snow. She'd leave for Lake Placid right after school tomorrow to make it in time for her first four-to-seven training session, but for now, there were treats to serve up. She felt the mud squish under her work boots, heard the scraping of Natalie's trowel as she scooped more packed snow into the end of the trough for the next batch.

And as she inhaled the sweet maple steam from the pitcher, another thought occurred to her. She wasn't sure she wanted a second home.

CHAPTER 6

"Watch."

Andrei Groshev pushed off onto the ice. Three long strokes and he was skating as fast as Claire had ever seen anyone skate. He turned, planted his toe pick, and vaulted into the air, revolving three times before he landed on the opposite foot.

He skated up to the bench where his students sat. "That was three. We will work on two today. Within a few years, you will be going for three revolutions. At least, some of you will." His eyes drifted down the line, past Tasanee, Meghan, Stevie, Alexis, and Hannah, on to Claire, and past her to Abby and Luke.

"Time to warm up." Groshev clapped his hands, and the eight of them spilled out onto the ice. Claire took off quickly, with strong, smooth strokes that carried her around the rink fast enough to blow her hair back off her face.

"Hey." She caught up to Tasanee and was going to ask about the schedule, but Tasanee shook her head.

"No talking during warm-up. It's one of Groshev's rules."

"Sorry," Claire whispered and then skated silently alongside Tasanee.

Be on time. No giggling. No talking. How many more Groshev rules was she going to learn about? Mary Kate's only rule was "Do your best," and she loved laughing as much as Claire and Natalie did.

"Focus now." Groshev was suddenly at Claire's side. "And watch your edges." He reached out for her hands to adjust her posture. She was thankful for her gloves, imagining how her palms must be sweating already.

Claire tried to hold the position, but it felt off, like she was wearing somebody else's clothes that didn't quite fit. Groshev came by twice more to take her hands and tip her in one direction or another. "Better," he said finally, just before the whistle blew them into line for instruction.

"To my knowledge, only one of you has mastered the double toe loop, so I will ask for a demonstration."

Claire looked down the line, at the jut of Alexis's chin, the determination in Meghan's eyes, and wondered who it was. Maybe Stevie. With her dad being a skater, she'd probably been training since birth. No, Claire decided, probably Luke. He was an incredibly talented skater, tall and thin but muscular. Or Alexis; she was so intense she'd probably try over and over again until she got it, no matter how many bruises she got in the process.

"Claire . . . ," Tasanee whispered, nudging her forward. Claire looked down the line and realized that everyone was looking at her. Including Groshev.

"Well?" he said.

"Me?" Claire squeaked. "I . . . I haven't mastered the double toe loop."

"Yes, you have. I've seen you land it twice now. It is why you are here."

The Maple Show. She had never landed a double toe cleanly in front of an audience before that day, and she had only landed one more since then.

"Come now." Groshev clapped his hands, and Claire's throat went dry.

"I . . . that was just . . . it was the first time I ever . . ."

Groshev's eyes narrowed, and Claire stopped talking. Her heart pounded so hard she thought it might burst right through her fleece, but she stepped forward. "Okay, I'll try." She felt everyone's eyes on her as she skated to the other end of the rink, made her three-turn, planted her toe pick, and hurled herself into the air. She barely made it one full rotation, landed on the edge of her blade, and fell on her side, skidding into the boards.

The rink was silent as she stood, and when she skated back to the group, her blades scratching the ice sounded like shouting in church. Before she reached them, Groshev flicked a hand out at her.

"Again."

She started skating again, but her right knee throbbed, and tears stung her eyes. She blinked them back. There was probably a Groshev rule against crying.

Claire picked up speed, made her three-turn, and planted her toe pick again. This time, she whipped her arms around even harder as soon as she took off, willing her body to spin faster before she hit the ground.

She spun faster, but not fast enough.

Her toe pick caught the ice in the middle of the second rotation, and the force of it threw her onto her hip and elbow.

She stood but didn't start skating back. She knew it was coming.

"Again."

Three more times she skated, took off, flung her body into rotation, and crashed. The last time, she couldn't even catch herself to keep her head from slamming back onto the ice. Dark spots danced in her eyes when she stood up.

"Come back," Groshev said. Claire skated over. She couldn't miss the smile playing at Alexis's lips, but she was past wanting to cry. She was just relieved she got to stop jumping.

She stepped back into the line, but Groshev motioned her to come forward. When she did, he looked her up and down. She brushed ice shavings out of her hair, wiped her runny nose on the sleeve of her sweatshirt, and waited.

"You are taking off," he said finally. "Again and again and again, you are falling."

Well, no kidding, Claire thought. She needed a fancy Lake Placid coach for this?

"Watch," he said, and took off, still talking. "I am gathering speed, as you did, maintaining that speed through my turn, and you did this, too." He turned. "But then I plant and"—he jumped, no, *sprung* was a better word—into the air above the ice as if he'd just bounced from a trampoline. After he was airborne, he rotated in the air, one, two, three times, before landing. He skated back to Claire.

"Do you see?"

She nodded.

"That's not enough. Tell me what you saw."

"You jumped. Really high. And then rotated."

"Yes. And *then* rotated. You must jump first. Get the launch. *Then* rotate."

Claire nodded and swiveled herself back into line, but Groshev shook his head.

"Again."

She felt Tasanee's hand on her elbow, half-comforting her, half-pushing her forward. She pushed off, stroking around the rink again. She had to get it this time.

Jump. And *then* rotate.

She tried to picture Groshev's jump, but she couldn't imagine herself getting that high, so instead, she pictured her own successful double from the Maple Show.

Launch first. High. *Then* rotate.

She made the three-turn, planted her toe pick, and jumped—not around, but up—and when she found herself airborne, when she felt as if she were flying, she tucked in her arms and turned, propelling her body around once, twice—all the way around and landed cleanly.

She skated back to Groshev, who nodded. "Better."

Claire, Alexis, and Luke all managed to land the double toe loop at least once before the session was over. Tasanee, Meghan, Abby, and Hannah were close. Stevie never got more than a single, and that surprised Claire; she'd figured someone with an Olympic star for a dad would be mastering triples by now. But Stevie seemed more interested in texting than jumping. Whenever Groshev was looking the other way, she'd pull her cell phone out of her jacket pocket and start poking at the keys. Then she'd skate a little, pull it out again, look at the screen, and laugh. Whoever was texting back was way more interesting to Stevie than anyone on the ice. Claire couldn't even imagine what Groshev would do if he caught her. If there was a rule about talking, there definitely had to be one about texting.

When they moved on to spins, Claire practiced with Tasanee but couldn't help sneaking glances at Groshev's private session with Alexis.

"Lower. You need to get lower. Like this." Groshev demonstrated a perfect sit spin, and Claire stopped skating to watch. Was there anything he couldn't do? It was easy imagining him with that gold medal around his neck; he was so strong, so solid. He came out of the spin and turned to Alexis. "Now you try."

She skated into the spin, lower this time, but not nearly as fast as Groshev.

"Good. Very good," Groshev told her. "Keep working on it." When he looked up at Claire, she realized she was staring. She jerked her head down and started in on a footwork sequence. But she couldn't help thinking, as her feet moved over the ice, that she could have done better. Sit spins were one of her strongest moves. Alexis didn't have that much power, and she was traveling. You weren't supposed to move from that single spot on the ice once you started spinning. Claire imagined what it would be like to just whip across the ice and launch into her own sit spin, right in front of Groshev and Alexis.

But she didn't. She practiced the footwork sequence a few more times and then went back to working on the toe loop.

With five minutes left in the session, Groshev blew his

whistle. "Change out of your skates and come back here before you go. We need to talk about some schedule changes."

"Schedule changes? It's the first day," Claire said to Tasanee as they slipped on their guards and started for the locker room.

"Get used to it." Tasanee pulled open the door. "He adds at least one practice a week. Usually two."

"You've got to be kidding!" What was she going to tell her parents? Her father had already rearranged his work schedule to get her here Mondays, Wednesdays, and Fridays. "More school nights?"

Tasanee nodded. "Weekends, too." She stood with her bag. "I'm going to the bathroom. I'll see you back out there."

Claire nodded, thinking about even more days in Lake Placid as she untied her skates. It was never going to fly. Not with everything her folks were trying to cram into their Saturdays on the farm to get caught up from the workweek. And when was she going to work on her math project? She'd scribbled a quick list of research questions, and Mrs. Cosgro had given her some books to use when she told her she was going to research Fibonacci, but she'd barely had time to skim through them.

"Nice job out there." Luke stood over her with his black skating bag slung over his shoulder and flashed her a smile full of braces and dimples.

"Thanks," Claire said. "You too."

He grinned and shrugged. "I've been skating at the college rink up in Plattsburgh most nights. My dad's an English professor, so our family has free access to the fitness facilities. I get a playlist going and skate for like two hours. Where have you been skating?"

"Northern Lights Rink, whenever I can. And then just on the pond." She stopped herself from calling it the cow pond.

"Well, you've obviously been working. You're going to fit right in here." He smiled, and Claire noticed his eyes. They were brown but not just brown; they were flecked with bits of green and gold, and they smiled along with the rest of his face. "Hey, we better get back out to the rink. Ladies first." He motioned for Claire to go ahead of him.

Claire stifled a laugh. That wasn't something you heard in Mojimuk Falls.

Stevie and Alexis were leaning against the snack machines in the hallway, waiting for Meghan to buy bottled water. Hannah walked toward them, too, a dollar bill in her hand. "Snack time, Hannah?" Alexis asked with a smirk.

Stevie stopped texting on her cell phone long enough to whisper something to Alexis, and they both laughed.

Hannah wheeled around and headed for the locker room without looking back.

"Hey, Luke!" Alexis stood up a little straighter. "Nice toe loop. You land your double flip yet?"

He stopped and shook his head, smiling. "Not quite. You?"

"I'm almost there." Alexis raised her eyebrows and grinned. "Want to make a bet on who lands it first?"

"Nope, too close to call. Plus we have some new talent, don't forget." Luke gave Claire a friendly nudge with his elbow. "She might end up landing it before either of us." He opened the door that led out to the ice.

Claire felt Alexis's eyes settle on her as she stepped into

the rink with Luke. She was thankful when the door closed behind her.

Tasanee was already in the stands, reading a new book that looked a lot like the one she had at orientation.

"More vampires?"

"This is the last one in this series." She looked sad but perked up. "But that lady who works at The Bookstore Plus called and said she set aside a new book for me. It's about homicidal fairies, so I'm all set for when I finish this one."

"Do you think this will take long?" Claire settled in between Tasanee and Luke and looked at her watch. It was ten after, seven, and her dad was probably already waiting in the parking lot.

"Nah—probably just practice times for Saturday," Tasanee answered as Groshev stepped through the door.

"Saturday?" Claire mouthed the question to Tasanee.

"Yes, Ms. Boucher," Groshev said, eyes fixed on her. Apparently, he could read lips. "We practice on Saturdays. Sundays sometimes as well. This Saturday, you'll be here at eight a.m. Will that be a problem?"

Claire shook her head.

"Good. I will also see you at four o'clock on Thursday. We will be working on routines for Friday Flair. Bring music." He blew his whistle, and everyone started to leave.

Claire tried to keep the shock from showing on her face. Training on Thursday, too? And what was this Friday thing? "We're doing routines for what?" Claire asked Tasanee.

"Friday Flair," Tasanee said. "It's just a casual show for the tourists who visit the Olympic Center."

"*This* Friday?"

Tasanee nodded.

"I can't be ready for a show in two days!"

"It's not a big deal. No formal judges or anything." Luke picked up his skating bag and started down the hallway. "Friday Flair is about showmanship. No required elements. Some people even do group numbers, for something different. Just do whatever routine is the most fun. Hey, Ab! Wait up!" Luke called to Abby, who was ahead of them. He turned to Claire. "I gotta run; Mom gets crazy when she has to wait. But listen . . . we all remember what the first week is like." He smiled. Those dimples again. "You probably feel overwhelmed, but it gets easier. All of it. You learn to do homework between sessions—and we all help one another out. I'm really good with math, and Tasanee's great at editing papers. You'll see. You'll get used to Groshev, too. See you tomorrow!"

"You too." Claire waved, but her head was still swirling. A show this Friday? Extra practice on Thursday *and* Saturday?

She turned to Tasanee as they headed down the hall to the back parking lot. "I can't believe this. I'm not ready to skate in a show. And then . . . the Saturday thing. I know my dad has to work, and the boys have hockey, and—"

"So stay with us Friday night." Tasanee opened the door, and a blast of cold wind cooled Claire's face. It felt good; her cheeks had been burning, her eyes stinging with tears that blurred the colors of the world flags flapping along the front of the building.

"You can come home with me after the Friday show," Tasanee said. "We'll go to practice together Saturday."

Claire squinted into the wind toward the lot. There was her dad, waiting in the truck, reading his newspaper. "Thanks, that's a really nice offer. I'll talk to my dad about it." She started to go, but Tasanee grabbed her arm.

"And Claire?"

"Yeah?"

"Be careful getting too friendly with Luke Collins."

Claire stopped. "How come? He seems really nice."

"Oh, he is," Tasanee said laughing. "Alexis thinks he's *especially* nice. And if he keeps paying more attention to you than her, you may need to watch your back."

CHAPTER 7

You got everything?"

"I think so." Claire's duffel bag sat next to her on the truck's bench seat. She hadn't even bothered to take it inside after last night's practice. The Thursday ice session had been a busy one with preparations for Friday Flair. Claire managed to rework the "Appalachian Snowfall" routine she'd skated for the Northern Lights Christmas show last year and felt a little better about the whole thing.

"Got your toothbrush?" asked Dad.

"Yep."

"Pajamas?"

"Yep. And homework, in case I have time to work on it." The Fibonacci books Mrs. Cosgro gave her made the bag even heavier when Claire hoisted it onto her shoulder.

Dad pulled out his wallet. "Take a twenty out of there for your dinner."

Claire shook her head. "I won't need it. Tasanee says we're going to help at her family's restaurant for a while tonight after our session, and we'll eat there."

"Since when do you know anything about cooking Chinese food?"

Claire laughed. "We're not cooking, just handing out menus and stuff. And it's not Chinese. It's Thai." Now that she was used to the idea of staying in Lake Placid, she was looking forward to spending the night with the Luangs. Tasanee's stories about chaotic weekends at the restaurant made Lemongrass Thai sound a lot like the sugarhouse.

Dad pulled into the parking lot, turned to Claire, and tucked a lock of hair back into her ponytail. "I'll see you tomorrow then. Mom's picking you up, and I'll be home around four."

"Sounds good. Bye!" Claire leaned in to kiss him on the cheek and hustled inside.

She found Tasanee in the locker room and plopped down to join her. Books spilled out of her bag onto the bench.

"Hey!" Tasanee said. "You're only staying one night, right? Looks like you brought your whole bookshelf."

"Kind of. I'm trying to sneak in homework time. I have a math project on Fibonacci numbers."

"Fiba-who?"

"Fibonacci. He was an old math guy who wrote about this sequence of numbers." Claire pulled a notebook out of her bag and flipped to her first page of notes. "Look."

0, 1, 1, 2, 3, 5, 8, 13, 21, 34, 55, 89, 144, 233, 377 . . .

"You start with zero and one, and then each number in the sequence is the sum of the two numbers before it. So zero plus one is one. Then one plus one is two. One plus two is three. Two plus three is five. Then eight. Then thirteen. Then twenty-one. And so on."

"Okay. But what's the point?" Tasanee tipped her head.

"Well, the numbers in the series are, like, special. They have all these cool properties." Claire's voice got a little louder. She couldn't help getting excited when she talked about this stuff. "Like if you take any ten Fibonacci numbers in a row and add them up, you can always divide that number by eleven."

Tasanee wrinkled her nose. "Why would you want to?"

"You sound like my friend Natalie. But check this out." Claire picked up one of her books from Mrs. Cosgro and flipped it open to the page of illustrations about Fibonacci numbers in nature. "Look at all these flowers. Lilies and irises have three petals. Buttercups have five. Cosmos have eight. Black-eyed Susans have twenty-one. Those are *all* Fibonacci numbers. Isn't that bizarre? And there are Fibonacci patterns in pinecones and pineapples and sunflower seeds—"

"And music." Luke was standing over the bench, looking down at Claire's book. "Some of the world's big composers— guys like Mozart and Beethoven and Bartók—used Fibonacci numbers in their compositions."

Tasanee laughed. "Okay, this is just weird. Are you two in some kind of math cult?"

Luke grinned. "Our math club had to put together a big bulletin board on Fibonacci last year. It's really interesting."

"You do math club, too? I just—" Claire looked up at him and completely lost her train of thought. Luke wore a leather jacket, with his hair slicked back as if he'd just stepped out of a fifties movie. "Why are you dressed like that?"

"Friday Flair." He ran a hand over his hair. "We're doing a fifties song."

Tasanee reached into her bag and pulled out a Hawaiian shirt—lemon yellow with red and orange flowers. "And I'm on a 'Surfin' Safari.'" She pulled the oversized shirt on over her leotard and started fastening buttons. Claire just stared. "My music is from the Beach Boys. Didn't you hear it yesterday when I ran the program?"

Claire nodded. She'd heard the high-energy surf music and admired Tasanee's rapid-fire jumps. And she'd heard Luke and Abby's Elvis Presley song, too. But nobody had costumes before. "We're supposed to dress up for this?"

Tasanee nodded. "And this is mild." She tilted her head toward the far corner of the room, where Meghan, Stevie, and Alexis were decked out in shiny gold bodysuits with black velvet vests.

"Make it floofier," Meghan told Stevie, who was spraying Gotta-Be-Glued hairspray onto her bangs.

Alexis sat on the bench, painting gold stripes down the middle of each red fingernail.

Claire's mouth hung open. "I didn't bring anything. I didn't know."

Tasanee pursed her lips. "Hmm . . . What's your music again?"

"It's that 'Appalachian Snowfall' song. I barely got my routine together yesterday, but I just brought my regular skating pants and fleece. I don't have, like, a snowflake costume or anything."

"You'll be okay," Luke said. "It doesn't have to be anything fancy."

"But I don't have *anything*!"

Tasanee started digging through her skating bag. "Oh, good, it's here!" She shook out a red skating skirt with silver and green sparkles. "Sometimes it pays to never clean out your skating bag. I wore this for the Christmas show. It's a start, anyway." She flopped the skirt over the wooden bench and pulled Claire's skating bag into her lap. "You do have tights in here, right?"

"I think so." Claire couldn't stop staring at the elaborate costumes. Hannah was dressed as a clown, complete with boot covers that made her skates look like giant clown shoes. She was painting her nose red. Claire turned back to Tasanee. "I can't do this. I'm going to look stupid not dressed up."

But Tasanee was grinning. "You're going to look perfect." Her lap was full of clothes from Claire's bag.

"I can't wear that." It was her outdoor winter skating stuff—a pair of thick, quilted blue mittens with fake fur around the edges, and the puffy purple-and-green-striped hat and matching wool scarf Aunt Maureen knitted for her last Christmas. Aunt Maureen was a lousy knitter, so the scarf was extra long and droopy. Claire only wore it on the coldest cow pond days, and never in front of anybody but Charlotte.

"You most certainly *can* wear this. It's perfect!" Tasanee handed Claire the red skirt she'd pulled from her own bag. "Put this on, and then add all the wintry stuff. You're going to be a country girl skating out on a pond in nature. It's perfect for your music, Claire!"

"You'll be great." Luke gave her a wave. "I need to find Abby. I'll see you out there." Claire couldn't see how her homemade hat and scarf could possibly amount to a costume, but she put everything on and laced up her skates. It was time for the run-through. In an hour, there would be people filling the stands.

"There." Tasanee looped the scarf around Claire's neck and stood back. "Perfect. Now let's go."

Claire followed Tasanee down the hallway to the rink, pulled off her guards, and stepped onto the ice. She took off into the cold air and felt the skirt ruffling against her thighs. She skated past the sign on the boards for WSLP, the Lake Placid radio station. *Music in the Mountains.* She already knew the slogan by heart; she must have skated past it two hundred times this week.

"Hey!" Meghan skated up with silver streamers hanging from her arms, ruffling out behind her. She reached out to touch Claire's scarf. "Your costume is awesome. Where'd you ever buy that getup?"

Claire shrugged. "Just something I pulled together."

"Well, the judges are going to love it." Meghan untangled one of her silver streamers. "We're skating to 'Dancing Queen' today so we did the disco thing. Stevie's dad got us the outfits. The judges either like really glittery or really folksy and cute. You'll do great in that."

"Hey, Megs!" Alexis skated up. "Well, how about that." She looked at Claire. "What's this supposed to be? *Little House on the Prairie?*"

"Oh, come on, Alexis. She looks cute." Meghan turned back to Claire. "It's perfect for your music. Such a homemade feel."

"Thanks." If they only knew.

"Hey!" Tasanee skated up in her Hawaiian shirt and made a hockey stop that sprayed snow onto the disco queens' bell-bottoms. "Come on, let's get a seat," Tasanee said, pulling on Claire's scarf.

"Easy on the costume!" Claire tossed the end of the scarf around her neck once more and winked. "This is one-of-a-kind, you know."

Claire slipped on her skate guards and followed Tasanee up into the seats so they could watch the first half of the show. Tasanee was in the middle of the lineup, after Luke and Abby; Claire had somehow ended up last on the list.

"Perfect," she said. "That way I have plenty of time to run to the bathroom to be sick while I wait."

"You're going to be fine." Tasanee reached over and stole Claire's hat to try it on. Only Tasanee, with her silky black hair and perfect skin, could make Aunt Maureen's hat look glamorous. "Remember, it's not a real competition. The judges are just people from the audience. They give them those stupid number cards, and they just hold up the highest numbers for whichever routine they like best. Nothing like the USFS judges at regular competitions."

"Yeah? Well, do they have clipboards?" Claire's stomach tightened just thinking about the judges at the Champlain Valley Open, making their little check marks every time she wobbled. She grabbed her hat back and pulled it down over her ears.

"No clipboards allowed at Friday Flair, I promise." Tasanee held up her hand as if she were taking an oath. "Besides, real judges don't use clipboards anymore, either. It's all computerized."

"Good evening, ladies and gentlemen!" One of those big, deep radio-announcer voices filled the rink. "And welcome to Friday Flair . . . where showmanship counts and *you're* the judge of that!"

Claire looked around until she found the source of the voice, an older balding man wearing a green-and-blue-plaid flannel shirt under a black fleece vest. "We have a faaaan-TAS-tic show for you tonight, Lake Placid! What do you say about that?!" He waved his arms at the crowd until they cheered.

"Who is this guy?" Claire whispered to Tasanee.

Tasanee laughed. "Everyone knows Bob-O around here. His real name is Robert O. Piddlemyer, but he always says, 'Call me Bob-O.' He used to be a local DJ, but he retired and now he announces shows and works in the Olympic Center skate shop."

"It's a beeee-YOO-tiful night for an ice show, isn't it?" More arm waving. "Our first contestant is Hannah Madison, and she's up to some funny business!"

Hannah skated to center ice and struck a pose on one knee, as if she were proposing marriage to someone. In front of Claire, Alexis whispered something to Stevie, and they laughed. Claire hoped Hannah blew them both away out there.

"What's her music again?" Claire whispered.

"Gary Lewis and the Playboys," Tasanee said, grinning. "It's this awesome sixties song, and she did a wicked job with the choreography."

When the music started, Hannah spun around on one knee and then sprang to her feet as the vocals began for "Everybody Loves a Clown."

Claire tapped her foot to the bouncy tune. Hannah had made a great choice; the tempo kept her moving fast and gave her some great opportunities for footwork.

"So far so good." Tasanee clenched her hands on the back of the empty seat in front of her, and her eyes followed Hannah around the ice. Claire wondered if Tasanee was nervous for Hannah or for herself, having to follow her.

When the key changed in the song, Hannah made a quick three-turn and launched into a toe loop. Claire gasped when she saw Hannah make not one but two perfect revolutions and land cleanly.

"Whoa! She only landed that once in practice. I thought for sure she'd just do the single tonight. Did she plan that?"

"Doubt it." Tasanee's grip on the seat relaxed, and she smiled. "It was awesome, wasn't it? Hannah says she's always great under pressure, so Groshev let her keep that jump in her routine even though she missed it at practice. Alexis was furious because whenever she's not landing her double salchow consistently, he makes her take it out."

Hannah nailed another double—this time a Lutz, which was even harder—before she sank back down to her clown-proposing-marriage pose for the end of the song.

"Woo-hooooo!" Tasanee cheered. "Perfect ten!"

That reminded Claire. "Where are the judges sitting?"

Tasanee tilted her head. "Right behind Bob-O."

Claire leaned forward and watched as a big woman in an I LOVE NY sweatshirt raised a number nine sign high over her head. The man next to her looked bored as he held up a number seven. The woman glanced over and then swatted him with her nine. Claire couldn't hear what she said, but the man put down his seven and found a nine.

The two people next to them, a younger couple with a baby, held up eights.

"That ought to be enough to keep her on the throne a little while, at least," Tasanee said.

"The throne?"

Tasanee pointed back to the far side of the rink, where Hannah was skating toward a big chair decorated to look like a throne. "You sit there until you get bumped off by somebody with a higher score. Whoever's there at the end wins."

Claire's stomach flipped again. Not only did you get judged here; you got judged and then thrown out of your chair if you stunk. And she'd have to skate pretty soon, too. Claire tried not to think about it. She counted the seats in the section across the ice to see if they were in a Fibonacci pattern. There were three in the first row, five in the second, then eight and thirteen—but the pattern didn't hold after that.

"All right, listen to Bob-O now, because I have a special treat for you. Did you know that the King of Rock and Roll is with us here tonight?" He waved his hands, and the I Love NY lady screamed, "Elvis!"

"That's right," Bob-O said. "Elvis Presley himself. The King is back! Here he is with his best girl . . . skating to 'All Shook Up!'"

Luke and Abby skated onto the ice holding hands. When they got to the center, Luke dropped Abby's hand to smooth his hair, and the audience laughed. If this contest was really all about showmanship, they were off to a good start.

When the swinging music started, Luke and Abby skated apart, toward opposite ends of the rink. They moved in unison, their footwork matching perfectly, even though they were nowhere near each other for the first part of the song.

When Elvis Presley got to the first refrain, Luke and Abby came together again, and he lifted her by the waist and tossed her, spinning, through the air.

Claire sucked in her breath, just as she had the first time she'd seen Luke and Abby do the move at practice. She'd seen plenty of tosses at professional shows like *Stars on Ice*, but she'd never seen kids her age pull it off.

Abby landed cleanly and spun back around to take Luke's hand for the end of the song. They did single axels in unison— Claire wondered if they'd started working on the double yet— and then simultaneous spins, freezing on the song's last note with huge smiles on their faces. There were those dimples again; Claire could see them all the way from the stands. If the audience applause was any indication, Hannah would be giving up her throne soon.

"That was great. Let's see now . . ." Tasanee leaned forward to watch for the scores. The I Love NY lady handed out another nine, and so did her husband. This time, he waited to see what she held up first. Claire clapped when the couple with the baby held up nines, too, and Luke and Abby skated toward the throne. Hannah skated off the ice, and one of the rink volunteers rushed out with a second chair. Luke gave Abby the throne and sat in the folding chair.

"Wish me luck." Tasanee stood and shook out her legs.

"You'll be great!" Claire didn't ask if Tasanee was going to try a double. She hadn't managed to land the double toe loop during her run-through earlier, even though she had pulled it off a few times on Wednesday. Claire had landed hers in practice consistently through the week, but she still wasn't sure if she'd try it tonight.

"All-righty!" Bob-O's voice echoed through the rink again. "Surf's up tonight, ladies and gentlemen! We have Tasanee Luang, skating to the Beach Boys' 'Surfin' Safari.'"

Tasanee skated out and picked up a surfboard—not a full-sized one, just one of those Boogie boards—that was leaning against the boards.

The music started abruptly, but Tasanee was ready. With the first chord, she jumped right onto the board on her skates and put out her arms as if she were balancing on the edge of a wave. When the opening lines ended and the drums kicked in, Tasanee stepped off the surfboard and skated a few quick figures around it before she scooped it up under her arm. She tossed it over the side of the boards and skated the lead-in to her first jump.

Claire held her breath, but this one was just a single Lutz—something Tasanee could do in her sleep. She landed it cleanly and followed it with a quick footwork sequence that fit the music perfectly before speeding up to prepare for another jump. Tasanee landed another clean single, and then another, and after a final spin, the music faded out, and she struck her last pose, lying back on the ice as if she were sunbathing.

Claire clapped along with the rest of the crowd. It was a cute routine, for sure, and artistry was the only thing that was supposed to count here. Still, Claire wondered if Tasanee would get lower scores because she stuck with the easier jumps. She leaned over to watch the cards go up, and sure enough,

Tasanee fell short—7, 8, 8, and 9. Tasanee waved and skated off the ice, away from Luke and Abby. They'd keep their seats for now.

"Nice job," Claire whispered when Tasanee returned to the seat next to her.

"Nah." Tasanee waved her hand as if she could brush away the compliment. "I wimped out on the jumps. I deserved those crappy scores."

"The I Love New York sweatshirt lady liked you," Claire said, and that made Tasanee smile.

"Only because I share her exquisite sense of fashion." She turned up the collar on her Hawaiian shirt.

"Ladieeees and gentlemen, are you ready for a real treat?" Bob-O raised his arms and waited for the crowd to cheer. "I bet you didn't expect to meet the Disco Queens when you came to Lake Placid, but here they are! Join me in welcoming Stevie Van Syke, Meghan James, and Alexis Rock, skating to a classic tune from ABBA!"

The three girls skated to center ice and joined hands to make a sparkly circle, and when the first notes of "Dancing Queen" filled the rink, they started spinning, faster and faster, until they were just a shiny gold blur with the ceiling lights shimmering on the fabric of their costumes. It was a wicked effect, and Claire wasn't surprised when the audience started clapping after just that first move. The I Love NY lady probably loved those shiny costumes.

Their skating, for the most part, was solid, too, but there were a couple bobbles. Stevie did a single when the other two were doing double salchows, and she also tripped during an easy spiral. Meghan fell at the end of her double toe loop but got right back up. Everything Alexis did was perfect, right down to the cartwheel she turned at the end of the routine, landing in a split between the other two girls.

Claire and Tasanee clapped, and Tasanee leaned over. "Hope Abby and Luke weren't too comfortable."

The scores popped up right away: 9, 9, 9, and 10. The Dancing Queens jumped up and down on the ice hugging one another and then skated over to the throne.

"Hey, you need to get up there!" Tasanee tugged Claire's sleeve. "You're next!" She had been so mesmerized by the shiny spinning she'd forgotten she still had to skate. Claire slid her skate guards off just as Bob-O announced, "And now, our final skater. Claire . . . Butcher, is it?"

It wasn't. It was pronounced Boo-SHAY. But Claire couldn't find her voice to correct him, so she just nodded.

"Claire is skating to 'Appalachian Snowfall.'"

She skated to the center circle and stood straight, arms at her sides, head bowed, to wait for the music. Her heart pounded, but she took a deep breath and tried to quiet it.

If the music would just start, she might be okay. She loved this song, really loved it. The way it started with graceful, tinkling notes that sounded like they were coming out of the music box at her aunt Maureen's house. The way the drums and strings kicked in with so much energy just a few seconds later, surprising everybody who thought it was going to be a quiet song.

Claire had designed her routine herself, to match that surprise in the music. She hadn't had time to choreograph anything new with Groshev yet; he'd just helped her fine-tune the jumps. He had insisted that she include the double toe loop at the end after she'd landed it the last time on Thursday. She'd nodded, knowing she could just change it back to a single once she got out on the ice, and that was exactly what she planned to do now.

Claire let her arms unfold, raised them above her head, and pivoted on the ice, as if she were a dancer on the music box playing the notes. And when the beat picked up, when the song kicked into high gear, she gave a sudden leap—a music box dancer breaking free—and took off around the rink.

Claire felt her scarf—Aunt Maureen's crazy purple-and-green-striped scarf—flying behind her, and it made her laugh a little. Here she was in Lake Placid, on the rink where who-knows-how-many world champion figure skaters had performed, on the rink where the 1980 American hockey team had beat the Russians in the Miracle on Ice. Here she was, skating in front of an audience that wasn't the Maple Show crowd, and wearing this loopy scarf.

Somehow, it made her forget about the cardboard number signs. And when the double toe loop came up, Claire forgot to change it back to a single. She planted her toe pick, took off, and made two complete revolutions. She landed cleanly on one foot and her smile broke open even wider when she heard the applause.

The next part of the song had lots of quick little notes, and Claire used them to show off her footwork. She and Charlotte used to make up the craziest steps out on the pond—crossovers and Rockette-kicks, and everything you could imagine. Claire's feet just took her along for the ride until the music transitioned into the last big push.

Claire had a single salchow planned for her final jump. She hadn't considered making it a double because she hadn't really landed it cleanly in practice all week, even though she'd come close a couple times. If she had stopped to think, she would have thought about the fact that she'd lose points for falling, that this was her first show and she ought to take it easy, that she hadn't even cleared the jump with her coach. But she didn't stop to think.

She jumped.

And she made two revolutions.

And a clean landing.

And then the music slowed, and she spun one last time. Slower, slower, slower still, until she stepped back onto the music box for a final pivot—a dancer recaptured by the last, lazy notes—and bowed her head.

There was a second of silence before the applause came in a great whoosh. Claire looked up and curtsied, and couldn't help staring out at the crowd. Not a crowd of people who clapped because they knew her and cut hay with her dad and were coming for pancakes later. A crowd of strangers, clapping because she had skated beautifully.

And they were holding up numbers.

9. 10. 10. And 10.

Claire started skating toward Tasanee, who was standing, clapping like crazy.

Coach Groshev intercepted her. "Absolutely stunning!" he said. "Tomorrow morning, we incorporate that double salchow into your program for the competition. Just stunning!"

"Thanks." Claire headed for the boards, but Bob-O's voice

stopped her. "Whoa-ho-ho there, young lady! Where do you think you're going? There's a throne over there with your name on it."

Claire turned. The seat was empty, waiting for her. The newly dethroned Dancing Queens were skating her way.

"Your . . . uh . . . your program was really good," Claire told Stevie as she skated past.

"Not as good as yours, apparently," Stevie said, and Claire's stomach flipped. "I didn't know you were landing the double sal."

"Yeah, well . . . me neither."

Alexis skated by her next. "Don't get too comfortable on that throne, Aunt Jemima. You got lucky tonight."

Then came Meghan. She whispered "Congratulations" and looked down at her skates, but not before Claire saw the tears pooling in her pale blue eyes. She skated over to the throne and took her seat. The guy who brought out the chairs before skated out to bring her the Friday Flair crown.

Glittery snowflakes adorned the top. It was so sparkly, Claire felt like a five-year-old in a Halloween costume when she put it on, but still, as she looked out over the empty ice, the cheering crowd, the bright lights, she had to admit—the Maple Princess had come a long way.

CHAPTER 8

Claire stayed back to get an extra copy of the training schedule from Groshev so her dad could keep one at work. When she clunked her way back into the locker room on her skate guards, Tasanee was already changed and waiting.

"That," Tasanee said, grinning, "was one amazing skate from the girl who was worried that she didn't have a costume."

"Thanks." Claire sat down on the bench to start unlacing.

"I never saw you hit that double salchow at practice. When did you start landing it?"

"About fifteen minutes ago." Claire pulled a terry cloth towel from her bag and wiped down her blades.

"Seriously?"

"Yep." Claire slid the skates into her bag. "I have no idea what I was thinking. Groshev is probably furious with me; I never cleared it with him."

Tasance shook her head. "He's only furious when you miss."

Claire stood and reached for her locker to get her regular clothes. A strong chemical smell hit her as soon as she pulled open the door.

"Whoa." Tasanee noticed, too. "Did you leave your nail polish open in there or something?"

Claire shook her head. "I don't even use nail polish." She pulled her sweatshirt down from the hook. Her other clothes had fallen onto the floor of the locker, and when she reached in to get them, she felt something wet and sticky.

"Oh!" She pulled back her hand as if she'd been bitten. Her fingertips were bright red. She reached back in and pulled out the black pants she'd brought to wear to the restaurant. They were covered—smeared everywhere with red and gold nail polish.

Tasanee drew in a sharp breath. "Looks like you've made yourself an enemy."

"What do you mean?" Claire asked.

"Who do you think?" Tasanee looked at her.

"Alexis?" Claire whispered.

Tasanee nodded. "That would sure be my guess."

Claire stared at the pants, still crumpled in her hands. "Maybe it was an accident or something. . . . Maybe . . ."

"Claire, look." Tasanee took the pants from her and held them up so Claire couldn't miss the angry red streaks. "This doesn't happen by accident."

"No." Claire felt her stomach drop, right down to the locker room floor. "No, I guess not." She bit her lip. "Should I say something to Groshev?"

Tasanee didn't hesitate. "No. He won't do anything."

"Seriously?"

"Whenever anybody complains about something with another skater, an argument or whatever, he puts his hand up and cuts the conversation off. He says it's not his job to deal with the drama. He's here to coach skating and doesn't want to hear about anything else. He'd just tell you to work it out yourself." Tasanee sighed and folded up the pants. "Just leave your skating tights on for now, and we'll stop at my house on the way to the restaurant. You can borrow a pair of my pants."

Claire followed Tasanee out of the locker room. "Why would she do this? Alexis can't possibly think I'm a threat. She's been skating here so much longer. She's Groshev's favorite. Isn't she?"

"Well," Tasanee said, "she used to be."

 ∞

By the time Claire and Tasanee walked the four blocks from the Olympic Center to the Luangs' house, found clothes for Claire, and made it back to Lemongrass Thai on Main Street, there was a line out the door. The people at the end zipped their coats and turned up their collars against the cold mist spritzing down from the clouds.

"Nissa's going to be furious if she's on alone." Tasanee opened the door, and Claire walked into the warm air, swirling with unfamiliar spices.

"Nissa's your sister?"

"One of them," Tasanee said as her eyes scanned the room. Two couples sat waiting on the red bench by the door, and every seat at the bar was full. "There's Kanita and Mae, too, but Kanita's fifteen and always manages to be busy somewhere else. And Mae is really too little to be much help."

"Sounds like my brothers," Claire said. "If you give them a job, they end up making a mess that takes twice as long to clean up."

"Exactly." Tasanee leaned forward to look into the dining room. A girl with a long black braid and an embroidered silk skirt balanced a tray of plates. "Looks like it's just Nissa tonight—and now us, too. Are you up for this? We're going to be hustling."

Tasanee handed Claire a stack of menus and a table chart from the counter. "Everything's full right now, but table seven's having coffee, so you'll seat . . . let's see . . ." Tasanee grabbed a clipboard from the counter. "The Hobbs party of two there, and it looks like the two four-tops by the window will be done soon, too, so then you can seat Schirmer and James. Schirmer's a party of five, but you can pull up a chair from another table."

Tasanee reached under the counter for an apron, tied it around her waist, tucked an order pad into the pocket, and headed toward the main dining room.

"Wait!" Claire stood holding the menus. "Aren't you host-essing with me?"

Tasanee shook her head. "You're okay, aren't you? Nissa's alone with eight full tables right now. I'm going to make sure Mom's okay in the kitchen and then help in the dining room."

Tasanee disappeared into the noisy, steamy room behind the swinging door. Claire had guessed right; this place wasn't such a far cry from the sugarhouse with its strong smells and bustling noise. It was at least as busy. And restaurant season lasted all year long, not just a few weeks.

No wonder Tasanee always looked like she was drinking in her time on the ice, enjoying every second of spotlight. Here, she was a butterfly stuck in a beehive.

"Excuse me." A man with blond hair and funky glasses tapped Claire's arm. She startled, and he stepped back. The ski passes hanging from his jacket zipper fluttered. Under the jacket, he wore a royal blue button-down shirt open at the collar and khaki pants, perfectly tailored. If Jake and Christopher were here to play Who's That Guy? he'd be pegged as the dad in an L.L. Bean Christmas catalog. "Sorry, I was just wondering if you know how long the wait might be at this point?"

Claire looked at the clipboard. She squinted into the dining room but couldn't remember which one was table seven or which one was supposed to be done after that.

"Um . . ."

"It's James," he said, pointing to the third name on the list. "Party of three."

"Oh!" said Claire. "Right. So . . ." She looked into the dining room again. "It'll be about five more minutes," Claire guessed.

"Perfect." He flashed her a smile and turned back to the bench. "Won't be too long."

"Good. I'm starving."

Claire recognized the voice. "Meghan?"

"Claire!" She jumped up, smiling. "Oh my gosh, hi! My dad came up from the city, so we decided to go out. It's so cool you're here. Are you helping Tasanee's family tonight? Are you staying over in town?"

"Uh . . . yeah." Did Meghan know what Alexis had done? Claire searched her face, but all she saw were big eyes and a bigger smile.

"That's great!"

"Excuse me, miss?" An elderly woman tugged Claire's sleeve. "How much longer?"

"Sorry." Claire turned from Meghan and her family and looked at the clipboard again. "Your name?"

Thank goodness Tasanee swept in then juggling two stacks of plates she'd cleared. "You're a party of two, right? Your table should be all set in just a couple minutes." She turned to Meghan's family then. "And your table for three is ready now. Right this way."

Meghan's mother picked up her purse and took off after Tasanee before Claire could even get a look at her. Mr. James put an arm around Meghan and led her to the table.

Claire seated the next table and the seven parties that came in after that. Finally, just after nine o'clock, Mrs. Luang came out of the kitchen. She wore a long, patterned skirt and a mustard yellow shirt, and her black hair was knotted into a loose bun. Her face was broad without a single wrinkle. She didn't look old enough to be Tasanee's mom.

"My goodness, Claire," said Mrs. Luang. "Please accept my apologies. We invite you into our home and immediately put you to work. I hadn't expected it to be so busy. There must be a hockey tournament in town."

Claire smiled. "It's no problem, Mrs. Luang. This was fun, and I appreciate your offer to let me spend the night."

"Well, you're welcome to stay with us anytime, dear." Mrs. Luang pointed to the kitchen. "Tasanee, it's quieting down a bit, so go ahead and put in an order for some tom yum soup, pad krapow, pad thai, and chicken satay. And sticky rice. We need to feed this girl."

"Really, I don't need all those different—" But Tasanee

had already disappeared behind the swinging doors, and Mrs. Luang had darted behind the counter to take a customer's credit card.

"Hey, why don't you join us for a few minutes?" Meghan appeared beside Claire. "We're just having some tea. My parents would love to meet you."

"Sure." Claire followed Meghan to a table by the window where her L.L. Bean dad sat next to her mom, a blond woman in a deep green cashmere sweater.

"Hello." She nodded at Claire over the rim of her wine glass.

"Hi, I'm Claire."

"I know." The woman put down her glass. "We saw you skate this afternoon. You did a lovely job. It was a very *clean* program." She raised her eyebrows at Meghan, who looked down at her tea. "I'm Meghan's mother, obviously." She stuck out a hand. Claire reached out to shake it, expecting long, elegant fingernails. Instead, they were bitten and ragged, but painted pink.

"It's nice to meet you."

Meghan's mother turned to her husband. "I'm exhausted. Let's take care of the check while the girls chat."

"Oh, come on, I think I'm up for another drink." He took the check and sauntered over to the bar. Meghan's mother stood and followed him, her arms folded tightly in front of her. Her father leaned in and said something to the woman working behind the bar, and they both laughed. Meghan's mother turned away.

Meghan watched, twirling her fork. "My mom gets migraines. She's tired, but my dad loves to be social, you know?"

Claire nodded, even though she didn't know. She could no more imagine her father flirting with a bartender than she could imagine him landing a triple axel.

Meghan picked up the miniature teapot. "This is still hot. Want some?"

"Sure." Claire held out her cup for Meghan to fill.

"How do you like training with Groshev so far?"

"I hear he's the best. It's just . . ." Claire pictured his piercing glare, and that alone was enough to make her shiver. "He's so intense."

"Everybody feels that way when they start. And just wait until the competitions." Meghan blew into her cup to cool her tea. "But I bet you're great under pressure. You have so much confidence out there."

"Confidence?" Claire laughed a little. "You want to see confidence? Ask my friend Natalie what I looked like at the Champlain Valley Open last year."

"You were there? So was I. I'm surprised we didn't meet."

"I wasn't in shape to be meeting new people." Claire took a sip of tea. "I got so scared I ran for the bathroom before they called me. I never even skated."

Meghan raised her eyebrows the tiniest bit and tipped her head. "*You* get nervous? You looked so cool out there today."

"Nervous? Terrified is more like it. Anytime there are judges."

"There were judges this afternoon."

"Well, *real* judges. Real judges make me want to run the other way. I don't count that I Love New York lady."

Meghan laughed. "No, I guess not."

Claire leaned forward. "I wasn't even going to compete anymore. But I kind of have to now."

"You'll love it once you get used to it." Meghan looked out the window. The lights of the Olympic Center lit up half the block. "Groshev seems pretty impressed with you."

"You think?"

Meghan nodded. "The Silver Blades Scholarship program is totally his thing. He thinks he's going to pluck a star out of some small-town rink. One of the girls he coached during the Salt Lake City Olympics was supposed to be a shoo-in for the gold, but she totally choked. Groshev's been looking for his next big talent ever since."

"He has?" Claire's mouth felt dry. She reached for her tea.

"Sure. I mean, he's got Alexis now. And she took second at regionals last year, but he's after more than that. He wants Olympic talent." She smiled at Claire. "Looks like you're it."

"What?" Claire almost dropped her cup. She fumbled to catch it, but not before a wave of tea splashed over the rim into a big, splotchy stain on the white tablecloth. "Oh, sorry!"

Meghan slid a napkin over the spill and smiled. "Don't worry—you *want* people talking about you around here." She finished her tea. "You're going to do great."

The kitchen door swung open, and Tasanee backed through it, carrying a huge tray of steaming plates. Nissa came behind her with a second one. They spotted Claire with Meghan and headed for the table.

"Just make sure you keep landing those jumps. Trust me. You *don't* want to see Groshev mad," Meghan said. She stood and turned toward the bar, where her mother was tipping

back the last of a glass of wine and her father was still talking
with the bartender. "I'll see you in the morning. Have a good
dinner!" she said over her shoulder.

"Told you Meghan was the friendliest of that bunch."
Tasanee said, setting plates in front of Claire. "There you go."

"Thanks," Claire said. Her mind raced. No wonder Groshev was so intense at training sessions. He couldn't really be
thinking she was Olympic material, could he? He hadn't said
anything to Claire about her being his "next big talent."

But here she was, and when she stepped back onto the ice
in the morning, everyone would be watching to see what she
could do. What if she fumbled on one of her jumps? She remembered how Groshev looked at Meghan when she stumbled.
Claire was pretty sure a look like that would freeze her insides
so she couldn't even move, much less skate. She picked up her
fork and rearranged noodles on her plate until Tasanee was
done eating.

"Are you sure you've had enough?" Tasanee asked, eyeing
Claire's plate.

Claire nodded. She couldn't have eaten a bite if she'd tried.

CHAPTER 9

Bend your knees!"

Groshev spent the first half of Saturday's session shouting at Claire.

"Let's work on the double salchow." He pointed her toward the corner. "Go ahead." But every time Claire got ready to jump, her muscles clenched, and instead of springing high into the air, she barely hopped forward. She struggled to land even a single.

"Keep your shoulder down!" Groshev shouted. "Again!"

Finally, Claire landed a clean single salchow. What happened to the girl from the Friday Flair show? The one with the perfect, high jumps? It was as if she had vanished.

"Okay." Groshev motioned her over to the wall. She slid her skates back and forth, staring at them as he spoke. "That was slightly better. Now double." He flicked his hand, as if she were a piece of tape or something that got stuck to his finger. "Go."

Claire started skating a circle on the ice—at least she thought it was a circle.

"You are skating an egg!" Groshev shouted. "No egg! A circle!"

Finally, when she thought she had the right shape, Claire jumped.

She meant to try a double. She really did. But at the last second, her whole body protested, pulling back. She did a single and didn't even manage to land that cleanly.

She skated toward Groshev, but he flicked her away. "Again. Double this time."

She circled again. Tasanee skated past, but Claire had to look away. She'd lose it if she didn't just focus. She had to get it this time, but already, she could feel her muscles tensing.

Double salchow. Double salchow. He's going to be mad if you don't look like you're trying. Just try the double. Try it. He won't be as mad if you try.

But she was already picturing the fall in her mind, and again, her whole body froze. She couldn't make herself jump at all, and the momentum of her lead-up sent her stumbling. She was lucky to stay on her feet.

"Come here." Groshev's voice wasn't loud, but his tone was like cold, gray slate. Claire skated over and made a T-stop, opening her eyes wide so they wouldn't look so full of tears.

Groshev crossed his arms and looked at her. "Why . . ." He paused. "Why are you looking so . . ." He held his hand out in front of him, as if he were waiting for her to place the right word in his palm. "How do you say it . . . you are like a string pulled tight about to break . . . ah . . ."

"Tense?" Claire squeaked out. She was about to break, all right.

"Tense, that is it. Why? You cannot skate like this."

"I just . . ." She tried to force down the lump in her

throat. How could he stand there yelling at her and then ask why she was tense? How could he drag her all the way down here with his big-shot scholarship—a scholarship *she* never even asked for—and then be mad when she didn't turn out to be the "next big thing" he wanted her to be? She wasn't just tense; she felt like she was going to explode. But she took a deep breath. "I guess I need to concentrate," she said finally.

"No," said Groshev. "You need to skate." He turned away from her, toward the far end of the ice, where Meghan and Alexis were working on sit spins. "Meghan, time for your lesson!"

☙

Claire felt queasy all through school Monday. She tried to concentrate when Natalie was going on and on about how Denver Moon talked to her in math class.

"And so he asked me if he could borrow my notes since he missed class Friday for his saxophone lesson, but he sits totally on the other side of the room and could have asked Jeremy or Gavin or anybody really, but he came over and asked *me*. Isn't that awesome?"

"Yeah . . ." Claire looked at the clock. She wished she could make school last longer so she wouldn't have to face Groshev again so soon.

"And did I tell you my bees were out over the weekend? It's really early for them, but it's been so warm and there's tree pollen around, so they should be fine. They're still really ornery, though. And I'm starting to have trouble with mites."

"Hmm." Claire bounced her pencil off her paper, still picturing all those failed jumps from the weekend.

"Claire, are you even listening? What's up with you today?" Natalie frowned at her across the table they shared in study hall.

"Sorry. I'm okay. Just overwhelmed." Claire said, pulling out her Fibonacci notes. She needed to finish her outline, but she could barely read half of what she'd written in the truck. Those roads through the mountains were so bumpy. "And I'm tired from all the training. It's a lot of time, I guess."

"No kidding." Natalie waved her script for drama club. "You said you'd help me run these lines, but I hardly saw you last week. Where have you been at lunch?"

"In the library, trying to get caught up on homework."

"And you never even called me back about going to open skate on Sunday."

"Sorry." Claire pretended to look for something in her backpack. When she sat up and Natalie was still looking at her, she left to sharpen her pencil.

She turned the handle, fighting back tears as the sharpener's teeth chewed up her pencil. What was she supposed to do? Lie to Natalie? She'd gotten the message but couldn't imagine getting onto the ice a second before she had to, and she knew Nat wouldn't understand.

But Claire, she imagined Natalie saying, *you always want to be on the ice. Always.*

A few weeks ago, that was true. But now . . .

Claire pulled out her pencil. It was sharp, but she put it back and turned the sharpener handle some more. Finally,

when Natalie had given up and moved over to practice her
lines with Riley, Claire headed back to her seat.

∾

When Claire got home from school, Charlotte's e-mail was
waiting. Charlotte was the one person who might get all
this, who might understand. Even though it was almost time
to leave for practice, Claire tossed her backpack on the floor
and sat down to read.

> Claire,
>   So glad you're making friends. I've met a ton of people
> at our skating group at school, too. It's been a blast, even
> though the new skates I just got are killing me—I can't
> wait until they're broken in.
>   Don't let your coach freak you out. ALL the coaches
> in Lake Placid are intense. My friend Naomi, who skates
> with me here, said she had this coach who used to kick
> the wall every time she messed up. You'll be okay—hang
> in there.
>   And have fun!
>
> —C

At least Groshev didn't kick walls.

Yet.

Claire checked her watch. She only had ten minutes to
get her stuff together before it was time to leave, but she des-
perately wanted to tell Charlotte more. Maybe Charlotte would
know how to deal with Alexis. With everything.

Claire took a deep breath and poised her fingers over the keyboard. She couldn't just start crying in her e-mail; she'd try to be positive.

> Charlotte,
> The skating's going really well. I won first place in this thing they do on Fridays with costumes. (Well, everybody else had a costume. I skated in my winter stuff, which they all thought was a costume, but that's a whole 'nother story!)
> Anyway, Coach is okay, too, but one of the other skaters . . .

Claire's stomach felt like a lead weight as she thought of the nail polish on her pants, the glares, the way Alexis and Stevie had beaten up Hannah with only words and a mean laugh. But if she started typing all that, she'd probably start crying, and she didn't have time.

> One of the other skaters—her name is Alexis—is really supercompetitive, just like you said. I kinda think she hates me.

"Claire!" Her father's voice called up from downstairs, and she could hear his car keys clinking.

"Coming!"

> Gotta go. Thanks for writing back. I miss you.

> —Claire

"You done at seven tonight?" Dad glanced over at Claire as he turned down the radio.

"Yep." Claire stared out the window as piles of highway sand sped past along the road. She loved how winter lasted longer in the mountains. How even at the end of April, snow-drifts clung to the roadsides for dear life. It made the Champlain Valley Open in June feel farther away.

"Listen," her dad said, twisting in his seat to stretch his back. "I'm not going to be able to drive you on Wednesday and Friday this week."

Claire's hopes leaped at the thought of staying home.

"But your mom's arranging a ride."

"With who? I'm the only one from Mojimuk Falls. Dad, it's really okay with me if I have to miss—"

He shook his head. "Claire, we'd get you here to skate even if one of us had to quit our jobs. We know what an opportunity this is, and we're so proud of you." He flicked on his signal to make the left turn into the Olympic Center parking lot. "Mom's already touched base with a parent in Plattsburgh whose kids skate, and you'll ride along with them. You know a Luke and Abby somebody?"

"Collins? They skate pairs." Claire's heart fluttered at the thought of time with Luke in the car, but then her stomach lurched almost immediately. Alexis would have a brand-new reason to hate her.

"Well, see? You'll be all set then." Her father parked the truck and pulled her skating bag out from behind the seats. "I'll be back to get you at seven. And hey . . . we're here plenty early. You take your time and make sure you hang up your clothes in your locker, okay? Mom had a heck of a time with that nail polish."

"Okay. Bye." Claire stepped out of the truck into a muddy puddle and ran to the building, pulling her coat tighter around her against the early spring wind blowing down from the mountains. She felt a gust of guilt, too, for lying to her parents about the nail polish. She'd told them that she was in a hurry, that she dropped her pants on the floor rushing to get out to the ice, that she hadn't noticed the spilled nail polish until she went to get dressed. She couldn't tell her we're-so-proud parents she'd already made an enemy.

∞

"Hey, Claire!" Meghan called from the locker room bench. "How's it going with the double salchow?"

Claire shook her head as she sat down to put on her skates. "Not good." She tried pushing her heel down into her skate but couldn't wiggle it in. She picked up the skate to loosen the laces. "I can't even get myself to *try* a double right now. I'm having trouble with singles."

Meghan watched as Claire finally wedged her foot into the skate. "Looks like you're due for some new skates."

Claire shook her head. "No, these are fine."

"I want new ones, but my mom says I have to wait." Meghan sighed and pulled on a skate that already looked brand new. "I'm going to ask my dad, though, when he comes back up. I want to get those new Graf boots; they're really, really light and they have these hinges inside so they're better for landings. And then for blades, I want Paramounts—you know Paramount, right?"

Claire nodded. She'd seen them in Charlotte's skating magazines. They could run a thousand dollars a pair.

"You ought to get them, too." Meghan tugged her laces tighter. "Then we'd match."

"Maybe." Claire just wanted to end the conversation. "You ready?"

They stood just as Luke and Abby crossed the locker room toward the door. Luke held it open for all three girls. Alexis was ahead of them, already heading into the rink.

"So are you a peanut butter or chocolate chip girl?" he asked Claire.

"What?"

"Mom always gets granola bars for the trip down after school, and I hear we're giving you a ride Wednesday. You like peanut butter or chocolate chip?"

"Chocolate chip, I guess."

Luke turned to Abby as they stepped into the rink. "Told ya."

Alexis was standing at the boards, looking at Claire in a way that froze her insides, but Luke just kept on talking.

"So we'll bring snacks, and I'll make us a killer playlist. You bring music, too, if you want, okay?"

"Sure," Claire said. "Go on ahead. I'm going to tighten my skate." She bent down and pretended to tighten a skate that was already squeezing the middle of her foot. It was better than having Alexis find out she and Luke were carpool buddies.

Once everyone else was skating, Claire slid off her guards and stepped onto the ice to focus on stroking class, the part of training where they skated laps around the rink to work on power and speed. It felt good to skate fast. The cool air of the rink somehow cleared out the gunk she felt like she'd been carrying around inside her chest since Saturday.

She flew around one of the curves and saw Groshev talking to a tall bald guy who looked familiar. Claire took a closer look her next time around. It was Claude Van Syke, from the corn-flakes box! She'd never seen Stevie's dad in person before, but she knew he was the chair of the Silver Blades Scholarship com-mittee and must know she was the new recipient. They were still talking when she skated past the next time, and Groshev was waving his hands out toward the ice.

When stroking was done, Claire left the ice. They had a five-minute break before individual coaching sessions. She bent down to relace her skate and heard men's voices pass-ing by.

". . . waste of my time."

"But she has talent."

"Pfft. Talent is not enough." Claire knew that voice, and she knew the hand-flicking gesture that went with it, even though she couldn't see it with her head down. Who was Gro-shev talking about? Her skate was laced, but she stayed down where she wouldn't be seen.

"She's capable of doing the advanced jumps. You've seen her."

"I am not seeing the jumping now, and I do not have the time for skaters who do not perform."

Claire's throat tightened. Were they talking about her? She stared at the popcorn crumbles on the cement floor and tried to quiet her breathing. The voices grew more distant.

Mr. Van Syke said something she couldn't hear, but she heard Groshev's response just fine.

"Fine. She will stay. For now. But I still think it is a waste of time and money. She does not belong here."

Claire's heart raced.

Stop it, she told herself. *You have no idea who they're talking about.* She wasn't the only one here on scholarship, and she wasn't the only one struggling with jumps, but still . . .

Claire swallowed hard and stepped back onto the ice.

"Hey!" Tasanee skated up to her. "You want to run through some jumps with me? It looked like you had a rough lesson Saturday."

"Rough is an understatement." Claire looked at Groshev, back on the ice and waving his hands around as he talked with Stevie. "He tells me I'm too stressed out, but then he stands there staring and yelling and *making* me tense. And then I can't jump."

Tasanee looked at her for a minute. "You know that deep breath you just took?"

Claire nodded.

"Do that when you're skating. The sports psychologist who gave a presentation to us last fall said it can calm jiggly nerves. Try it. It might help you with the mind games you're playing on yourself."

"I'm not playing mind games with myself." That wasn't fair. It was Groshev playing the mind games, offering her a scholarship and then expecting her to be better than she really was. Maybe even saying she didn't belong here. *Had* he been talking about her?

"Breathe. . . ." Tasanee said again.

"Fine," Claire said. Groshev's sharp whistle called her to the boards across the rink for her lesson.

She took deep breaths all the way there. She was ready to try the double again. Nerves aside, her legs felt strong, and she couldn't imagine them betraying her like last time.

"How are you feeling?" Groshev asked when she skated up to him.

"Fine," Claire answered. And she waited, sure that he'd make her try again right away.

"Very good." He flipped a page on his clipboard and pulled out a pen. "Let me see a backspin with the two changes of legs."

A backspin? Claire didn't need to work on backspins. She could do them in her sleep. "Eight revolutions. Go." Groshev clapped his gloved hands, and Claire skated to the center of the rink. She did the spin and skated back to him.

"Good. Now a sit spin with the change of legs."

"But I can already do that."

"I know. Today, we do what you already know. It is good for the head. Go."

Claire skated out again and crouched into her sit spin. Normally, she loved the way the lights of the rink blurred when she spun. With perfect balance, she switched legs, made her last four revolutions, and finished, one leg extended behind her, her arms out straight, but she couldn't enjoy the feeling.

Why was she spinning? Spinning was her strongest skill. She didn't need to practice spins, and he wasn't even coaching her. What was with all the clipped compliments? Good. Good. Good. When was she going to start her real lesson?

"The arms!" Groshev barked from the boards. Claire extended her drooping arms back into position. She tucked them into her chest when she started to spin, tucked them in so tight that nothing stopped her from twirling faster and faster. She loved this spin and barely had to think about the technique anymore, she'd done it so many times on the cow pond with Charlotte, always wanting to spin faster.

Claire finished and returned to Groshev for another "Good."

"Another sit spin now." He waved her back to the center of the rink, and she spun.

"Okay." He glanced at his watch when she returned. "That is all for today. Alexis, come!"

"What about my double salchow?" Claire blurted out.

"What about it?" Groshev raised a thick eyebrow.

"Well . . . what should I do? I mean, aren't we going to practice it? Don't you even want me to try it?"

Groshev flipped a page on his clipboard as Alexis skated up in a hockey stop. Her blades threw a spray of snow at Claire's shins.

"I need first, for you to skate," Groshev said to Claire. "Saturday, you did not skate. Today, you did. It is . . . in the mind. You cannot go forward until you remember that you are a skater. So you skate. You are not to jump for two weeks."

"Not in lessons? Or not at all?"

"I said you are not to jump. At all." He turned to Alexis. "Let us begin with a single axel."

CHAPTER 10

For two weeks, Claire did not jump.

She rode to skating with Abby and Luke and their mom. They ate granola bars and talked about Abby's pet tree frogs and listened to Luke's classic rock playlist until Claire knew every word to "Rock and Roll Never Forgets."

On the second Friday, Claire brought a CD of her own, handed it up to the front seat, and held her breath, waiting for Luke to make fun of the acoustic guitar and folk music lyrics that sang out from the speakers. Instead, Luke bounced his head a little. "I kinda like this . . . who is it?"

"The group's called Crossing North." Claire let out her breath and handed him the CD case. "It's actually just Uncle Bruce and his friend Jen. They've been playing at our pancake breakfast every spring since I was born."

They sang songs about how hard it is to feel like you don't fit in anywhere you go. How hard it is to be away from home and missing the smell of biscuits and such with nothing going right.

Claire understood those songs better than ever now.

For two weeks, Claire stole bits of time for her Fibonacci research. She learned about special shapes that were tied to

Fibonacci numbers—golden rectangles where the ratios of the sides were Fibonacci numbers. Those rectangles showed up all over the place in architecture and art—all the way back to the Greek Parthenon and Leonardo da Vinci's *Mona Lisa* painting. She learned about golden spirals with those same Fibonacci numbers connected to the measurements of their curves, and how those spirals showed up everywhere, too, like in seashells and animals' horns.

For two weeks, she tried to find a time to call Natalie for a milk-shake night, but homework and skating—usually skating—got in the way. And when she finally decided she could afford a regular lunch period in the cafeteria, Natalie had moved to a different table with Riley and Maya and Denver Moon. They had their drama scripts out, practicing and laughing. Claire took her sandwich and went back to the library.

For two weeks, while Claire was grounded on the ice, she watched Alexis's jumps get higher and stronger.

"So, Mrs. Butterworth," Alexis said one day when they were leaving the ice after practice. "What's up with you lately? You ever going to try that salchow again?"

Claire mumbled something about focusing on her spins and walked away. She had hoped Charlotte might have some advice about dealing with Alexis, but the e-mail she'd sent back was short.

Hey, Claire!
Sorry it's taken me so long to write back. HUGE projects due b/c it's almost the end of the semester. The good news is I got that grant to study in London this

summer. I'm leaving right after finals. Can you believe it?
London!!

Claire knew she should be happy for her; Charlotte had always wanted to study abroad, but did it have to happen now? And did she have to leave right after finals so she wouldn't be home at all? Claire sighed and kept reading.

Glad to hear you're skating well. As for that Alexis girl,
I'm sure she doesn't hate you. She's probably just
ultracompetitive, and you're really talented, so it's natural
that she'd see you as a threat, as much as that stinks.
Competitive skating's like that. If you're good, they're
going to be jealous. Keep skating well, and eventually
you'll earn her respect. Until then, ignore the nasty looks.
Wish I were there to give you a hug. Hang in there!
Headed to the library now—talk to you soon!

—C

For two weeks, Claire tried to ignore the nasty looks. She locked her street clothes and skating bag in her locker while she was on the ice. The only day she forgot, she found a bunch of grapes smooshed in the bottom of the bag, as if somebody had put them in and then jumped up and down on it. At least the bag had been empty. Claire rinsed it out in the sink and held it under the hand dryer before she put her stuff back inside with shaking hands. She had wanted to deal with Alexis on her own, but this felt like too much to handle.

"Do you think I should say something to Groshev?" she asked Tasanee, who had finished her last vampire book and moved on to the homicidal fairies.

She answered without looking up. "No."

"I mean, I don't want to rat on her, but she keeps—"

Tasanee put down her book. "Claire, I hate to break it to you, but skating isn't just competitive; it can be cutthroat. And where Groshev comes from, this is no big deal. He was in the '94 Olympics—the year Nancy Kerrigan got her knee smashed with a metal pipe because she was better than somebody else. Trust me, he's not going to be impressed with a few grapes in your skating bag."

For two weeks, Claire steered clear of Alexis and Stevie as best she could. She laughed with Tasanee and helped Meghan with her math homework in the locker room. She cheered like crazy when Hannah landed her first double axel.

And for two weeks, Claire skated. She worked on spins and inside edge work and outside edge work and new choreography for her program, and never once did both of her blades leave the ice at the same time.

⁓

Finally, on a warm, sunny Monday in May, her two weeks of being grounded were up. Claire practically skipped into the Olympic Center. She breathed in the cool air, hurried onto the ice, and skated up to Groshev at the boards.

"Well?" He crossed his arms and looked at her. "What will you work on today?"

She'd been dying to try the double salchow again—even a

single salchow—but now it felt like something had a grip on her voice deep down in her throat and wouldn't let it out. How did he just suck the air out of her like this? She swallowed hard.

"Well?" Groshev asked.

Claire cleared her throat. "I guess I need to jump today."

Groshev shook his head. "You need to do nothing except skate. If you jump in the skating, then that is good. You jump. But whatever you do, you need to skate. So what do you wish to start with?"

"Well . . . should I try the single first?" Claire's voice was shaky.

Groshev folded his arms. "You decide."

"Okay," Claire said. "I'll try the single." He probably wanted her to get back to the salchow after waiting two whole weeks.

She skated out, taking deep breaths. She counted her strokes, held her arms high and stiff, turned, and took off. She launched immediately into the spin, afraid she wouldn't make it all the way around. Instead, she overrotated and stumbled.

She skated back to Groshev. "Should I try again?"

He let out a sharp huff. "Enough with the questions." His stare made the ice look cozy and warm by comparison. "You are not being the skater I chose for Silver Blades. You are not the girl from the . . . what was it . . . the maple syrup show. She knew how to skate."

"Well, I can't very well skate if you won't tell me what you want me to *do*." Claire's voice broke. "You're my coach. What do you want me to do?"

"I do not care. You spin. You jump. You whatever. But enough of this. Skate."

Claire bit her lip. "Well, should I try—"

"Stop." Groshev put his big hands on her shoulders pushing her to stand straighter. "You are acting like . . . what do you call it . . . the opposite of a person?"

The opposite of a person? thought Claire.

"This . . ." Groshev waved his hands around, as if he were trying to shake the word loose. "How do you say, automaton."

"Like a robot?" Claire said.

"Yes, robot. Enough of the robot."

Claire tried to take a deep breath, but it caught in her throat. Not only could she not jump or talk coherently. Now she was skating like a robot, too.

"Bella!" He called up to the sound booth and spoke quickly in Russian. Then he turned back to Claire and pointed to the ice. "Go."

She turned and took a deep breath. She would just have to do something, more spins maybe, and in ten minutes her lesson would end. She breathed in, and the air cooled her hot cheeks from the inside out. Across the rink, Alexis should have been warming up for her own lesson. Instead, she stood next to Stevie, arms crossed, smirking.

In an instant, Claire went from nervous to angry. She was a skater. She could spin faster than Alexis and probably faster than anybody here, and she could jump, too. She could. She'd landed plenty of jumps before Groshev got her all worked up.

She'd start with a sit spin. That's what. She was good at that.

But just as Claire started skating in the circle that would lead her into her spin, staccato violins played from the giant black speakers that hung over the ice like booming gods.

It was Vivaldi.

"Autumn."

Claire slowed and then stopped, and she looked over at the boards, where Groshev gave her a sharp nod.

She listened for a moment, took a deep breath, and picked up the routine leading into the first flying camel. The other skaters gathered at the boards to watch.

Claire kept breathing, let the cold ice air fill her lungs, and she skated. She breathed in the rich music, felt the whole length of her body as her leg stretched back and up in a spiral that carried her all the way down the rink. She landed one—two—three waltz jumps in perfect time with Vivaldi's rhythm.

She didn't think about jumping. She just skated. Her feet flew over each other with the playful notes, and she was home. On the ice.

The jump was coming. The double salchow. She could do it; she knew she could get it today.

When the music told her to, she turned, tucked in her arms—and hesitated just long enough that she knew she couldn't make it.

Instead, she made a single revolution and landed.

It wasn't clean—she put her second foot down for a split second—but at least she didn't fall. And at least she knew she could jump again.

She let the last quiet notes of the song settle her into her final pose.

There.

She had skated.

CHAPTER 11

We picked up food because there's no break tonight. You want an Italian mix or turkey?" Luke held up two wrapped subs as Claire tossed her skating bag and social studies notebook into the van and climbed into the middle seat next to Abby, already halfway through her veggie sub.

Claire sighed. What she wanted was her mother's roast chicken with the crispy, salty skin. She was glad her jumps were coming back, but honestly, the schedule was wearing on her. They'd been training straight through dinner—from four to eight—every session for the past week because some of the kids were skating in a Memorial Day weekend competition in Saratoga Springs. She hadn't even had time to study for her social studies test; somehow, she needed to memorize the Preamble to the Constitution by fourth period tomorrow.

"I'll have whatever you don't want. Thanks."

Luke tossed her the turkey sub and settled in with his Italian mix. "Abby, we gotta work on that single-double combination tonight."

"Ugh. I know. I'm not getting enough height on the second jump. If I don't have it by the end of my session today, I'm going to see if Hannah can help." She turned to Claire. "Have you seen her doubles lately?"

"She's amazing." Everyone, including Claire, had been surprised by how quickly Hannah had nailed the new jumps she was learning. She was the only one landing a double-toe-double-toe. "She's going to do great in the competition. That move's worth a ton of points."

"How about you?" Luke twisted in his seat so he could see Claire. "All set for Saratoga this weekend?"

Claire shook her head. "I'm not competing in Saratoga. I don't have anything till the Champlain Valley Open in June."

"Really?" Abby said. "That seems like forever. Maybe you could talk to Groshev about doing something sooner."

"Oh, no," Claire said. "June is plenty soon." *As a matter of fact*, she thought, *June couldn't stay away long enough.* She'd like to just freeze time, and then tomorrow's social studies test wouldn't happen, either. She opened the notebook. "Just ignore me if I'm mumbling back here, okay? I gotta get this memorized."

Luke looked back at her. "What is it?"

"The Preamble to the Constitution."

"Ah, yes." Luke sat taller and put on a serious face. "We the people of the United States, in order to form a more perfect union, establish justice, insure domestic tranquility . . ."

"You know it?"

"We did that unit in September. Actually . . ." He reached for his iPod and pushed a few buttons. "Here you go."

Claire's heart skipped a beat when his fingers brushed hers, but what she heard on the iPod was even more exciting.

"Somebody made the Preamble into a song? That's perfect!" It was catchy, too. "Luke Collins, you are my absolute hero."

"Aw, shucks."

"Thanks." She handed back his iPod when the Constitution song was over.

"Anytime. You still working on that Fibonacci project, too? I could give you a hand if you want. I like that stuff."

"Actually, I'm doing pretty well. I'm making a slide show, so I've been taking pictures around the farm now that the flowers are out. I'm trying to find more examples of the numbers, in places other than nature and art."

"Don't forget the music." Luke held up the iPod. "You can listen to that Bartók on here later if you want."

"I found that on iTunes when you talked about it before. But I was thinking about Fibonacci in figure skating. Those numbers are everywhere. They must be in skating, too, don't you think?" Claire leaned forward in her seat. "Any idea whether or not the rink is a golden rectangle?"

"Hmm . . . it might be a little long. We could check. But what about the lead-in to our spins?" He traced a spiral in the air with his finger.

"Oh my gosh!" Claire bounced a little in her seat. "I bet you're right! I bet it'll be a golden spiral. That would be perfect!"

Luke's eyes lit up. "We can test it out later. I'll do a scratch spin right after the Zamboni comes out, and we'll check the tracing on the ice."

Abby sighed a dramatic sigh. "Luke, this is the saddest attempt to impress a girl in the history of the world. You are getting geekier by the minute."

"I don't have to take that from a girl whose best friends

are amphibians." Luke leaned back and punched her lightly on the arm. "You're just jealous that you don't share my mathematical awesomeness."

"You mean your Fibo-nerdiness."

Claire laughed. "Aw, go easy on him, Abby. I'll take all the help I can get. If I can manage to get this project done with my skating schedule, it'll be a Fibo-miracle."

∽

Traffic in Lake Placid held them up a block from the Olympic Center, so there was no time to check on their Fibonacci spiral theory. Claire, Luke, and Abby had to rush onto the ice.

Claire fumbled with her skates in the locker room. "Go ahead, I'll be right there," she told Luke, pulling the right one off to loosen the laces again.

The locker room door swung open as Claire was pushing her heel into the boot. When she heard a loud sniff, she looked up.

"Hannah, what's wrong?"

Hannah squeezed her eyes shut, as if that could stop them from spilling any more tears. She shook her head, sank onto the bench, and buried her face in her sleeve.

Claire stood—one skate on and one off—and limped over to sit next to her. "What is it?" She put an arm around Hannah's shoulders.

Hannah shook her head, still buried in the crook of her arm. Her whole body shook with quiet sobs.

"Did you get hurt? Are you okay?" Claire glanced up and down Hannah's body but didn't see anything wrong. She was getting snot all over her skating dress, though. Claire hobbled to the paper towel dispenser and tore one off. "Here. Sorry it's not softer."

Hannah took it and blew her nose. Her cheeks were all blotchy red, and her green eyes still shone with tears.

"Do you want to talk about it?" Claire glanced at her watch. They were definitely late now. She hoped Groshev wouldn't flip out on Hannah the way he had on the first day. Whatever was wrong, she didn't need that, too. "Can I help?"

"No." Hannah blew her nose again. "I just . . ." She took a deep breath. "I kept thinking that it would get better once I got used to everyone here, that it would start to feel more like my rink at home. But I don't belong here. Not even a little."

"Hannah, you do *so*! You skate—and *jump*—better than anybody here."

"Hmph." Hannah bent down and started unlacing her skates. "Don't let *them* hear you say that."

Claire felt as if a snowball had landed in her stomach. "Alexis?"

Hannah nodded. "And Stevie." She pulled off her skate and started unlacing the other one.

"Stop that." Claire pulled her hands away from the laces. "Just . . ." She tried to think of how Tasanee had calmed her down. "Just take a deep breath, and then you can go back out there."

"I'm not going back out."

"But why? What did they do? Did they say something?"

Hannah snapped at her. "You *know* what they say. Don't pretend."

Claire was quiet. Hannah wasn't fat—not by a long stretch—but she was shorter and a little huskier than most of the other girls. Claire had heard Alexis and Stevie make jokes about Hannah's weight, but she never dreamed they'd say those things to her face.

"Do you think it matters that I can't always hear them? Do you think I don't notice their laughs when I land a jump? I heard them just now. 'Check out that crack in the ice. Hannah-the-size-of-Montana must have been practicing jumps again.' Do they think I'm deaf?"

"Hannah, you know you're not fat." The words stung Claire, and they hadn't even been aimed at her. Alexis and Stevie reminded her of the hornets that nested in the split rail fence next to the sugarhouse. They weren't like Nat's honey-bees that only stung when they felt threatened. Hornets came buzzing after you while you were minding your own business.

"Why can't they just leave me alone and let me skate? I've never done anything to them." But she had.

Watching Hannah skate, Claire knew that her energy, her speed, her passion, were all threats to Alexis. "Oh, Hannah, I'm sorry they were so rotten today."

"It's not *today*. It's every day, Claire. Today was just . . . I don't know . . . it's been piling up and piling up and that one comment made it all too much to carry around anymore. Every day, my mom drops me off here after school, and every day, I put on my skates and my sparkly dresses and I tell myself it doesn't matter that I don't look like the rest of you because I'm *good* at this. I tell myself it doesn't matter that I have a blotchy round peach for a face instead of high cheekbones like Tasa-nee. It doesn't matter that I don't have a tiny waist like Alexis and Stevie or perfect hair like Meghan or long legs like you, because I'm *good* at this."

"You are! And none of those things matter!" Claire took Hannah's arm, but she yanked it away, pulled off her second skate, and threw it against the locker.

"Yeah," she said. "They do matter."

Claire stayed while Hannah called her mom to pick her up. Hannah pulled everything from her locker—the extra fleece, her hairbrush, her spare tights—and crammed her skating bag full. The only thing still in her locker was a left-over program from Friday Flair, torn at the corner and damp.

Claire tried again. "You don't want to do this. You're a skater, Hannah."

Hannah whirled around. "Well, you know what? I can be a skater somewhere else. Groshev acts like this is the only ice in the state, but it's not. And I'm tired of showing up some-where every day where people treat me like this and nobody cares." Hannah sank down on the bench and wiped her eyes with her sleeve.

"Well, I care." But Claire knew that wasn't enough. She sat next to Hannah and rested a quiet hand on her back. Groshev was going to be looking for her, but she couldn't just leave.

Finally, the cell phone in Hannah's hand rang, and she stood. "Thanks for waiting with me." She walked out of the locker room without looking back.

When the door clicked shut, Claire finished lacing her skates and walked slowly down the hall to the rink.

⟳

"Over here!" A gloved hand tugged her sleeve. Meghan motioned to the seat next to her in the stands. "Just scoot in really fast, and you should be okay. He started before four, and I don't think he's seen who's here yet." She nodded toward Groshev, who was out on the ice talking Luke and Abby through their single-double combination.

"Thanks." Claire peered past Meghan, expecting to see Alexis and Stevie, but the seats were empty. "Where is everybody?"

Meghan pointed up to the sound box. "Dealing with music. We're running all the programs today. Did you take your CD up already?"

Claire shook her head. "I don't have my routine ready yet. I'm not competing until the Champlain Valley Open."

"Then you've got plenty of time."

"Thank goodness for that," Claire said. "I'm still popping all my doubles."

Meghan gave a little smile. "Don't you hate that? I went a *month* last fall when I couldn't land a jump for anything. Has Groshev been a bear about it? I bet he's frustrated."

"*He's* frustrated?"

"Well, you know, the scholarship and all. Stevie told me that her dad said the scholarship committee wasn't all that hot on taking a second skater, so Groshev kind of stuck his neck out to get you here. And there's always so much pressure on scholarship skaters anyway. When Alexis first got here, she had trouble with some of her jumps and Groshev wanted to let her go after just a month. She turned it around fast, though, thank goodness."

No wonder Alexis was so protective of her scholarship, Claire thought. She was used to fighting for it.

"Anyway," Meghan went on. "I hope things go better for

you today. Groshev's not exactly the most patient guy if someone's not performing."

Claire flashed back to the conversation she heard between
Groshev and Mr. Van Syke. Maybe she *was* the one who didn't
belong. But no, he had seemed happier with her lately. She still
hadn't tried any of the doubles, but these last couple weeks,
her singles had been strong and clean. She was actually plan-
ning to try the double salchow again tonight.

Out on the ice, Groshev clapped his hands and shouted up
at the sound box. "Okay . . . again, Bella! From the beginning!"

A ghostly whisper filled the arena, a man's voice calling
for his angel to come to him.

The low bass notes started pounding as Luke and Abby
skated to center ice. "Angel of Music" was Claire's favorite
song from *The Phantom of the Opera*. She'd never seen the
musical, but Charlotte went when it was in Montreal and
played the soundtrack over and over.

She watched Luke and Abby skate faster and faster, doing
their crossovers in unison as the music grew more intense.
Their single-double combination was perfect. Whatever Groshev had said to Abby while he was waving his arms out there
worked.

It was a beautiful routine, but Claire couldn't enjoy it.
When Luke skated past with his head tipped up to the lights,
she could just barely make out those speckled brown eyes
under the mask that covered half his face.

She snuck a glance at Alexis, leaning on the railing with
her chin on her hands, her blue eyes clear and quiet, a tiny
smile on her face as she watched Luke and Abby swirl past on

the ice. She didn't look like someone who would smoosh grapes in your skating bag. Was there another side to Alexis, or was it just a mask?

Who were these people?

They skated like angels—all of them—but they had so many sharp edges—and keeping track of them all felt like more than Claire could handle.

The phantom voice returned as Luke and Abby spun in unison, faster and faster, in the frenzy of the song's high-pitched ending.

"Good. Good." Groshev said. "Claire—you are next. Bella has your music."

Claire shook her head. "I didn't bring music."

"You left it last time." He motioned her to get up.

"Okay . . . but I thought the people in this weekend's competition were the priority tonight. I can wait."

"No, you cannot." Groshev flipped a paper on his clipboard. "You need practice in front of judges. So I have decided that you will compete this weekend, too."

CHAPTER 12

Hey!" Claire found Natalie at her locker right before lunch. "It's Free Lunch Friday. Want to go get something?" When the weather got nice in the spring, the seventh and eighth graders who didn't have any discipline write-ups were allowed to leave school grounds for lunch on good weather days. Most of them just took their school pizza to the park or got sandwiches across the street, but it was nice to be outside. This was the first one of the year, and Claire had stayed up late to get ahead on her homework so she'd have time to eat with Natalie. If anybody could convince her she'd be okay competing this weekend, it was Nat.

"Okay." Natalie shoved her books into her locker and pulled out her backpack. It was covered with buttons from Broadway musicals.

"Hey! That one's new. Did you see that show?" Claire pointed to a button for *Wicked*. A big green witch face covered the whole thing.

"I got it when my aunt took me to see the show in Montreal two weeks ago." Natalie looked at Claire and sighed as they headed out the front door of the school. The Falls Deli was right across the street. "I told you in science, but you must not have been listening."

Claire wanted to argue, but she knew Natalie was probably right. Even when her body wasn't at skating, it felt like she left her brain there half the time.

"The usual?" The woman behind the deli counter wiped her hands on her apron and smiled at Natalie and Claire.

"Yep," Natalie said. "Egg salad on sourdough, please."

"I'll have turkey with Swiss on whole wheat, and do you have honey mustard?" The woman nodded, and Claire turned back to Natalie.

"So you're not going to believe this. On Monday, there's this Memorial Day competition at—"

"What happened to peanut butter and strawberry jam?"

"Huh?"

"And since when do you eat whole-wheat bread?" Natalie gave her a playful shove and made her voice snooty sounding. "And do you have honey mustard? Or maybe some nice Grey Poupon?"

"Oh." Had it really been that long since she'd eaten lunch with Natalie? "I guess I switched to turkey because I've been eating in the car so much. PB and J doesn't travel very well. The bread gets mushy from the jam."

"Geez, anything else I should know? Do you still like milk shakes? Or have you moved on to those frozen coffee things?"

"Cut it out." Claire laughed and paid for her sandwich. "I could so go for a milk-shake night."

"What about tonight?" Natalie surprised her. "My mom and I were going to get something quick to eat because Dad's golfing after work. You can come with us."

Claire's heart jumped. "Actually, skating is early today because of some weird scheduling thing with the ice. I'm leaving after seventh period, and we're skating from two to four, so I'll be home for dinner for once."

"Well, yay!" Natalie tipped her head up to the sunshine as they walked across the street to the park by the river. "We'll do pizza and then get shakes. Although . . ." A playful smile grew on Nat's face. "Does your fancy new coach let you drink things like that? What would he say?"

"He'd say . . ." Claire made her voice low and grumbly. "'What is this . . . this . . . how do you say it . . . this milky shake you are drinking? I am thinking that you care more about the chocolate and the ice cream than you do about the skating!'"

Natalie laughed, and they plopped down on the grass, as close as they could get to the water without sitting in mud. Too close for comfort, apparently, for the spotted frog that had been sunning itself on the bank. It hopped into the river.

"I've been dying to talk to you," Claire said. "They're making me compete on Monday. I just found out."

"No way!"

"Yep." Claire watched the frog kick off into the current. "And I'm so not ready. Forget the butterflies. I feel like I have frogs flopping around in my stomach these days."

"You'll be okay," Natalie said, unwrapping her egg salad. "Your jumps must be getting there; you've been practicing so much. I feel like we haven't hung out in forever."

"I know." Claire stretched her legs out in front of her and leaned forward to pick a dandelion, twirling it in her fingers. "How are your bees?"

"They've been better. I'm still having trouble with mites. One of the orchards down the road brought in commercial bees and they're all infected. There's nothing I can do to keep them from mixing with mine." Natalie swallowed and reached for her lemonade. "Plus, my guys are still mean as all get out. I ordered a new queen, but she hasn't come yet."

"You *ordered* a new queen?"

"Yeah, from apiary.com. When she gets here, I have to go in and find the old one and take her out. *That'll* be a fun afternoon. I'm going to have to smoke the bees like crazy to keep them from going nuts."

"So you can just get rid of the old queen and get a new one?" Claire couldn't help thinking of Alexis. Just get rid of the old queen and bring in a new one. Wouldn't it be nice if you could pull that off with people? "And that'll make all the bees . . . nicer?"

"Well, yeah. Honeybees only live about a month, so when the old worker bees die off, the new ones born from the new queen will have different genes. Friendlier ones, I hope."

Claire grinned. "I hope so too."

∽

After seventh period, Claire signed out in the office and got into the Collinses' car to head for Lake Placid. It felt weird to be zipping off down the highway while math was going on back at school, but Claire had already touched base with Mrs. Cosgro and was actually on schedule to have her project done for Tuesday, even though she wasn't scheduled to present for a while.

Even with her time crunch with skating, she was excited

about the way her slide show had turned out. She'd stayed late at the Olympic Center one day last week and found out that Luke's hunch was right; the shape skaters made going into a spin was almost a perfect golden spiral—Fibonacci all over the place. The actual tracing on the ice didn't show up in her picture, so she took a second photo of Luke leading into the spin and figured she'd explain when she gave her presentation.

"You excited for Monday?" Luke asked over his shoulder from the front seat.

Claire just grunted. "Ugh."

"Aw, come on, Claire. You've come so far the past couple weeks. You'll be great." He fiddled with his iPod, took out the earbuds, and handed them to her. "Here. Motivational music." He always had something for her to listen to on the way down now, and Claire couldn't decide what she liked more—his songs or the fact that his fingers always brushed hers when he handed her the iPod.

Today it was "Born to Run."

"Gotta love The Boss," Luke said over the music.

"Shouldn't that be 'Born to Skate'?" Claire handed the earbuds back as they pulled into the Olympic Center parking lot.

"I'm going to the outlets to look for some shorts. I'll pick you up at four," Mrs. Collins said. "Call me if you're done sooner."

"Think we'll get out early?" Claire bounced a little as she walked. As nervous as she was about the competition, she still felt light today, knowing she had plans with Natalie.

"Maybe." Abby pulled open the door to the locker room. "Sometimes he gives us a break before a competition."

Claire headed for her locker and found Tasanee lounging on the floor with her new book—this one had rose petals on the cover that looked like wings—using her skating bag as a pillow.

"Hey, how come you're not getting ready?"

Tasanee sat up and heaved a sigh. "Because I don't feel like sitting around in my skates for two hours. Coach didn't catch you outside?"

Claire shook her head. Her shoulders slumped.

"Our ice time changed again. There's some Disney show here this weekend and their contract with the Olympic Center included setup time on the 1980 rink all afternoon. We can use the 1932 rink but not until four."

Claire didn't say anything. She pulled her cell phone from her bag, sat down on the bench, and started to call Natalie. But before she finished, her eyes started stinging and she knew the lump in her throat would keep her from talking. Natalie wasn't going to understand. Claire closed the phone and let out a shaky breath.

"Hey, what's wrong?" Tasanee closed her book and joined Claire on the bench. "You'll still have time to practice for Monday. Just a little later."

"It's not that. I had plans with my best friend at home tonight." Claire blinked away tears. "I'm okay. It's no big deal." But it was. She wondered how long Natalie would even be her best friend when she was never around.

"Oh, Claire. That stinks." Tasanee put an arm around her. "You're so good that I forget sometimes you're new and still getting used to this schedule. You don't really get to have a life outside of this place."

Claire sighed. "I just wanted one regular day, a regular skating session and then a regular day with Natalie like I used to have. But nothing is regular anymore."

Groshev pounded on the door. "Ladies! We need you in the gym, please. We'll have a general fitness session while we wait for our ice."

After an hour of cardio and Pilates, Claire managed to pull herself together to call Natalie, who sounded disappointed but not all that surprised.

"It's fine," she said. Claire knew it wasn't.

"Have dinner without me, but I'll come by the house when I get home, okay? Maybe we'll still be able to do milk shakes?"

"Sure," Natalie said. "Whatever."

By the time they finally got onto the ice and ran everyone's routines, it was almost six. On the way home, Claire called her parents to let them know Mrs. Collins was going to drop her off at Natalie's house. She was late, but she still wanted to see Nat.

☙❧

When they pulled into the Rabideaus' driveway, Natalie was heading down the porch steps in her white beekeeper's jump-suit with her smoker in her hand.

"Thanks for the ride." Claire waved and ran to meet Natalie. "Hey! Did your new queen come today?"

"No." Natalie sat down on the bottom step to put on her rubber boots. She pulled the elastic at the bottom of her pant legs down over them. "I'm dealing with the mites."

"How do you . . . deal with them?"

She picked up a frame, like a tray, from the lawn. "Put in a new frame with bigger cells so the queen will lay drone eggs. The mites like drones for some reason, so they'll lay eggs in there, too, and then I'll pull the whole thing out and put it in the freezer to kill them." She paused and looked at Claire. "How was skating?"

Claire tried to smile. "Natalie, I'm so sorry about tonight. I really still thought I'd be home sooner than this, but we got on the ice so late. And Saratoga's on Monday, so we couldn't just leave early."

Natalie looked back at the porch where her leather gloves sat, flopped over a step. She turned and picked them up. "Of course you couldn't." Her voice was flat.

"Well, do you . . . still want to hang out tonight?" Claire looked at her watch. "We could get shakes, maybe?"

"No thanks. I need to do this now. It's important." She started pulling on the gloves. "If you really want to hang out, you can grab my dad's gear and come with me." She tipped her head toward the porch, where Claire knew the other jumpsuit and veil would be hanging from a hook by the door. She had walked by them a million times on her way into Natalie's house but never even thought about putting them on.

"Well?" Natalie raised her eyebrows. She knew the bees made Claire nervous and usually just teased her about it, but here she was, waiting for an answer.

"Okay, I guess." Claire forced herself up the steps, dropped her skating bag on the porch swing, and lifted the suit from the hook. She sat down, pulled it on, and zipped it. Mr. Rabideau was only a little taller than she was but way stockier, so the thick canvas bunched out all around her. She took off her sneakers and put on his big boots, pulling the pant legs down over them. The elastic left big gaps; she tried not to think about bees flying in there and up her leg. She pulled on the gloves, but they were so big and bulky that she had trouble using her hands. "Um, Nat? Can you help with the veil thing? I can't figure it out."

Natalie set down the smoker and pulled the hood over Claire's head. She zipped the zipper that ran all around the neck until it looked like a space suit. "There. That should be okay. If one gets inside your veil, just squash it so you don't get stung." She picked up the smoker and frame and started toward the orchard.

If one gets *inside* the veil? Claire took a shuddery breath and followed Natalie out to the two hives that sat between the rows of apple trees. They looked like big white wooden dressers, each with three fat drawers that Natalie called supers. That's where the bees lived.

Natalie stuffed some dried grass into the smoker. It was the shape of a lantern with a little bellows attached to the side and a lid that looked like the tin man's hat from *The Wizard of Oz*. She struck a match, held it to the grass, and blew on it until it caught. She closed the lid, stepped toward the first hive, and used the bellows to puff smoke into the holes. An angry buzz rose from inside. Natalie set the smoker down on the ground next to the hive, picked up the new frame, and handed it to Claire. "Hold this, okay?"

The evening air swarmed with bees flying in from around the orchard, and every once in a while, one bumped into

Claire's suit. Her heart raced, thinking of those gaps around her ankles, and she squeezed her eyes shut every time one flew close to her face. Her forehead was dripping with sweat under the hood, and she tried to take deep breaths, but it didn't calm her down. She could *hear* them close to her, even when she couldn't see them. What if one got inside her suit?

"Natalie, I'm not sure I can do this. How about if I meet you back at the house?"

Natalie picked up a crowbar and wedged it under the super on top. "You can leave if you want. But I'm going to be a while, so if you want to talk tonight it needs to be here." She lifted the super off the top of the hive and carefully lowered it onto the grass. More bees buzzed around her as she stood back up. "I know skating's *your* whole entire world right now, but this is part of *my* world and it's just as important. At least to *me* it is."

"Natalie, that's not fair. You know I—"

"I'll tell you what's not fair." She reached for the frame, practically yanking it out of Claire's hands. "Expecting me to just be here waiting whenever you finish with your skating friends. You're almost never here anymore, and when you are, it's like you're not even paying attention. You're somewhere else, and we used to do everything together and now you've just . . . dumped me." Her voice broke, and she swiped at her tears through the veil. "*That's* what's not fair." She turned back to the hive, leaned the frame against the bottom, and started prying inside the super with the crowbar.

"Natalie, I haven't dumped you. I miss you like crazy. You have no idea what it's like there."

"You're right," Natalie shot over her shoulder, pulling a frame from the hive. It was sticky with wax combs and drips of honey and coated with a thick layer of bees. "I have no idea because I never even see you anymore to hear about it, Claire. Can you not even see what you're like now?" She turned too fast and bumped the frame into the edge of the hive. Bees swarmed everywhere, so fast Claire couldn't keep track of them. Three flew at her eyes, and she felt them push the veil in so it touched her face. She wanted to run but was afraid they'd chase her. She stood still and closed her eyes and felt the veil fold into her face every time a bee hit it.

"Shoot. Hold on."

Claire opened her eyes and saw Natalie lunge for the smoker. She puffed the bellows over and over, blowing great clouds of smoke down into the bees that were covering the top of the hive. If anything, it seemed to make them angrier. They buzzed louder until the whole hive sounded like it was sizzling in the hot night. Claire gasped and took a step back.

"Just hold on," Natalie said. "The smoke makes it hard for them to communicate. It masks the chemical signals so the rest of them don't get angry, too. And they don't like it, so they try to get away from it." Natalie puffed the smoker again, and the sizzling got louder. It sounded like bacon on an extra-hot griddle.

But she was right; even as the bees got louder, they disappeared deeper into the hive. They stopped dive-bombing Claire, and she could breathe again. She stood silently while Natalie added the new frame and found a spot for the old one in the other hive. When the hives were back together and the bees started to quiet down, Claire's voice finally returned to her. She could think of only one thing to say. "I'm sorry, Nat."

Natalie sniffed and bent down to pick up the smoker. "Let's just go back to the house. My mom can give you a ride home."

Claire nodded and started walking. When she felt far enough away from the bees, she pulled off her gloves and reached up to unzip her hood. Back on the Rabideaus' porch, she peeled off the jumpsuit and stepped out of the rubber boots as Natalie's mom opened the kitchen door.

"Claire!" she said. "You're just about the last person I expected to see in a bee suit. I thought you liked to keep your distance."

"I did," Claire said. "But Natalie . . ." She stopped. She wasn't about to tell Mrs. Rabideau that Natalie *made* her go out to the bees, even though that's exactly what happened. Claire's eyes welled up.

"Claire, is something wrong?" Mrs. Rabideau's concerned face just made it worse. "Did you girls have a fight?"

"We're fine, Mom," Natalie said briskly, pulling open the kitchen door. "Claire's just tired. She's been busy."

Mrs. Rabideau didn't look convinced, but she pulled car keys from the pocket of her shorts. "Come on then, Claire. Get yourself a drink of water, and I'll drive you home. You coming, Nat?"

"Nope. I'm going to get ready for bed." She looked tired, too. Tired and sad and still angry. Did she mean for Claire to be so scared out there? Had she insisted that Claire help with the bees to punish her for not being around? Claire couldn't believe the Natalie she'd known since preschool would do something like that.

But then, a lot had changed in the past couple months. An awful lot.

CHAPTER 13

The one good thing about competing at Saratoga was that it gave Claire almost no time to think about her fight with Natalie. The beginning of the weekend passed in a blur of editing music, sewing more sequins onto Charlotte's skating dress from regionals four years ago, and trying to land the double salchow over and over and over again.

"Arms up!" Groshev shouted on Saturday morning. "Bend your knees as you go into the jump! Arms up!"

For what felt like the hundredth time, Claire slid across the ice on her hip, covered in snow. She'd be covered in bruises soon, too.

The thought of competing in Saratoga was just . . . ugh. She wasn't ready. And even when she *was* ready, competitions made her feel like she was about to pass out. Nobody understood that except Natalie. And now she didn't even have Natalie.

"Come on. Up! Again!"

She wasn't ready. Why was he doing this to her? "I can't do this." She skated up to Groshev. "When I land, I'm just . . . crumbling. I'm too weak in my legs or my abs or . . . something. I can't stay solid on this landing."

"It is not your legs or your abs. You are . . . how do you say it . . . crumbling . . . because you are not solid here." Groshev tapped the top of her head with his finger. He took a deep breath. "Focus. Single salchow now. Go."

Claire forced herself to keep going. Forced herself to get up again and again, and little by little, the ache in her muscles took away some of the ache in her heart. By the end of the morning session, she was landing the single again. At least she had that.

"But I still don't think I should be—"

"Enough!" Groshev held up a hand. "You are competing. It is what you need."

What she needed, Claire thought, heading back out to the ice, was another few months to get her jumps under control. How was throwing herself into a frenzy to compete on a few days' notice going to help anything?

"Let's go. Again." Groshev waved his hand at her, and Claire worked through the single four more times. She landed every one cleanly.

"Good! That's good!" Groshev called. He looked at his watch. "Again now, and keep going into the sit spin."

"Coach?" Meghan skated up. "I think I've almost got that footwork sequence down. Do you think I could get another five minutes with you before we—?"

He held up a hand. "Not now. I am finishing with Claire, and then we have to be off the ice for the hockey at noon." The Zamboni was already growling in the corner as he turned back to Claire. "Do the routine—the full routine—right now with the single in place of the double salchow. Skate it. Do not be the robot running back and forth and waiting for the jumps. *Skate* your program. Go."

Skate. Just skate. This time, she didn't let herself worry about the jumps before they came. She willed herself to skate only in the moment, to feel the cold air on her face as she spun, the rhythm of her music. It was the only thing that took away the sting of Natalie's words. She skated. And she landed every jump.

"It is good. You are ready." Groshev almost smiled when she skated up to the boards.

And for the first time in weeks, Claire thought she was ready, too.

༄

"What do you think?" Claire held up the dress so the skirt swished against her bare legs. Grateful for a free Saturday afternoon, she'd spent it helping her mom put in the tomato plants, and her knees were still caked with mud.

"I think you better get that dress away from those filthy legs. The dry cleaner is closed by now."

"Good point. But really, look. . . ." Claire held the dress out from her body and turned it in the late afternoon light. "Do I sparkle enough?"

"You always sparkle when you skate. But we should probably sew on a few more just for good measure."

Claire picked up a blue sequin that fell out of the package and held it up to the window. She'd tried calling Natalie, but her mother said she was at her Champlain Valley Beekeepers meeting. Maybe she'd still call back. Claire sighed, louder than she meant to.

"You nervous?" Her mother touched her tongue to the

frayed end of a length of thread, twirled it between her fingers, and held the needle up to the light.

"Not really. It hasn't sunk in yet." Her mother missed the eye of the needle twice. "Want me to do that?"

"Yes, please. It's a job for younger eyes than mine."

Claire threaded the needle and handed it back. "You know, it's not nervous I feel right now. It's more . . . overwhelmed. Skating takes up so much time, and I still have school, and I don't see Natalie and she's all mad about that, and now all of a sudden I'm competing again. I mean, I'm learning a ton and it's a fantastic opportunity and everything." She didn't want her mother to think she wasn't grateful for all the rides to training. "But it just feels like this happened so fast."

"Well, sure." Her mother held a silver sequin to the thin fabric and pushed the needle through. "I'd imagine it's a lot to take in. You're living a dream here." She tipped her head toward the package on the table. "Can you find me another blue one?"

Living a dream. Claire poked through the sequins. Did it matter that she had never once dreamed about skating in another competition? She found the right shade of blue and handed it to her mother.

"What was your dream when you were my age?"

"Hmm . . ." Her mom looked out the window, where Dad was watering the kitchen garden, turning every so often to spray the boys with the hose. "I'm not sure I knew what it was back then. I mean, Grandma and Grandpa always told me I should be running some great big company when I grew up. I was so bossy when I was little; they thought I was a natural, so I kind of got that in my head as a dream." She motioned for another sequin.

"And you went to school for business, right?" Claire fished another blue one out of the package. She already knew this story, how her mother went to Cornell University and met a cute, quiet environmental studies major and went home with him to visit his family. She came on Maple Weekend, one of the sunny perfect ones where the steam from the sugarhouse made the only clouds in a bright blue sky, and said she couldn't imagine going to work in a tall building in some smoggy city after that. Mom always said she fell in love with Dad and the North Country all at once. "Are you ever sad you *didn't* get to run a big company?"

Her mother smiled. "No, because by the time I graduated, *this* was my dream." She tipped her head at the window, where the boys had commandeered the hose from Dad. All three of them were soaked.

Claire didn't let it go. "But what about that first dream?"

Her mother tied off a knot. "Well . . . I guess a dream isn't so hard to let go when it wasn't entirely yours to begin with." She handed the dress back to Claire. "Go take a shower and then try that on. I bet you'll sparkle like crazy."

೧೨

The sequins scratched against Claire's arm as she draped the dress over her shoulder on her way into the Saratoga Ice Rink on Monday morning. She hadn't felt even a little nervous until she stepped inside.

"Whoa." She stopped so fast that Luke and Abby almost crashed into her. The hallways were lined with bright booths, where vendors displayed everything from tights and sequined skirts to tall stacks of skating books and DVDs. Girls with perfectly braided hair and sparkling dresses held up outfits to show their mothers. Claire was suddenly self-conscious about the sweatpants she'd worn on the ride down. She figured she'd wait to change into her competition outfit after practice; she was so afraid of messing up Charlotte's dress.

"Over here, I think." Abby pointed through the crowd to a row of tables. The registration area was already mobbed, and it was only a quarter after seven. Luke's mom had picked Claire up before five, just as her dad was getting up for his early shift at the border.

"Sorry I can't make it, sugar." He'd kissed her on the top of her tight braid. "And Mom, too." He sighed. "But she's got the boys at hockey, so . . . next time. Grandpa's going to drive down later if he can."

"It's fine," Claire had told him with a wave.

Now, she wished they were here. Her eyes even searched the crowd for Natalie, but of course, Claire knew she wasn't here, either. She was probably out with her mean bees or off practicing drama stuff with Riley and Maya. Too busy—or angry—to return Claire's phone calls.

"Over here." Luke's mom led them toward the registration area. "*A* through *K* are here. You and Luke wait together while Abby and I find some drinks."

"And I'll be right back," said Luke. "I gotta find a bathroom."

Claire edged into line behind three girls that looked just like the Ice Queens, decked out in matching turquoise dresses with full skirts and sequined tops held up by thin silver straps. When the tall one turned, though, she saw a girl with bangs and a friendlier smile than Alexis's.

"Hi!" the girl said. "I'm Jackie. Welcome to Saratoga Springs . . . home of the never-ending registration line."

Claire smiled. "Is this your home rink?"

"Yep. All three of us—me and Steph and Justine"—she nodded toward her friends—"are on the synchronized skating team."

"That's great. So you always compete as a team?"

"Yep." Jackie, Steph, and Justine joined arms and laughed. "On our own, we're a mess, but together, we're unstoppable."

"Well, good luck." Claire smiled as they inched closer to the registration table. She felt a twinge of jealousy. It must be nice not to be out there getting shouted at all alone.

"Come on—I thought you'd have us all registered by now." Luke joined her in line and pulled his iPod from his pocket. "We're okay. Our practice ice is at eight, and then the juvenile competition starts at nine."

"Ugh." Claire wrinkled her nose.

"Lighten up. You need to laugh, Claire. It's good for your skating."

"Okay. Make me laugh."

"Let's see . . ." Luke moved up as the line moved forward a little. "What would make Claire laugh?" His face lit up. "Here's one. Where does a baby mathematician sleep?"

Claire made a face at him. "In a bed with a number blanket?"

"Nope." He grinned. "In a crib-o-nacci!"

"Oh. My. Gosh. That was bad." Claire rolled her eyes.

"Oh, I have more where that came from. Anything to

cheer up a fellow Fibo-nerd. Let's see . . . What does a baby mathematician wear?"

She couldn't help smiling. "What?"

"A bib-o-nacci."

"And do you know what the mathematician did onstage when his script turned up missing?"

"Tell me."

"He had to ad-lib-o-nacci."

Claire laughed. But then thought about Natalie. She hadn't even had time to ask Nat about drama or how things were going with Denver.

"You're going to do fine. Just keep thinking positive," Luke said. He whirled his finger around on the iPod wheel. "Here, listen to this one. Perfect skating competition song."

He leaned over and put one of the earbuds into Claire's ear. His hand brushed against her neck, and she shivered.

Low piano notes trilled, and then Gloria Gaynor launched into "I Will Survive." Claire laughed again, and this time, it made her feel better. "Okay, I'll survive. I promise," she said when the music faded out.

"Good." Luke took his earbuds back, caught her hand, and held on. His hand was warm, a warmth that traveled right up Claire's arm and into her cheeks. "You're going to be great, you know."

She nodded. "Thanks."

Her stomach was still turning flips when he let go.

∞

Claire didn't find anyone else from Lake Placid until five minutes into their practice time, when Tasanee hurried in from the hall and plopped down onto the bench to rummage through her skating bag.

Claire skated up to the boards. "Hey! Where have you been?"

"Reading. I lost track of time."

"Homicidal fairies?"

"No, I finished that book. This one has bloodthirsty pixies." She held up a book with barren trees, silhouetted against a girl's pale neck. She had glittery gold lips.

"Nice lipstick," Claire said.

"It's pixie dust."

Claire laughed. "Don't you ever feel like just reading about normal middle school stuff? Like school and crushes and girls fighting with one another?"

"With skating, I get enough of *that* drama in real life. This is my escape." Tasanee put the book back in her bag, stepped onto the ice, and swung a leg up onto the boards to stretch.

"You ready?" she asked Claire.

"Not really. I still wish I didn't have to do this competition."

"You'll be fine. You were landing everything Saturday. Just don't try anything too fancy."

"Don't worry." Claire started skating to warm up. She'd pretend it was just another practice. She ran through her routine twice, tried the single salchow both times, and had two clean landings. Meghan skated up just as the whistle blew to clear the ice.

"Great dress!" Claire reached out to touch the shimmering fabric. It flickered between deep red and shimmery midnight black and glittered with sequins that seemed to catch every light in the rink.

"Thanks." Meghan smiled and moved so her skirt swished around her thighs.

"Are your parents coming today?"

Meghan stopped swishing. "My mom is. My dad was supposed to but says he has to stay in the city. Again." Her face drooped, and Claire felt bad for asking.

"Is your dress new?"

Meghan started swishing again. "No. But it's the one I wore last year for the Jamestown Invitational. I came in first there, so I figure it's good luck."

"You don't need luck," Claire said. "I'm the one who needs a four-leaf clover. I had a good practice session, though, so if I can just keep landing the jumps, I should be fine."

Meghan smiled as they started skating. "I bet you'll land that double salchow perfectly."

Claire shook her head. "No, I'm only doing singles today."

Meghan stopped, her skates spraying up ice shavings. "You are?"

Claire stopped next to her. "Yeah, Groshev says it's a good idea for me to ease back into the jumps."

Meghan frowned a little. "Really?"

"Yeah. Why?"

The lines in Meghan's forehead deepened. "I'm surprised he has you backing off. I hope he's not, like, testing you or something."

"What?"

"You know . . . to see if you've got the guts to go for the double."

"Well, that's dumb. Wouldn't he *tell* me if he wanted me to try the double?"

"Probably," Meghan said slowly. They started skating again. "I wonder if you should try it anyway, though. I bet you'd land it, and you could show him for sure that he didn't make a mistake with the scholarship."

"No way. I haven't landed a clean double in weeks."

Meghan held up her hands and shook her head as if she could erase the whole conversation. "You're right. That was a dumb idea. I shouldn't have said anything." She turned to skate the other way around the rink.

Claire felt her chest getting tight. *Should* she try the double? She tried taking a deep breath, but it caught in her throat.

"Hey!" Luke called from the boards. "There you are. I was looking all over. You guys are in locker room five. I'm in eight, right down the hall. I'll see you before you go out for real." He looked at Claire. "All set?"

She nodded. But that old awful competition feeling was back in her stomach. She couldn't imagine for a minute that she'd be able to skate.

CHAPTER 14

When Claire and Meghan stepped into locker room five, Alexis and Stevie were lacing skates. Tasanee was pulling a new pair of tights from its package. "Figures I landed right on my toe pick in that last fall. Look." There was a gaping hole in her tights.

"At least you have extras. I practiced in my sweats so I wouldn't have to worry about my tights for the competition." Claire unzipped her bag and pulled out the new tights her mother had picked up in Plattsburgh, took them out of the package, and stretched the Lycra over her hand. "I'm trying these thinner ones because my skates are a little snug."

"You know, that might be your problem with the jumps," Meghan said.

Tasanee looked up from lacing her skates. "She's not having problems with her jumps."

Meghan's eyes narrowed. "I was talking to Claire. And anyway, you sort of missed the first part of the conversation."

Tasanee shrugged. "I don't really see how it matters. Either way, your jumps were gorgeous today, Claire."

Claire shook her head. "Just the singles."

"Isn't that what you have in your program? I thought you took out the doubles for now."

"Well, I did but—"

The door opened, and a woman with a frizzy brown ponytail popped her head into the room. She had a blue staff badge pinned on her fleece and a pencil stuck behind each ear. "Fifteen minutes until juvenile skaters need to be out. Don't forget the lineup has changed since we had a skater drop out."

Hannah. Claire hadn't heard a thing from her since the day she walked out of the Olympic Center. *Wherever she was*, Claire thought, *Hannah had it easy today.*

"Let's go use the bathroom while we have time," Meghan said. "I can help with your makeup if you want."

Claire nodded. Her heart was pounding and her stomach churned. Maybe if she let Meghan help her look the part, she'd feel better about skating.

She and Tasanee followed Meghan through a maze of lockers and benches and skating dresses in the color of every gemstone ever discovered. On an ordinary day, Claire would have loved looking at the outfits, but today, they were too bright. Too sweet. Like eating too much candy on Halloween.

"Oh, nuts!" Meghan's hand flew to her hair just as they reached the bathroom. "I forgot my hairspray. Be right back, okay?" And she quick-stepped on her skate guards back into the sea of costumes.

"Are you okay?" Tasanee asked Claire as they headed into the bathroom. "You seem stressed. Is it just because this is your first competition in a while? You really are ready, you know."

Claire nodded. She was grateful when one of the stall doors opened and she could shut herself away from the world, the colors, the noise, and the ice that waited outside. She pulled her sweatshirt up over her mouth and breathed in. It still smelled like wood smoke from home.

Claire heard Meghan come in. "It's a zoo out there!" She heard the *pffffft* of hairspray and knew their ice time was getting closer. She couldn't hide in the stall forever.

Meghan met her at the mirror with a puffy makeup brush. "Let me get your cheekbones." She whisked blush onto Claire's face. "There. We better go. You still need to get dressed."

The frizzy ponytail lady was waiting back at the locker room. "Five minutes. Five."

Meghan and Tasanee stretched while Claire pulled out her skating dress and tights.

"That's *so* pretty." Meghan leaned over to finger the fabric of Charlotte's dress, a light, shimmery purple blue the color of the lake at sunset.

"Thanks, it's my cousin's. She's in London right now, but she usually skates in Pennsylvania at school. Or with me when she's home." Claire smiled, remembering Charlotte twirling in the dress so the flowing layers of its skirt flared out. She pulled off her sweatpants and put her right foot into her tights, day-dreaming about the last time she and Char had skated together on the pond. Charlotte had worked and worked with her on that double toe loop, until she'd fallen so many times she was sure she was going to just fall right through the ice onto the frogs asleep on the bottom. But she hadn't. She'd finally gotten it, and they'd gone in for hot chocolate and—

"Oh, no!" Claire stared down at her tights, pulled halfway

up her left leg, her fingers snagged on the edge of a huge hole above her knee. "These were brand new!"

"Two minutes, ladies," the ponytail lady called.

"What am I going to do? This is my only pair!"

Meghan rushed to her locker. "Here, take my backup pair."

"Thanks." Claire ripped open the package. Her stomach felt like a wet towel someone was wringing out. She peeled off the torn tights, flung them toward her locker, and started pulling on Meghan's.

They were way too small.

Of course they were. Meghan was a full six inches shorter than Claire.

"Oh, no!" Claire jumped, tugging the top of the tights. She reached down to her ankles, pulling at the fabric, willing it to stretch more, but the crotch of the tights came just halfway between her hips and her knees.

Meghan bit her lip. "Maybe you could run out to one of the vendors."

"One minute, girls." The ponytail lady stood by the door but didn't notice Claire's disaster.

"There's no time." Tasanee climbed over the bench and reached down to start unballing Claire's first tights. "You'll have to put these back on. It won't affect your score. It happens. The judges know that."

Claire almost fell over, trying to squirm herself out of Meghan's tights. When she pulled her ripped pair back on, the hole gaped, and the chill at the back of her knee reminded her how flawed she was. She slowed down to step into Charlotte's dress—nothing was worth tearing it—and stomped into her skates, fingers flying as she tied them.

When she finished and looked up, Alexis was standing there, her hair in a perfectly smooth bun. "Newbie mistake," she said. "You should always bring an extra pair."

"Okay, ladies, let's head out." Ponytail lady waved her clipboard.

"Hold on!" Tasanee grabbed Claire's shoulder and stopped her long enough to zip up the back of her dress before they stepped out into the hallway.

Luke was the first one out of the locker room down the hall. "Hey!" His eyes lit up when he saw Claire. "Great dress! You look awesome."

Hot tears streamed down Claire's cheeks, and she turned away. She let the sea of skaters carry her down the hallway to the rink.

"Up here." Thank God for Tasanee's hand on her elbow because she could barely see, certainly not well enough to make out which coach among the shouting grown-ups was theirs.

Claire breathed in, and it came out all shaky and shivery, as Tasanee led her up into the stands and planted her on a seat.

"Listen, Claire," Tasanee whispered in her ear. "I know you hate competitions, and I know you're freaked out about skating, and it stinks that your tights ripped, but just . . . pull it together. All you have to do is skate the show you just did on the practice ice, and you're going to be fine."

Claire stared up at the ceiling lights. They blurred like fuzzy stars through her tears. Tasanee was wrong. She wasn't going to be fine. What if Meghan was right and Groshev was testing her? She couldn't put the doubles back in, could she?

What if Groshev decided to yank her scholarship because she wasn't skating the way she skated when he chose her?

"Try to relax." Tasanee tucked a curl back into Claire's braid. "Our sports psychologist always says, before a competition, you should think of things that calm your mind. So what makes you feel peaceful?"

Claire took a breath. It came out less shaky this time. What made her peaceful? Sticky, wet, late snow on the trees. The sound of sap dripping into a bucket. The rich bronze gold color of it, poured out as sugar on snow. The smell of corn chowder and the sound of Uncle Bruce's lazy guitar notes drifting in through the sugarhouse windows. Natalie's laugh, back when they used to laugh together. And the cow pond and Charlotte. With Charlotte, even double toe loops felt peaceful.

Claire didn't answer Tasanee out loud, but she nodded and took another deep breath as she heard the announcer's voice echo through the arena.

"From Lake Placid, skating to Vivaldi's 'Autumn,' we have Claire Boucher." He pronounced it wrong, just like Bob-O, calling her Claire Butcher. Claire concentrated on that as she stepped up to the rink so she wouldn't have to think about skating. *They really should have somebody review the names with the announcer*, she thought, pulling off her guards. And since when was she *from* Lake Placid?

Claire skated out to center ice, struck her opening pose, and waited. When the opening notes from the strings erupted from the speakers, they were so loud that Claire felt as if she'd been fired out of a cannon when she took off. She skated fast—maybe faster than she had at practice all week, and she felt as if she were flying the length of the ice when she straightened her back leg into a spiral. Every muscle in her body was as tense as it could possibly be, but she made it through the quick footwork moves, too, keeping every step measured and precise and in time with the staccato notes of the piece.

She skated down the ice and almost missed her cue for the waltz jumps, but she caught herself and leaped—not too high, though. If substituting a single for a double might get her dumped, then falling in competition would do it for sure.

Her sit spin was textbook-perfect, her upper body tight and strong. Was she actually going to get through this program? For a second, coming out of the spin, Claire felt a rush of relief. It was almost over, and she was doing okay.

But then the music slowed, and she heard the long, high notes that meant it was time for her to gather speed, to cross over faster and faster until she was ready for the jump at the end of the program. She forced her skates to move faster. Her heart pounded. The cold air on the back of her neck wasn't enough to keep her face from burning. What was she going to do?

The ads on the boards blurred past as she circled the end of the rink. Maybe she could make it a double. She had to at least try, didn't she? But the program had been perfect so far. She hadn't even stumbled, so maybe if she just kept the single, even though it wasn't what Groshev wanted to see, her score would be high enough that he wouldn't—

Oh, but the difficulty affected scores, too! She could probably skate a perfect program with that single and still be at the bottom of the list here, with all the moves girls like Alexis were doing. The single wasn't going to be enough.

She'd try the double. She tried to feel the music, tried to let it carry her into the last turn, but the sound of her skates scratching the ice seemed magnified—like somebody dragging a full sap bucket across the flagstone porch—and it gave her chills. She could feel the wind on the back of her leg; the hole in her tights must have gotten even bigger.

The notes came faster, sharper, into the final crescendo of the piece—the one that was supposed to lift her off the ground and send her spinning, defying gravity—and on the last stroke before she was about to take off, she knew she wouldn't be able to do it. She couldn't land the double.

She launched herself into the single, saw the blur of the boards as she turned, and tightened the muscles in her right leg to land.

She made it all the way around.

She was high enough.

But the momentum of her twisting body took her too far. Instead of landing cleanly at the perfect moment—landing solidly on one foot with the other extended behind her—she kept turning. She could feel it happening.

No! Too much! Too much!

But she couldn't stop.

The music went silent for Claire, and the faces of the crowd blurred in the lights as she tightened her muscles to try and save the landing. But she was too far gone. She came down on the side of her boot and slammed to the ice, skidding four or five feet before she was able to get back onto her feet. She picked up her last series of dance moves halfway through, did the final scratch spin, not half as fast or strong as the first had been, and finished in her lunge.

She stood to acknowledge the judges and the crowd, and they clapped.

But she'd blown it. Everybody knew.

The applause was supposed to make her feel better, but it didn't. It pushed her right over the edge, from quiet tears to sobs that she could barely keep down in her throat as she left the ice and headed for the locker room. Every sharp clap felt like a slap in the face.

"Hold on there, butterfly girl." She couldn't see him through her tears, but Claire knew the voice, and she let her grandfather fold her into a hug. "Hey, now . . . I know you wanted to be perfect, but you looked beautiful out there. Just beautiful, and I'm proud of you." He gave her an extra squeeze.

She leaned in and wiped her tears on the rough wool of his jacket, then stepped back. She couldn't bear to stand there waiting for her scores. Hearing it out loud would just make everything worse. "Thanks, Grandpa. Let me get changed and I'll see you after, okay?"

"Sure thing. And chin up, okay? You'll get that jump next time."

Claire took a shaky breath as she turned toward the locker room.

She wondered if there would even be a next time.

CHAPTER 15

This looks terrific," Mrs. Cosgro said, paging through the printed-out slides Claire turned in at the end of class. "I know all about Fibonacci in nature, but I hadn't read nearly as much about the patterns in music. And you have sound clips embedded at this part for when you present?"

Claire nodded. Her mom had helped her download the audio files from Mozart and Bartók that Luke had told her about and put them into the slide show so they'd play when she got to that part of the presentation. "You can't really hear how the Fibonacci plays into the music," Claire admitted, "but I still thought it was cool."

"It is!" Mrs. Cosgro flipped through the last few slides. "And the appearance of the golden spiral in figure skating is just fantastic."

"Thanks." It felt good to have done something right. With Groshev yelling in one ear all the time and Alexis snipping at her in the other, Claire had almost forgotten that she was ever good at anything.

Mrs. Cosgro smiled down at the page with Luke's photo on it. "And it looks like you had a coconspirator to help with the project."

"That's my friend from skating. He does math club in Plattsburgh."

"Speaking of that . . ." Mrs. Cosgro hurried over to her desk, the beads on her skirt clicking against one another. "I want to give you paperwork for the school MATHCOUNTS team for next year. Our eighth graders often make it to the state competition, and I think you'd be great. We're going to hold a few sessions with the new members before summer break—you know, so you're comfortable with the kinds of challenges you'll face in competition next winter."

Claire stared at the forms in Mrs. Cosgro's hands. Last fall, before her life was so full of car rides and skating, she'd heard about the eighth grade MATHCOUNTS team on the announcements. They'd taken second place in Albany and had a pizza party in the cafeteria when they got back to celebrate. Back then, she had wondered if she was a strong enough student to be invited, and she had hoped . . .

"I'm sorry." Claire shook her head and picked up her backpack. "I can't. I'm skating three nights a week, and I just can't do any more after-school stuff right now."

Mrs. Cosgro frowned a little. "Well, maybe I could talk with your coach. Riley and Maya worked it out so they can split their time between MATHCOUNTS and softball."

Claire shook her head and tried not to laugh. Groshev would eat Mrs. Cosgro and her jingly skirt for breakfast if she ever showed up and suggested that math problems might be as important as his skating sessions. "Thanks, though."

"Well, maybe in the fall, you'll consider joining us, if your schedule's any different?"

Claire nodded. "If I still can, that would be great." And for

a minute, she let herself think about August, when her scholarship would be over and she'd get her old life back. And she
could play Indiana Jones with the boys again and make up
with Natalie and do homework at her desk in her bedroom
instead of on a locker room floor.

She just had to make it through another few months with
Groshev first.

◌◌

"Are you going to be around the Olympic Center during practice tonight?" Claire fidgeted with the zipper of her fleece
jacket as the truck idled at the stoplight Wednesday afternoon.

"I thought I'd get a cup of coffee and read my paper, since
it's only a couple hours. Not much sense in going home." Dad
glanced over at her. "How come?"

"I just wanted to make sure . . . you know . . . in case I
need to reach you or something."

What would Groshev say after her performance in Sara-
toga? Thinking about it made Claire long for the days when
skating was just for fun. She missed her old coach like crazy.
Whenever Claire failed a skating test to move up a level, Mary
Kate had been right there with a hug and a Hershey's bar.
Groshev was going to be a different story.

What would he do? Claire had played out today's practice
in her head a thousand times on the drive down. About half
the time, it ended with Groshev telling her to get out. Just
leave. And even though a part of her longed for her old life, her
old schedule, something itched deep inside when she thought
about leaving now. She wasn't ready to give up. Not yet.

She kissed Dad on the cheek, climbed out of the truck,

and pulled open the athletes' entrance door. There were still no alarms, but if they were ever going to toss her out, this would be the day.

Claire chose the bench at the far end of the locker room, focused on her skates, and rushed out to the rink before Tasanee was even finished getting ready. Her stomach felt as if she had swallowed lead weights.

She stepped onto the ice, ready to face the fire, but Groshev was already busy with Abby and Luke. She stood for a moment watching until his eyes landed on her.

"Warm up. You will be skating with Kalina today." He nodded over Claire's shoulder toward a bench just outside the rink where a woman with short-cropped hair and long legs was folded over herself, lacing up skates. Claire watched her slender fingers pulling the laces tight. Her skates were the padded ones they give little kids so they're more comfortable. She didn't look like a coach.

Claire skated around a couple times to warm up. She paused near Groshev, waiting for him to say something about her performance, but he was still working with Luke and Abby. He probably had high hopes for them at regionals since they'd won the Saratoga competition. Figures he wouldn't have the time of day for Claire, who couldn't even land a single without falling anymore.

"Sorry to hold you up!" The woman from the bench stepped gingerly onto the ice, as if she hadn't skated in a long time. "I don't usually work *on* the ice, but I figured I'd take a spin with you since we haven't met before." She steadied herself on the edge of the boards for a couple seconds and then held out her right hand. "I'm Kalina Banks. It's nice to meet you, Claire."

"You too." Claire shook her hand but didn't know what to say. How was this woman supposed to coach her? Was this Groshev's clever way of telling her how awful she was? So bad she deserved a coach who couldn't even skate?

"Mind if I skate next to the boards?" Kalina ducked behind Claire. "That way I can catch myself."

"No problem," Claire said, "but . . . are you . . . are you coaching me today?"

"Oh gosh no!" Kalina's deep laugh rang out over the ice. "I'm sorry. I thought your coach had talked with you. I'm a sports psychologist, Claire. I give seminars for groups and sometimes I work with athletes one on one if your coach thinks I might be able to help. I guess you could call me a coach, but I'm not here to help you with your skating in the traditional way. I'm more of a brain coach—I get people thinking in healthier, more positive ways. Of course, then they skate better, so I guess I am a skating coach after all."

Tasanee glided past them in a spiral. She was lifting her leg so much higher than even a couple weeks ago. She looked great, but instead of being happy for her, Claire felt her heart droop. Everyone else was getting better. She was getting worse.

"I've always wanted to try that," Kalina said, lifting her back leg off the ground a few inches. She wobbled and quickly put it back down. She grabbed the boards to steady herself and took a slow, deep breath. So that's where Tasanee got it. Kalina was the deep-breath lady. She let go of the boards and tried again, but her leg was only up for a second before she wobbled and put it down. "How do you keep your balance when you do that?"

"You have to be going faster," Claire said. Not that she was in a position to be teaching anybody anything these days. "Look," she said, skating alongside Kalina, "I don't know what Coach told you, but I don't really think there's much that you can do to help me. He signed me up for this scholarship based on a fluke, a jump I landed at a tiny little show up at my home rink, and I haven't skated that well since I got here. I—I don't belong here." There. She said it herself.

Claire's eyes fell, and she watched her skates pushing along with tiny strokes that her new not-a-coach could keep up with.

Kalina skated with her quietly for a minute, then said, "Do you like skating?"

What kind of question was that? "I love skating. I'd rather skate than anything." Claire heard the words come out of her mouth. They used to be true. "I mean . . . I felt that way before. Now, I just . . . I get so stressed out, and Coach said . . ." She paused. He never actually *said* he wanted her to try the double, and he hadn't *said* anything after she bombed the jump. It was what he wasn't saying that was the problem. "I just . . . need to focus."

"I think I can help you." Kalina skated to one of the circles and started trying some slow crossovers. "I used to be able to do these, with my left foot over my right, but not the other way."

"Everybody has a dominant leg," Claire said, following her and crossing over, too. "Everybody's got strengths and weaknesses."

"What are your strengths?"

"Mine?" Claire passed Kalina and made a three-turn so she could face her skating backward. "Probably spins. I'm pretty good with sit spins, and I was working on—"

Kalina shook her head. "I asked you the wrong question. I mean where do you *find* your strength? What makes you feel strong?"

Claire had a sudden image of herself out in the woods with Dad, lifting sap buckets into the truck, and she laughed a little. "Collecting sap makes me feel strong, till I'm back in the house later that night and my arms feel like they're about to fall off."

"Sap? Does your family have a farm?"

Claire nodded. "We tap around seven hundred trees every March."

"Really?"

"Or real early in April if the thaw comes late. It's crazy busy when the sap starts running because it only lasts for so long, you know, and everybody pitches in to collect it and then boil it down to syrup. The sugarhouse is like a beehive with the whole family buzzing around all sticky." It made Claire think of Natalie and her grumpy bees; she wondered if they'd gotten any friendlier.

Claire stopped. "We should change direction now if you ever want to cross over the other way. You need to practice with your weak leg, too."

"You're a pretty good coach yourself," Kalina said, smiling. Her right-over-left crossovers were slower and clumsier.

"Thanks. I'm a junior coach for the Basic Skills program. I used to be, I mean."

"Not anymore?"

Claire shook her head. "No time."

"Do you miss it?"

"I will when it starts up, I bet. I love little kids."

Claire watched Tasanee glide by in another high spiral, a huge smile on her face. She was just like Ivy and Jenna—full of confidence and I'll-try-anything hope. It made Claire want to smile and cry at the same time. How come she couldn't be like that?

She blinked fast when she felt her eyes starting to fill. "You're not picking up your foot enough," she told Kalina. "You can't just slide it over; you need to pick it up and put it in front, and then you'll be able to push and get going faster."

"And what if I don't want to get going faster?" Kalina smiled. "Actually, I think I'm about done for now. Will you come talk to me in my office for a bit? You'll have time to skate for maybe another hour when we're done."

Claire nodded and stepped off the ice. "Should I change out of my skates?"

Kalina shook her head. "Just put your guards on. It's right down the hallway."

୬୦

Claire followed her to a door not far from the vending machines; she'd walked by it a dozen times in the past month but never noticed the lettering: DR. KALINA BANKS, SPORTS PSYCHOLOGIST.

Kalina opened the door. "Have a seat. I'm going to get some water. You want anything?"

"No thanks." Claire stepped into the office and plopped down in an overstuffed chair with a faded denim slipcover drooping off its arms. The place was small; three chairs and a desk filled it up, and the walls, covered with posters, made it feel even smaller.

The posters weren't what Claire expected. She figured a sports psychologist in this place would have life-sized figure skaters plastered on the walls, but there wasn't a Sasha Cohen to be found. Instead, the posters featured scenes from nature and more extreme sports. One showed a mountain climber hanging off the edge of a ledge so high above the ground it made Claire dizzy just looking at it. PERSEVERANCE was written in big letters at the bottom. *That guy better have perseverance,* Claire thought, *or he's going to have a heck of a long fall.*

Another poster showed a circle of thirteen skydivers in free fall, all holding hands as they plummeted toward a beach with turquoise waters rippling offshore. Claire wondered if they knew they were falling in a Fibonacci number. Probably not. They had other things to worry about. The quote on that one said, TEAMWORK: WHEN WE ALL WORK TOGETHER, WE ALL WIN TOGETHER.

Hmph, Claire thought. Whoever designed that one didn't know squat about figure skating in Lake Placid. She wanted to write that poster designer a letter and tell him about Hannah leaving, about Alexis and her mean comments and nail polish. There was no teamwork in figure skating, unless maybe you were one of those synchro girls.

"Something funny?" Kalina twisted the cap off her bottle of water and took a drink.

"Nothing," Claire said. She hadn't meant to hmph out loud.

Kalina followed Claire's gaze up to the poster. "That's one of my favorites."

"Well, maybe it's true for some sports." Claire looked away

from Kalina to the small end table that stood between her chair and the wall. There were a bunch of stress balls on it—those cushy foam balls you could squeeze to relax yourself. They had different faces on them. One had a big smile and bright eyes. One had worry lines in its forehead and a wavy line for a mouth. One had really wide eyes and an open mouth like it was scared. One had a frown, with eyebrows furrowed tight. It looked angry. No, not so much angry as pressured. Claire picked that one up and squeezed it.

When she turned back around, Kalina was nodding. "You feel like figure skating's pretty cutthroat? Every man for himself—or woman for herself, I should say?"

Claire half-laughed. "If you win, somebody else loses. Doesn't that kinda kill the whole teamwork theme? And then people like Alexis—" She stopped.

"People like Alexis what?"

"Nothing." Claire remembered Tasanee's advice about keeping her troubles with Alexis to herself. "Some people are just supercompetitive."

Kalina nodded slowly. "You can talk about stuff here, you know. It's private, so you're not being catty if you want to bring up issues with the other girls. And I know pretty much everyone, including Alexis."

"You work with Alexis?"

"Well, saying so would be against confidentiality rules, but I can tell you that I work with just about everybody here at some point, Claire. Sometimes because they're having a family crisis or their parents are stressing them out. Sometimes because they're putting too much pressure on themselves. And sometimes because this figure skating opportunity is the first positive thing that's ever happened to them, and they're so terrified of losing it that they don't know how to respond to competition."

Claire picked at the flap of the stress-man's foam hat. It had never in a million years occurred to her that Alexis could be afraid of anything.

"So back to you now," Kalina interrupted. "And back to the posters. Which one do you like? If you think the team-work one is bogus, which one feels true?"

Claire scanned the posters again and finally pointed to the one closest to the door, with a picture of a long pier jutting out into a perfect turquoise sea. DESTINY IS NO MATTER OF CHANCE. IT IS A MATTER OF CHOICE. —W. J. BRYAN. "I like that one, I guess."

Kalina nodded, looking at the poster as if she were seeing it for the first time, too. "Yeah? So what's your destiny?"

What was her destiny? When she closed her eyes to picture a future-Claire, she always saw herself in high school and col-lege, then working in a bright elementary school classroom with really fun bulletin boards. Or lately, in a high school math classroom, getting kids excited about math like Mrs. Cosgro did. Wherever she ended up, she had always wanted to be a teacher. And on weekends, she wanted to coach kids who were learning to skate, kids like Ivy and Rory. She still saw herself crunching through the snow in the March maple stand, breath-ing in sap-steam, too. But she couldn't say that. Everybody at school talked about getting out of Mojimuk Falls to live some-place with tall buildings and city lights and subways. It was as if you weren't allowed to admit you liked living there. What was her destiny *supposed* to be?

Claire glanced up at the picture again. "I don't know.

I just liked the water in that one. Look"—she leaned forward, elbows on her knees, and passed the foam head from hand to hand—"you don't need to do a big sports psychologist exam to figure out that I choked on Monday. I was going to try a double, and at the last second I held back and did a single instead, only I overrotated, and that's why I fell."

Kalina tipped her head. "You think that's why you're here? To find out why you fell?"

Claire nodded. Why else would she be here? She put the angry foam head down and picked up the happy one.

"I'm not a skating coach, Claire. Andrei will teach you all about overrotating later on, I'm sure. I'm supposed to help you figure out what's going on up here." She tapped her temple with her finger.

"What's going on there," Claire said, "is that I got this scholarship and everybody—including me—thought it would be great. But now that I'm here, it's . . . not what I thought. I should have known better. I mean, I freak out when I have to skate for judges. I've always had a problem with that. The only other time I tried to compete, I got so many butterflies in my stomach I almost threw up."

"That would have been colorful."

"You know what I mean. Butterflies, like churning and nervousness and stuff."

Kalina smiled. "I know. I was making a joke. A lame joke, but a joke. Smiling can help you relax, you know."

Claire tried to smile. Kalina was being nice enough, but she didn't see the point of all this. If the point of giving her the scholarship was to train a new Olympic star, it was pretty obvious by now that Groshev had made a mistake.

"Claire? Did you hear my question?"

"Sorry." She hadn't.

"Do you *want* to keep skating in competitions?"

Claire opened her mouth to answer, but nothing came out.

Did she? After last year's Champlain Valley Open, she had never wanted to go back. And after that disaster at Saratoga, it should have been easy to walk away from anything that involved judges. To just say no thanks. But she couldn't help picturing the other Claire—the Maple Show Claire, the one who landed doubles and smiled on the ice—and wondering what that Claire could do if she ever made it onto the ice at a competition.

Slowly, she nodded. "I think I do."

"Good." Kalina smiled. "So now I can help. What strategies are you using to manage your stress before you skate?"

"Well . . . Tasanee told me to take deep breaths." Claire looked down at the foam face in her hand and gave it an extrahard squeeze.

"Breathing's good," Kalina said, "but it's not enough."

"No kidding. It doesn't make the butterflies go away."

"Oh, you don't want that."

"Yes I do! How can I compete if I get queasy every time someone holding a clipboard watches me skate?" Claire plopped the smiley foam face onto the table so hard its cheeks bulged out for a second.

"We don't want the butterflies to go *away*." Kalina leaned forward in her chair. "That feeling—nerves or adrenaline or butterflies or whatever you want to call it—that's what allows a skater to shine on competition day. Those butterflies can give you that extra something you need to jump a little higher or spin a little faster when it really counts. Trust me, you want the butterflies to stick around."

"Maybe." Claire sighed.

"You'll see." Kalina looked at her watch. "And I can't make them go away, anyway. But I can do something even better. Next time we meet, I'll teach you how to make them fly in formation."

CHAPTER 16

For the next two weeks, Claire felt as if she had two coaches instead of one—and her two coaches weren't always sending the same messages.

"The arms! The arms!" Groshev shouted across the ice, and Claire held them higher. "It's all in the arms," he said.

"It's all right up here." Kalina tapped Claire's temple as they stood together, leaning on the boards, watching Tasanee finish her routine at practice one day. "When you go out there next, you need to see yourself skating—skating the way you want to skate—no, the way you'd like to see yourself skate on television, how's that?"

Claire gave a little shiver. If she couldn't skate in front of a dozen judges, how could she even think of skating in front of a bazillion people on television?

"You're really making progress," Kalina told Claire when she skated up to the boards halfway through practice the first week in June. "You're skating calmer and cleaner because you're visualizing all the right things. Visualizing makes things real."

"I should visualize a nice hot bowl of corn chowder right now." Claire rubbed her hands together; she'd forgotten gloves. "I could visualize myself some warm hands and a full stomach."

Kalina laughed. "Get on out there. You're almost done for the day. And you're doing great. Really great."

"You are doing all right, but not great," Groshev told her, not ten minutes later as practice was winding down. Claire had to follow him instead of escaping to the locker room. She'd left her orange fleece right next to his clipboard on the bench.

"I'm feeling a lot better about all my singles," Claire said, reaching into her sleeve to pull it right side out. "I'd like to get back to trying doubles soon."

Groshev nodded. "Okay. If I see more height on your single salchow, your single toe loop next week, then we look at the doubles again. I think you are ready."

☙❧

"I'm ready." Claire volunteered to go first as soon as Mrs. Cosgro announced it was time for presentations. With the Champlain Valley Open coming up this weekend, she wanted to get her math project finished now. She went to the classroom computer, opened her file, and took a deep breath.

"Fibonacci numbers are named after an Italian mathematician named Leonardo of Pisa, who—"

"So shouldn't they be Leonardo numbers?" Henry Noogan

called from the back without looking up from the paper he was folding.

"Well, he went by Fibonacci as, like, a pen name. It's actually short for filius Bonaccio, which translates to son of Bonaccio. That was his dad's name." Claire surprised herself, remembering all that even though it wasn't in her notes.

"Thanks," Henry said. He waved to her with what looked like an origami cat.

"Well done, Claire," Mrs. Cosgro said and looked at Henry. "We'll save any other questions for the end of the presentation."

Claire advanced to the slides about patterns in nature. She had drawn arrows to show how the rows of bracts on pinecones came in Fibonacci numbers. She found herself using her notes less and less; she'd ended up loving this project after all.

The only time she paused was when she got to the slide about Fibonacci numbers in the lives of honeybees. Because male bees had only one parent and female bees had two, if you charted it all out, you ended up with a kind of strange-looking family tree where the number of ancestors at each level was a Fibonacci number. When Claire had read that part at home on her computer two weeks ago, she'd reached for the phone to call Natalie and tell her about it. She'd dialed the first three numbers before putting down the phone. Natalie had barely said a word to her since Memorial Day weekend. She was probably busy, anyway, and besides, it was too late at night for a phone call.

"Claire? Is there more?" Mrs. Cosgro brought her thoughts

back to class, and Claire wrapped up her presentation with the figure skating slides at the end.

"Is it time for questions now?" Maya asked.

Mrs. Cosgro nodded.

"Who's the cute guy?"

The class laughed, and Claire explained Luke away as a skating friend. But she realized she was starting to think of him differently, like she used to think of Keene. No, not like that. More the way Natalie thought about Denver, who loved drama club as much as she did.

When the bell rang, Claire stopped at Natalie's locker for the first time in weeks.

"Hi," she said when Nat arrived with an armload of notebooks. "I just wanted to see how you've been. I . . ." She took a deep breath and just said it. "I miss talking to you."

"Me, too," Natalie said, reaching for her drama club folder. She turned to Claire. "Did you do your Fibo-Rama project yet?"

"Just now. It went pretty well. And there's a thing I learned about honeybees that I've been dying to show you. Maybe . . . later or something. How's drama?"

"Good. I'm going to be the evil witch in the play."

"And that's a good thing?"

"*Very* good." Natalie grinned. "Denver Moon is the evil wizard." The hall was emptying. "Hey, do you have skating tonight?"

"Yeah, I do."

"Oh."

"We have the Champlain Valley Open this weekend. I'm hoping it goes better than last year. Hey—" Claire paused. "Do you want to come? I know you could ride over with my mom."

"I don't think I can. I have a beekeeping thing. But good luck."

"You too. I mean, have fun." Claire watched Natalie bounce down the stairs to the drama room, where her evil magician was waiting.

∞

When Claire stepped out of the locker room in Lake Placid later, she found Groshev and Kalina together, waiting for her.

"I'm getting double-teamed?" She joked, but her stomach twisted into a knot. She was just starting to feel better about the competition. Why were they both here today? Were they that worried about her performance?

"We go back to working on the doubles today," Groshev said. "The double salchow first. Go warm up some, then come back here."

Claire pushed off and stroked around the rink three times before stopping in front of them again. "Can I try some doubles now?"

"Here is what you do." Groshev reached out for her chin and turned her head directly toward him to make sure she couldn't escape from his directions. "You go out. You make the loop. You do the three-turn."

"And then you jump—but only in your head," Kalina said. "But jump nice and high in your head."

Claire raised an eyebrow. "I skate the lead into my jump?"

"Yep." Kalina grinned.

"But I don't jump. I just . . . stay there?"

"Your feet stay on the ice, but your mind goes through the rest of the jump—every step, every moment of it, the takeoff, pulling in your arms, and it needs to be so real that you feel the landing."

"Go ahead." Groshev gave that little flick of his hand that meant the conversation was over.

Claire skated to the center circle and started with the backward crossovers that would lead her into the jump. She turned as if she were about to jump and even got her arms ready but stopped herself and coasted back toward the boards. "Like that?"

Kalina shook her head. "No. Not like that."

"I did what you said. I did the lead into the jump."

"But you didn't jump."

"You told me not to jump."

Kalina shook her head. "I told you to visualize the jump, to jump in your mind. And you didn't."

How could *she* tell if Claire jumped in her head or not? She could have just done a triple axel up there for all Kalina knew. Claire opened her mouth to protest but before she could, Groshev flicked his hand at her.

"Again. Go."

Again she skated, speeding up, turning at just the right second, tensing her body, and forcing herself not to take off. She turned toward the board and could already see them frowning.

"I can't do this." Claire stopped. Her blades threw up a shower of ice shavings and her words followed. "I can't jump in my head. If you want me to jump, I'm ready to try it again. I've been dying to try the doubles again, and I'm ready. I am. But I can't do this . . . imaginary jump thing. Do you know how hard it is to lead up to a jump and not jump? Can I please just do it?"

They stared at her. It was probably the most she'd ever said to either of them.

"No," Kalina said finally. "You can't just jump. But you can just think. Come off the ice."

Claire skated to the gate and stepped onto the rubber matting that edged the rink. Kalina waved her over to a spot next to them at the boards. "Lean over and watch yourself on the ice."

"I thought you wanted me off the ice."

"I do. I want you to stand right here and watch yourself on the ice. Your perfect-skating-day self. Imagine it. What do you look like?"

Claire sighed and squinted toward the empty rink. "I'm landing my doubles."

Kalina shook her head. "You need to buy into this, Claire, or it won't work. Start at the beginning of your routine, and really *watch*."

Claire couldn't imagine it would help, but she leaned out over the ice and tried to imagine herself . . . let's see . . . the best skating day she could think of was the Maple Show, as pathetic as that sounded. So she put imaginary-skater-Claire in her Maple Show costume and pictured her in her opening pose.

"Okay," Claire said. "I'm standing at center ice with my shoulders back and my chin tilted up, and I'm waiting for my music to start."

"Good. And now it starts . . . and . . . ?"

"I'm skating, extending my legs and keeping my arms up." She stared hard at the ice, trying to picture herself going into the first jump sequence. Then Alexis skated past and almost crashed right into her imaginary-Claire.

"Alexis—off the ice until four thirty!" Groshev shouted. "This is Claire's solo session."

Alexis skated up to them. "But she's not even on the ice." She crossed her arms and leaned toward the boards. "I'm so close. Can't I just practice my double axel a few times until she starts?"

Groshev shook his head.

"But if I don't get this jump down—"

"Enough. She has started. I will see you at four thirty." And he flicked his hand toward the stands.

Alexis looked so angry her eyes might have burned holes right through the ice. Kalina raised an eyebrow at her, and she skated back to the boards.

"Now." Groshev turned to Claire. "Go on."

"Focus," Kalina said.

Claire settled her eyes and her brain on the circle at the center of the rink and imagined herself there, starting her routine. Her eyes followed her imaginary self in a wide loop, into the first sit spin.

"What do you see?"

"I'm spinning," Claire said, "with my head up and my arms tucked in. Really fast," she added. Her eyes lifted when imaginary Claire finished the spin and started skating toward her first jump. "I'm getting ready for the double salchow. I'm turning and—"

"Coach, can I get out there now?" Meghan stood next to them, tugging on her skirt. "I really need some time to work on that new spin."

Groshev didn't even look at her. She got the hand flick. "When Claire's session is over."

Claire wished he'd just let them skate.

"Claire, come on," Kalina said gently. "Get yourself back out there."

Claire sighed and leaned out again, but she couldn't focus.

"This isn't working." She dropped her head to the boards. "I can't concentrate. I can't get back there."

She felt Groshev's hand on her shoulder.

"Hold on . . . Bella!" he shouted up to the sound box. "The Vivaldi, please! Now," he said, turning to Claire. "Listen. And watch."

Claire stared out at the ice and listened, and when the first notes of her skating music fluttered down from the speakers, she could finally see what they wanted her to see.

She took a deep breath, and a shadow of the Maple Show Claire came to life. She watched the strength of her very first strokes, felt the exhilaration and speed of her spins.

Her eyes followed her journey around the ice, traced the path of her routine, and lifted with the first jump. The double salchow. She watched herself launch without a thought of hesitation. It was high and tight and clean.

It was perfect. And when Claire saw herself land, she saw something else she remembered about Maple Show Claire.

She was smiling.

Maple Show Claire skated the rest of the routine, spinning, jumping, dancing in a perfect, light footwork sequence. By the time she finished, a smile played at the real Claire's lips, too.

"Well?" Kalina's voice broke the quiet. "Did you land them?"

Claire nodded. "Every one."

Groshev raised a dark eyebrow. "Every one? You'd better

show us." He stretched a long arm forward and unlatched the gate so she could step onto the ice.

She didn't need to warm up again. She was already there. She headed straight for the center of the rink and struck her opening pose. She didn't need to ask for the music. They knew. And when it started, somehow Claire was watching herself again, even though she was out on the ice and not leaning on the boards. Somehow, she was both places. She was both Claires, skating, spinning, spiraling, launching, and jumping. She landed the double salchow and the double flip, bobbled a little on the double toe loop but kept going, and at the end, did a clean single axel to finish the routine.

Frozen in her final pose, she heard applause. Just one set of hands. She looked over, expecting it to be Kalina, but it wasn't. It was Groshev's big hands, clapping for her. "Well done," he said.

"Really?" Claire skated up to him. She felt better than she had since her first day here. Better than that, actually. If only she could bring this feeling to the competition. "You think I might be able to put one of the doubles back in my program for Saturday?"

"One of them?" Groshev raised that eyebrow again. "We are putting them all back in."

"But I didn't land the double toe cleanly; I just—"

"That is why you are trying it again right now. You will have it back by Saturday." He flicked his hand at the ice. "Go on now. Jump."

CHAPTER 17

The bridge to Vermont looked like a lazy sea monster, stretching up out of the shallow water with its smooth, curved back. When Claire was younger, she always thought she might be able to look over the railing from the bridge and see Champ, the real Lake Champlain monster of legend. Today, the lake was still and quiet.

Her mother glanced over at the passenger's seat. "Are you nervous?"

"I'm okay," Claire answered. And it was the truth. Groshev had been right about Claire getting the double toe loop back in time for the weekend. By the end of Friday's session, she had it down clean. And today, she felt calm as the water's surface, at least for now. She felt ready.

Claire watched the beams of the bridge whoosh past her window as they crossed into Vermont. Below, the water was blue gray, and a kayaker paddled through the reeds close to shore. He scared up a blue heron that pumped its wings and flew off over clusters of purple loosestrife, pointing its toes behind it.

How did it get to be June when she wasn't looking? It felt as if no time at all had passed since she was crunching around the woods pulling sap buckets off naked maples. Now the trees zoomed past her window in thick, humid, mosquito-summer greens. The marina next to the bridge was crowded with boats. Usually, Uncle Bruce had invited them out on the lake on his boat by now. Had he forgotten this year, or did her parents and the boys go out with him one day while she was in Lake Placid? She missed everything now.

Her summers had always been made of lazy afternoons with Natalie. Sleepovers and blueberry pancakes. This one would be different, like everything else. Claire's schedule would be packed with skating, even if Natalie did still want to spend time with her. Claire had joined Natalie and Maya and Riley for lunch a couple days after they talked at their lockers this week, but Nat hadn't said anything else about getting together.

Claire wondered . . . If all the things she had to give up had been listed in Groshev's paperwork that day at the rink, would she still have come to Lake Placid? She was pretty sure she knew the answer, but it didn't really matter now. She needed to skate today. She didn't just need to; she *wanted* to. That was new.

"Is Dad coming later?"

"Maybe. He's not sure when the boys'll be done with their game. Grandpa's coming." Her mother turned into the rink parking lot. It was right along the Burlington Bike Path, and they had to watch for bicycle traffic as they crossed the path to the sidewalk.

Her mother pulled open the rink door, and they stepped in out of the heat. "I'm going to register and head right to the locker room." Claire gave her mom a quick hug. "Our warm-up is in an hour."

Meghan, Alexis, Stevie, Abby, Luke, and Tasanee would all be here. Hannah's name had been on the list for this competition once, too, but yesterday, Claire had seen over Groshev's shoulder it was crossed out, just as it had been in Saratoga. *Was she even skating anymore? If she wasn't, she must miss it,* Claire thought. She was so great out there.

"Hey! You're in three with me!" Tasanee called to her from down the hall, already dressed in a pink halter top with sparkles splashed over one shoulder and a swirly satin skirt. She had a book tucked under her arm as usual.

"You look great!" Claire called and stopped to wait for her.

"Thanks, I'm skating that new routine to the 'Pink Panther' with the double-double combination."

Claire nodded. Tasanee had been working on the combination jump all week and had the bruises on her hips to prove it. She'd landed it consistently on Friday, though, so Groshev gave her the go-ahead to put it in her routine.

They walked down the usual row of vendors, an explosion of sparkles and sequins, tights and skater dolls and books.

Claire handed Tasanee a book with a girl spinning on the cover. "Need a break from your vampires?"

"Nope." Tasanee laughed and put it back. They started down the hall again, weaving through skaters and moms and dress racks. "I'll keep my vampires and pixies—thanks. I need the magic. I love the idea that you can be an ordinary kid and just suddenly, magically, turn into something else. It makes me feel . . . I don't know. Hopeful."

Claire looked at the cover of Tasanee's latest book, a girl who looked like she was sprouting wings. It was by the same author who wrote the homicidal fairy book. "More killer fairies? How are killer fairies hopeful?"

"Well . . . when the main character outsmarts them, it makes me feel like anything is possible. I like that."

"Hey there!" The girls Claire had met in Saratoga—Jackie, Steph, and Justine, the synchronized skaters—called from a table piled with bright brochures and a laptop computer playing a video of their show.

"Oh, hi! I didn't know there was synchronized skating here."

"There's not," said Jackie. "Our club is just doing an information table. We've been getting a ton of new members. Here." She handed Claire a brochure with two circles of skaters, one inside the other, on the front. Claire couldn't resist counting the skaters in each circle; she was having trouble letting go of that Fibonacci project. Sure enough, there were eight skaters on the inside, thirteen skating around the outside.

"You guys look fantastic," she said as Tasanee started tugging on her skating bag. "Guess we need to get going. Great to see you!"

"So," Tasanee said, pulling open the locker room door. "What did Groshev decide you're doing for jumps today?"

"We put the doubles back in."

"All of them?"

Claire nodded. "The only one I'm not solid on is the toe loop, and I'm sure it's okay if I scale that one back to a single if I need to."

Tasanee nodded. "Awesome."

"Morning, ladies!" Kalina bubbled into the locker room

wearing a bright green fleece and carrying her travel coffee mug. Claire had never noticed the printing on the side before, a quote from Eleanor Roosevelt. NO ONE CAN MAKE YOU FEEL INFE-RIOR WITHOUT YOUR CONSENT. Claire couldn't imagine Kalina ever feeling bad about herself; she was all made of smiles and you-can-do-its and energy.

She straddled the bench while Claire laced her skates. "Ready?" Kalina's knees bounced up and down, wiggling the bench. Claire laughed. Kalina was probably just like Jake and Christopher when she was a kid—a never-sit-still machine. Sometimes Claire wished she could be more like that and not so nice and predictable. They were all boiling, bubbling maple sap, spitting out of the kettle. And her? She was sugar on snow, sweet and quiet and cool.

Claire finished with her laces and straightened up. "I'm ready. I just don't know about the double toe loop. What do you think I should do?"

"You should skate." Kalina nodded as if that settled it.

"Yeah, but what jumps? Groshev told me to put the dou-bles back in, but I don't feel great about the toe loop and I don't want him to be mad if I don't do what he wants."

"What he *wants* is for you to skate."

"Hey—I'm going to go find some water." Tasanee stood up. "You want anything?"

Claire shook her head. She wanted a lot of things, but none of them came from a vending machine. Wouldn't it be great if you could feed in your dollar and press a little button for GUTS or BALANCE or CONFIDENCE? "No thanks. I'll see you out there for warm-up."

She turned back to Kalina. "*What* am I supposed to skate?"

Kalina grinned. "Close your eyes and let's see what happens."

"Right now?" Claire looked around the locker room. It was one thing to close her eyes and pretend to skate when she was right next to the ice. But here? Two girls were chattering at their lockers along the next bench. Another one stood at the mirror, wincing as her mother painted her eyelids with a brush full of blue shadow. And Stevie and Alexis had just burst into the room, laughing. Meghan came behind them. She looked surprised to see Claire and Kalina on the bench but gave a quick wave and followed Alexis and Stevie to the mirrors.

"Yep, right now." Kalina pulled an iPod from her backpack, handed the earbuds to Claire, and poised her finger over the play button. "Listen to your music and do a perfect program in your head. Watch yourself and see what jumps you do. Just let it happen, and it will. Ready?" Claire pushed the white buds into her ears, closed her eyes, and nodded. She took a deep breath and tried to imagine herself out on the ice when the opening notes played. It wasn't easy, with the smell of hairspray fumes stinging her nose, but she did it.

She was getting better at this. She could feel the wind rushing past her face when she spun. She could hear the scratch of her blades as she turned, getting ready for the first jump—a double salchow. Imaginary Claire landed it beautifully, head up, arms out, and a smile on her face.

She listened and watched the rest of the program—sit spin, double sal, double flip, the death drop—sit spin combination, and at the end, a double—no, it was just a single—toe loop. But a clean one.

The music faded out, and Claire opened her eyes. "I think I'm all set."

Kalina smiled. She didn't ask what Claire had seen or what she planned to do about the toe loop. But she lifted her coffee mug as if she were making a toast with a champagne glass at some big fancy dinner. "Here's to a performance that matches your vision."

"I'll try." Claire smiled.

Stevie and Alexis clattered past on their skate guards. They had new ones that lit up every time they took a step, flashing purple and green like alien fireflies.

Meghan was a little behind them. She paused next to Claire's bench. "All set to warm up?"

Claire nodded. She was.

She turned back to Kalina. "Thanks," she said, and followed Meghan out to the rink.

⁖

"Come stretch with me," Meghan said after they'd skated around a couple times. She stopped near the audience's main entrance to the rink, where parents and aunts and uncles wearing shorts and fleece jackets were starting to wander up into the stands.

Meghan flung one leg up onto the boards and leaned over so her nose was brushing her knee. "Are you nervous?"

Claire swung her leg up next to Meghan's to stretch. "A little, I guess. No more than usual." But she realized as she stretched the back of her leg, that wasn't really the truth.

She was less nervous—way less. Maybe all that imaginary skating had helped.

"Wow. I'm surprised." Meghan's skate clunked to the ice as she switched legs. "I mean, with all that pressure from Groshev. It looks like he's watching you like a hawk these days. It's so great that you're just—"

"You're here!" Claire recognized her grandfather's red and black wool cap before he was through the door. She stood up from her stretch to wave, and he smiled so big and warm it's a wonder he didn't melt the whole rink. "Sorry," she told Meghan. "That's my grandfather."

But Meghan was looking past him. "And who is *that*?"

Claire's heart jumped when she saw not only her mother and Jake and Christopher trailing behind her grandfather, but Mrs. Rabideau with Natalie and Keene, too.

"That's my best friend, Natalie! Oh!" Nat *was* still her friend. She had given up her beekeeping workshop to come.

"Not her. *Him*." Meghan's eyes were fixed on Keene, shuffling along in his sneakers behind Natalie with his face buried in a paper plate of nachos. He didn't look quite as cute as Claire remembered.

"That's Nat's brother, Keene." He licked some cheese sauce off his thumb, then saw Claire and waved with the hand that wasn't holding the nachos. They all headed toward the boards, except Jake and Christopher, who ducked away toward the Zamboni in the corner.

"Well, there's my girl!" Grandpa leaned over the boards to hug her. Some of the sparkles from her costume came off on his brown jacket. He brushed it off, frowning. "Look at ya . . . all fancied up and drippy."

"Don't hug her anymore. You'll rub off her glitter," her mother said and reached over to straighten Claire's sleeve. "Who's your friend, Claire?"

"Oh!" Claire had been so happy to see Nat she'd almost forgotten about Meghan. "Mom, Grandpa, Natalie, Keene, this is Meghan James."

"Nice to meet you," Natalie said and then turned back to Claire. "You look fantastic. I can't wait to see you skate." She leaned over and gave Claire a huge hug.

"Thanks. I'm . . . excited, too. How are your bees?"

"Better. Fewer mites now."

"Oh." Claire picked at a sparkle on her skirt. She glanced over at Meghan, who had struck up a conversation with Keene, though Claire had no idea what they could possibly have in common. She turned back to Natalie and took a deep breath. "Listen, I didn't really have time to tell you in school this week, but I'm really sorry I haven't been around more." She gestured at the rink. "This was just all . . . more than I thought it would be."

"Is it fun?"

Leave it to Natalie to ask that.

"Well, yeah. It's not fun, laughing-goofy, sugar-on-snow fun like at home, but it's fun. More of a challenging, push yourself kind of fun, I guess."

"Well, that's good then," Natalie said. "Really, Claire, it's okay. And I'm sorry I was so bent out of shape before. I know your skating schedule's been hard on you, too. After we fought that day, I talked to my mom, and she said she actu- ally figured this might happen. You'd make new friends, and

I'd have to make some new friends, too. And I have been. It's okay."

"Well . . . thanks." Claire pictured Riley and Maya at Nat's lunch table, and Denver. She couldn't help feeling a little . . . replaced.

"Hey!" Tasanee skated up. "Is this the famous Natalie from home?"

"It is," Claire said, and then realized she'd never told Natalie a thing about Tasanee. "This is Tasanee, one of my friends here."

If Natalie thought it was strange that she'd never heard of Tasanee, she didn't show it. "Listen, we should let you practice. Good luck to both of you. And Claire . . . no butterflies in the stomach this time, right?"

"Well . . ." Claire hesitated. She was really more excited than scared. She knew what she had planned for jumps, and she knew she could do them. She'd use that extra energy to jump higher. "The butterflies are still there. But I have them flying in formation, so it's all good."

Claire's mother tapped her on the shoulder. "Go get warmed up now. And we need to get seats. Where have Jake and Christopher gone off to?"

Claire pointed toward the Zamboni. They had either found the gate unlocked or climbed over it because Jake was sitting at the steering wheel of the thing, and Christopher was hanging off the side.

"Oh, mercy! I'll meet the rest of you in the stands. Get a seat near the judges, okay?" Her mother hustled off toward the boys.

"They're a riot," Meghan said, moving her feet back and forth quickly on the ice. "Want to skate some more?"

"Yep." Claire took off alongside her. "Is your family coming today?"

It was as if a curtain fell over Meghan's face. "Sort of."

Claire frowned. "Sort of?"

"Mom's here, and Dad said he's coming. With Monica."

"Who's Monica?"

"His girlfriend from the city."

"Oh!" Claire thought back to the night she had met Meghan's parents at the restaurant. "Oh my gosh, I'm sorry, Meghan. That's awful. Well, I mean, not awful that he's coming but . . . it must be, just, really hard."

"It is." She sped up, then made an abrupt hockey stop next to Alexis and Stevie. "Hey. You guys ready?"

"Ready as I ever am." Stevie rolled her eyes and stretched her arms toward the lights. "I hope this doesn't go too late. We have a school dance tonight."

"I'm always ready," Alexis said. But her mouth was tight, and for just a second, the confidence left her eyes. Then she turned to Claire. "What about you, Aunt Jemima? Sticking with singles again today?"

Claire didn't have time to answer before the whistle blew, calling them off the ice. But as she reached for her guards, she felt something burning in her chest—not the usual heart flutters that hit her before a competition. Something new. Who was Alexis to mock her for one lousy routine? Alexis hadn't landed her double toe loop once all week. No wonder she looked nervous. But that was no reason to take it out on Claire.

"All set, lady?" There was Kalina with her Eleanor Roose-velt mug.

Claire nodded. She wasn't going to feel inferior. She was going to skate. And she knew she could do it. She already had.

⊕◦☉

"Our first skater in Juvenile Ladies Group A Free Skate is Claire Boucher from the Lake Placid Skating Club." The announcer wasn't Bob-O, but he sounded just like him and pronounced her name wrong, too.

Not today, Claire decided. Instead of heading to center ice, she skated right up to him. "It's Boucher," she said. "Boo-SHAY. And I'm from Mojimuk Falls—not Lake Placid." She skated out and waited for her music.

"My apologies, ladies and gentlemen, and my apologies, Miss Boo-SHAY, for the error. Our first skater is Claire Boucher, from Mojimuk Falls, skating to Vivaldi's *Four Seasons . . .* 'Autumn.'"

For just a second before the music started, Claire felt the butterflies trembling. "Dance," she thought. "Come with me."

And they did.

She let Vivaldi's strings carry her over the ice, smooth and light. She felt as if she were in the movie in her head again, skating but also watching herself skate—no, it was more like watching someone else. Watching one of those skaters on television on a show where you know everything is going to go perfect because it's on tape and you've seen it already and know how it ends.

Only the bright lights reminded her that she was in a

strange rink competing with judges, somewhere up there, tapping their pencils on their little electronic scoring pads. Otherwise, the cold air on her face would have tricked her into thinking she was home on the pond, with the wind cooling her cheeks, her ponytail flying behind her.

She landed the double salchow.

She landed the double flip.

The death drop–sit spin was perfect and fast.

And Claire knew what would happen next. She'd nail the double toe loop.

She'd seen the routine and knew how it ended.

For a split second, just as she was leading into the jump, another movie clip edged into her mind—the clip of her waffling, then stumbling and falling in Saratoga.

No, that was the wrong ending!

She felt her chest tighten, fought with herself to get the right vision in her head. Landing the double.

No, wait! It wasn't supposed to be the double today—she was doing the single. The single was what she had landed before. She just needed to do a clean single.

She planted her toe pick, but her mind was so jumbled, she couldn't gauge how hard a launch she needed. *Focus*, she thought. *Single. One revolution.*

She jumped—and pulled back at the last moment into what she thought was the right amount of twist for a single toe loop.

It was almost enough.

But not quite.

Her upper body didn't make it all the way around. She landed off balance and had to put her second foot down.

It was a stumble but not a fall.

Keep going, she thought. *Finish clean.*

And then the movie came back. The movie from the locker room.

She spun, fast and in perfect form.

She finished. And addressed the audience. And made herself smile.

And waited to hear her score.

CHAPTER 18

You did really well." Tasanee balanced a bag of popcorn on her book. "Really well. Isn't a 38 your personal best?"

"Well, yeah," Claire said, "but personal best doesn't mean much in my situation."

Tasanee shook her head. "38's good. I only had a 40, and that's my best score in weeks. Groshev's going to be happy with you, even if it isn't enough to put you in the top four."

"There's no way I'm going to be—"

"Just wait and see," Tasanee said. "Were you paying attention to the top four scores at this competition last year?"

Claire shook her head. She wasn't paying attention to anything except her stomach that day.

"Well, some girl from Maine took bronze with a 38. And the fourth-place girl had like a 36. You're in the running here." She held out the popcorn box again, and Claire took a handful.

"Who's next?"

"Alexis maybe?" Tasanee pulled out the program she'd been using as a bookmark and flipped through the pages. "No, it's that Marilee Allen girl—this is her home rink—and then Meghan and then Alexis."

Marilee Allen skated to a song called "Great Balls of Fire." She was good, full of energy, and she looked like she loved being on the ice. Claire found herself holding her breath when Marilee jumped, willing her to land cleanly. She breathed out when the routine finally ended. "She was great."

The judges thought so, too. Claire had watched them poking pencils at their electronic score pads, adding up the numbers.

"Marilee Allen's score for Juvenile Ladies Free Skate is 41," said the announcer. "Our next skater will be Meghan James of the Lake Placid Skating Club."

Meghan pulled off her skate guards and skated to center ice. She kept looking over her shoulder toward the stands. Claire waved and thought Meghan must have seen her, but she didn't wave back. Instead, her eyes landed on a couple just climbing into the stands.

Claire leaned forward to get a better look at them and drew in her breath. "Oh! I think that's Meghan's dad," she whispered.

Tasanee raised her eyebrows. "Well, that's not Meghan's mom."

"I know." Claire reached for more popcorn. It was Meghan's dad, for sure. Claire recognized him from the restaurant. He lifted the woman's fur coat from her shoulders and folded it carefully over his arm while she smoothed her skirt and sat down on the bench. "She told me her dad was going to be here. With his girlfriend."

Meghan struck her opening pose.

"She looks good," Tasanee whispered.

She did. Until she started skating.

Meghan's spins that had been so fast and clean yesterday at practice were sloppy and loose. On her first jump—it was supposed to be a double flip—she pulled back at the last second and only made it around once. She landed her second jump, a double salchow, but it wasn't as high as it should have been, and she had to put her second foot down to catch her balance.

"What's up with her?" Claire whispered. "She looks all uptight."

"Nerves." Tasanee put down her popcorn box and took a drink of her bottled water. "Nerves got her today."

Claire's stomach tensed as she watched Meghan's lead into her double toe loop. It was all wrong, and sure enough, she overrotated and landed hard on her hip, skidding across the ice. Meghan stood up quickly but missed the footwork sequence that Claire knew was supposed to follow the double toe loop.

Instead, Meghan skated one more circle and did the death drop that led into her last sit spin. She stumbled during the spin, then crouched into it again. The music ended while she was still spinning, so when she finally stood and raised her arms in the air, it felt too late and silly. Even from a distance, Claire could see the tears streaming down Meghan's cheeks.

Alexis was waiting at the boards. She gave Meghan a quick hug as she left the ice, then skated out for her own routine. It was her usual perfect show until the very end, when she fell coming out of a double toe loop and completely missed the single that was supposed to follow it. Claire knew she'd be furious about the points she lost for that, and sure enough, when the score was announced, it put Alexis in fifth place.

"Only two more skaters—another girl from here. . . ." Tasanee flipped through her program. "Her name's Maggie Rupert, and then there's one, Isabel Sorensen, from New Hampshire. She's supposed to be pretty good, but it really depends on what she has in her program. If she has, like, a double axel or something and she pulls it off, then you're probably done, but if not, then you might have a chance. And if she falls, you'll totally get the platinum. Maybe even the bronze."

Tasanee looked so excited for her that Claire smiled, but it still felt weird to be waiting for someone else's performance to see how you did. She already knew how she did. She'd bobbled the single a little, but landed her doubles and scored better than she ever had before. Shouldn't that be enough?

The Vermont girl skated onto the ice next, a green, fluttery skirt flaring out behind her. She skated to a song Claire didn't know—something classical—and skated well. At least Claire thought so.

But Tasanee shook her head as the girl struck her final pose. "Her compulsory spins weren't fast enough. And she only had one double. She won't be able to touch you."

Claire watched the judges poke at their score screens. One judge leaned over to another, who cued up a replay of one of the girl's jumps on his computer. Claire shuddered. It was a good thing she hadn't been able see all this consulting and thinking and poking while they'd been judging her.

"The Free Skate score for Maggie Rupert is 36.4."

"See?" Tasanee nudged Claire. "You're still in fourth! And I'm still silver as long as this last one isn't too good."

"Our final skater is from the Merrimack Valley Skating Club," the announcer said. "Please welcome Isabel Sorensen!"

They clapped, and Tasanee leaned forward as the girl began her routine. "You know, we really have a shot at this today, Claire—both of us. And then we'll go to regionals and maybe even nationals. Don't you just dream of being up there on a podium with people from all over the country?"

Claire smiled, but she didn't answer. Sure, she'd thought about what it would be like to win a medal, and it would be great, but there were lots of other things she wanted, too. She wanted time to hang out in the woods with Jake and Christopher. They hadn't played Indiana Jones in ages. She wanted to get milk shakes with Natalie. She wanted to junior coach. She'd love to be on that MATHCOUNTS team Mrs. Cosgro talked about.

Claire watched Tasanee, leaning forward in her seat, her eyes glued to the next girl taking the ice. Her hopes were so focused, so clear. Claire felt as if her own dreams were all spread out, as if she had more pieces to herself than she could keep track of.

"She's doing well." Tasanee's knee bounced up and down nervously as her eyes followed the girl on the ice. "This is going to be really close."

As Isabel skated, Claire tapped her foot to the beat of "Stars and Stripes Forever." Isabel's outfit was pure silver on top and seemed to catch every ray of light in the place. The skirt was made of red, white, and blue scarves that flipped and mixed and twirled around her when she spun.

"Oh my gosh! That was just a double axel! That's the only one today, isn't it?" Claire clapped with the rest of the audience as Isabel landed with just a hint of a wobble. It wasn't perfect—she hadn't quite made it all the way around for the full two and a half revolutions—but she managed to stay on her feet.

When her routine ended, Isabel skated around, scooping up the stuffed animals her friends and family tossed from the stands as Claire clapped along with the crowd. "She'll place for sure, don't you think?"

Tasanee didn't answer right away. Her eyes were fixed on the judges and their poking pencils and huddled whispers. Finally, she shook her head. "I don't think so. I was watching them view that replay of the double axel, and I don't think she'll get credit for it because it wasn't a true double. She didn't have the full two and a half revolutions. Plus, she stumbled on one of her other jumps, too. I think we're safe."

Claire didn't want to be safe. For sure, she'd love a medal, but . . . there was something just wrong about this girl not getting any credit at all for what was pretty close to a double axel, even if it wasn't perfect. Shouldn't she get some credit for trying? Nobody else even tried a double axel today.

"The score for Isabel Sorensen is 38.8."

"Yes!" Tasanee's fist pumped into the air.

"That concludes our Juvenile Ladies Free Skate competition for this afternoon. The awards ceremony for all categories will be back here this evening at seven."

"See??" Tasanee pulled Claire into a hug. Her hair smelled like carnations. "That's it! We're both going to be on that podium tonight, Claire! Ohmygosh!!"

Claire looked for her family over Tasanee's shoulder. Had they been doing the math, too? Had they figured out she placed fourth and would be at the ceremony later?

Nah. They probably had no idea. They probably left to get hot dogs already. Which wasn't a bad idea. Claire pulled loose from Tasanee's death-grip hug. "I'm going to see if I can find my mom and get something to eat. Want to come?"

Tasanee shook her head. "Not right now. I want to see if Coach has my score sheet yet. I'll see you in the locker room later, though, say . . . six? That way we'll have time to get ready."

"Aren't we already ready?"

"You need to change out of that until later." Tasanee nodded down at Claire's dress. "You can't be spilling ketchup all over it before the awards ceremony. And we'll need to redo our hair, too. Oh!" She waved to Groshev, talking to another coach over by the boards, and rushed over.

☙❧

When Claire pulled open the locker room door, Alexis and Stevie were already changed out of their costumes, wearing sweats, and plowing through an enormous bag of cheese puffs.

Claire hurried past them to her locker so she could get out of there quickly. She'd forgotten her combination lock at home, but thankfully everything was just where she'd left it. She changed into her wind pants and warm-up jacket, then hung up her dress so it would be ready for later, and headed for the exit.

Meghan came flying through the door and headed straight for the toilet stalls. The door slammed and sobs spilled out from underneath.

"Meghan? You okay in there?" Claire heard toilet paper being unrolled. A big wad, from the sound of it. Meghan blew her nose.

"No." Her voice was muffled.

"You need . . . help or anything?"

The door swung open. "I'm done." And Meghan pushed past her.

"Done . . . crying?" Claire followed her past Alexis and Stevie to her locker.

"No." Meghan flung open her locker, yanked out her skating bag, and reached back to unzip her dress. Her words were quiet and tense. "Just done." She tugged at her zipper, but it was stuck on the fabric.

"Want some help?" Claire reached for her, but Meghan turned away and wrenched the zipper free with a ripping sound that made Claire's stomach drop.

"Easy, Meghan, you're ripping—"

"So *what*? It doesn't really matter, does it? I'm *not* going to need this dress later because I'm *not* going to be at the award ceremony because I completely blew my routine. It doesn't matter because my father, who was all set to stay and go see me at the awards ceremony and then take me to dinner with *Monica*, decided that they wouldn't have to stick around now for dinner after all because *Monica* was chilly, and wouldn't it be great because they could get a nice early start and get back to the city instead of staying overnight. He said he'll catch me next time. But you know what? There's not going to be a next time because I'm *done*."

She peeled the dress off, balled it up, and sent it flying into the lockers. The sequins pinged against the metal.

Meghan sat down and started tugging at her tights. Claire sat next to her. "Meghan, you're just upset right now. Maybe your dad—"

"Spare us, Mrs. Butterworth." Alexis walked up with her Diet Coke and took a long drink. "Everybody has bad days; just leave her alone. And don't think you're something all of a sudden just because you'll have a medal around your neck later. The only reason you placed is because the rest of us screwed up worse than you did."

Meghan buried her face in her hands, and her back shook with sobs.

"Aw, I didn't mean that. You just had a tough show, Megs. It'll be okay." Alexis put a hand on Meghan's shoulder and gave it a squeeze. She looked up at Claire. "Just go. *We're* her friends. We'll take care of her. Go knit yourself a new scarf or something to wear at your big awards ceremony."

ᘓᘔ

"There you are!" Claire's mother was balancing a tray full of hot dogs, french fries, sodas, napkins, and ketchup packets. "The Rabideaus had to leave, but Natalie said to tell you what a great job you did. Grandpa's headed home, too. I don't know where the boys went. They ran off while I was in line here. I got you a hot dog and fries, and there are cookies in my bag." She nodded over her shoulder at the paisley bag Aunt Maureen had quilted for her. "But can you just take a look and see if Jake and Christopher snuck back in there with the Zamboni?"

Claire nodded and headed back into the rink. Jake and Christopher had gotten past the gate again, but this time, they appeared to be checking out the Zamboni with the driver's blessing. He was talking with them, pointing to different parts of the machine.

Good. It would give her a minute to breathe. She waved to the boys, then leaned over the boards and looked out at the empty ice.

The surface was scratched, and little curves of ice shavings told the stories of the eight skaters who had just performed there—scratches from spins, sharp cuts from takeoffs, skid marks from the falls. Claire took a deep breath and closed her eyes to remember her own routine. She skated it again in her head—right up to the double—no, single loop at the end. It had been close to perfect except for that last jump, and she knew why. She had seen a negative image in her head, and it had started to come true. It was scary, how powerful thoughts were.

Over at the edge of the ice, four men in work clothes were setting up risers for the awards later on. Soon, Claire would be on one of those risers, with a medal around her neck. The thought made her feel the funniest mix of flutters in her heart—excitement and a little fear and a little . . . was it sadness, maybe? When she thought about herself out there, she couldn't help thinking about the girls who wouldn't be there. Some of them, like Meghan, seemed to want it—need it, even—so much more than she did.

"Hey! Can we go with Rudy?" Jake tugged at her sleeve and pointed to the side of the rink, where the Zamboni guy was waving. "He's going to let us ride on the side."

Claire knew what her mother would say. Too dangerous. Who was this Rudy character, anyway? And were there seat belts on that thing? "Sure." Claire grinned at him. "Just don't tell Mom. I'll let her know you'll be out to eat in a few minutes."

∞

Claire managed to force down half a hot dog, even though she didn't feel like eating. They sat on a blanket from the car, spread out on the thin strip of grass along the bike path, and watched people ride past.

"Hey—let's play Who's That Guy!" Christopher said through a mouthful of chocolate-chip cookie. "I'm first."

He fixed his eyes on the bike path until a man on a bright yellow racing bike appeared through the trees. "His name is Lance."

"You can't do that!" Jake said. "You can't name him after Lance Armstrong just because he's a biker. That's so lame."

"I wasn't naming him after Lance Armstrong."

"You were, too."

"I was not."

"Lame."

"Fine—he's . . . Ricardo. And he's training for the Burlington Bike Championship."

"That's lame, too."

"Jake, if you're going to play, let him finish." Mom zipped up the cookie bag and started collecting trash.

"Okay. But it was still lame."

"Was not. Who's next?" Christopher said as Ricardo disappeared into the trees.

"I'll do these two." Claire pointed up the path where a man who looked around her father's age pedaled slowly.

Alongside him, a little girl wobbled along on a bike with training wheels. "His name is . . . Ted Crandall, and that's his daughter, Emily."

"You need more than that." Jake reached into Mom's bag and snuck the cookies back out.

"I'm working on it," Claire said, watching them. The man was pedaling so slowly he looked like he was about to tip over. It looked frustrating, but he was smiling, and not a fake smile. "She's . . . five years old and likes to play with frogs at the lake. He's . . . I don't know . . . forty-two, I guess. He works in a bank, so he's happy to be outside in the sunshine. And this is her first time on the bike path on her own bike, and she's doing really well."

"Where's the mom?" Jake asked.

"On an expedition to the Arctic, and she's being held captive by angry penguins," Christopher said, grabbing the cookie bag.

"Penguins live in the Antarctic, dork, not the Arctic." Jake yanked the bag back. "If she's in the Arctic, it'll have to be angry polar bears."

"Or walruses." Mom held out her hand and waited for Jake to give up the cookies. She tucked the bag back into her purse. "But I'd much rather think that the mom is home, enjoying a lovely afternoon reading in the hammock with a tall glass of lemonade." She tugged at the blanket they were sitting on. "Now let's get going. It's almost six, and Claire needs to get ready for the big ceremony."

CHAPTER 19

When Claire got back to the locker room, it was empty
except for Tasanee, already dressed and brushing on sparkly
green eye shadow. She caught Claire's eye in the mirror. "It's
after six, you know. Are you redoing your hair?"

Claire shook her head. Her ponytail was fine. "I just need
to change." Something crunched under her sneakers as she
walked to her locker. The floor was covered with orange cheese
puff crumbles and empty ketchup packets. *Figures Alexis and
Stevie would leave their mess for somebody else*, thought Claire.
She picked up the ketchup packets, tossed them into the trash,
and kicked the crumbs into a pile.

She opened her locker, reached for her dress, and froze.

Charlotte's dress—her beautiful dress with the sparkly
sequins—was ruined.

No.

Ruined wasn't enough of a word. It didn't even look like a
skating dress anymore. It was an ugly, vicious mess. The
sequins were torn off; ragged threads poked out where they
used to be. Cheese-puff crumbs were ground into the velvet
of the bodice in ugly orange smears. And when she saw the

streaks of ketchup—angry, hateful slashes that covered half the dress—Claire could hear Alexis's voice.

Don't think you're something all of a sudden just because you'll have a medal around your neck later. The only reason you placed is because the rest of us screwed up worse than you did.

Claire sucked in her breath and heard Tasanee's skate guards clunking toward her on the floor.

"Oh, no." Tasanee stared at the mess.

"How can she be so awful?" Claire whispered into the locker at Charlotte's beautiful, beautiful dress. She tried to hold in the sobs, but they bubbled over.

Tasanee pulled Claire into a hug and let her cry. "I know," she whispered. "I think I was wrong before. You do need to talk to Groshev."

Claire pulled away, swiping at her tears. "No," she said. "Groshev *loves* Alexis. I'm not giving him a reason to get rid of me."

"Get rid of you?"

Claire hadn't meant to say that, even though the thought had nagged at her since she'd heard him talking with Mr. Van Syke. She waved away the words. "Never mind. But I'm not telling Groshev. I can't prove anything. It's not like she left a note. She'll just say somebody else made a mess with her cheese puffs after she left." Claire pulled the dress from the locker and tried to brush off some of the crumbs, but they just smeared into the ketchup.

"You're probably right," Tasanee said. "Look, I have my practice dress in my other bag in my dad's car. I know it's not what you wore for your routine and it's not nearly as pretty, but at least it's something. There's time; I'll have him run out and get it."

Claire breathed in a shaky breath and shook her head. "No." She was done running around trying to pretend everything was okay. She wasn't the problem here, and she wasn't going to feel awful because of Alexis. She skated better than Alexis today. Way better. And nothing Alexis did was going to erase that—Claire took another look at the dress—not even this. "Do you have a plastic grocery bag or something I can put this in so it doesn't get all over my other skating stuff?"

"I have one from my lunch." Tasanee walked over to the garbage can, pulled out the bag, and gave it a shake. "It's clean."

Claire folded the dress and slid it inside.

"But what are you going to wear out there?"

"This," Claire said. She stood up and zipped her warm-up jacket.

"Don't you think you should wear a dress? The judges will be there and everything."

"The judges saw me skate, and I already got my score. They can't change it, right? Is there some rule about what I can wear to pick up my medal?"

"Well, not officially, but—"

"Good." Claire stepped up to the mirror and wiped at her puffy eyes. She pulled her hair loose from her ponytail and let it fall over her shoulders. She turned to look at her back in the mirror to make sure it didn't cover the lettering on her jacket. She could read it just fine: NORTHERN LIGHTS SKATING CLUB, MOJIMUK FALLS, NY.

Maybe the announcer would get it right this time.

৩৩

"For the Juvenile Ladies Free Skate, in fourth place, with the platinum medal, let's welcome Claire Boucher from the Northern Lights Skating Club in Mojimuk Falls."

When Claire skated out in her sweats and warm-up jacket, everyone clapped. The local skating club woman handing out the medals gave Claire's outfit a curious look, but she smiled and lifted the medal to place it around Claire's neck.

It was heavier than she expected. Claire watched the third-place winner skate out in her silver dress to accept her medal. She smiled as Tasanee twirled in a blur of a scratch spin before taking her spot on the second-place podium.

"And finally, with our gold medal, Marilee Allen of the Champlain Valley Skating Club!" She skated out, fast and confident and smiling.

After they posed for pictures, Claire followed Tasanee back to the locker room. Alexis and Stevie were just leaving. There was no "congratulations." No "sorry I destroyed your dress." Just a locker door slamming.

Meghan was just finishing up, too. "What's with the street clothes?"

Claire shook her head. "Didn't have time to change." She didn't want to talk about it.

"Oh. Listen, I . . ." Meghan looked down. "I'm sorry I was kind of short with you earlier. I was upset about my awful score and then the whole thing with my dad. I . . . I just wanted to be alone."

"It's okay. I hope you have a better night." Claire grabbed her skating bag and gave Tasanee a quick wave. "See you guys on Monday."

∽

Claire went home and showed off her medal to Dad and Aunt Maureen, then collapsed into bed.

Sunday was the quietest day she'd had in ages, a day of homework, music in her room, and gardening with Mom. Later on, Dad put burgers on the grill and they ate at the picnic table out by the pond.

"Can we have a fire? *Please?*" Jake asked, and when Dad nodded, he and Christopher took off into the woods to gather kindling.

Claire heard them shouting over the sound of breaking branches. "Dude, you better watch out for tarantulas! Remember that time Indiana Jones got *covered* with them?"

The wood they brought back was dry, and Dad had a respectable bonfire going within minutes.

Watching her marshmallow brown over the embers, watching Jake use his roasting fork to poke pinecones into the flames, Claire felt the tension she'd been carrying around all day melt away.

This was the first dinner in a long time she hadn't eaten in the van with Luke and Abby and their mom.

She was tired of turkey subs and chips.

She was tired of a lot of things.

An owl called from the trees behind her.

It stared down as if it could see right into her soul. Could the owl tell that she had won a medal yesterday? That she was heading to Lake Placid to skate again after school tomorrow?

"Whooo!"

Could the owl's big night eyes see what she hadn't told anyone? Could it tell that a part of her didn't want to go?

☙

After school on Monday, Claire slopped jam on two thick slices of toast, wrapped them in a paper towel, grabbed her backpack and skating bag from the bench by the door, and ran to the van waiting in the driveway.

It didn't really matter what the owl thought about her last night. She needed to finish the summer session, finish up her scholarship. She didn't have to worry about any more competitions—just another two months of training. She'd even won a medal. At the end of August, her scholarship would run out. She'd be a stronger skater, and she'd get to go back to training with Mary Kate and junior coaching at the Northern Lights rink. She wondered if Ivy still carried Roger everywhere.

"Hey, fellow Fibo-nerd! Congrats again on your medal." Luke leaned over the seat, headphones in his ears, using two pencils to tap out a beat on the headrest. How come he never looked tired? He pulled out one earbud. "Ready for today?"

"Ready for a nap." Claire grinned and took a bite of her toast. As Mrs. Collins started to pull out of the driveway, Claire's dad came out the front door of the house, dressed for work at the border, with a big envelope in his hand.

He jogged up to the driver's side window. "Could you pass

this along to Claire's coach? He phoned last night and asked me to send it in today." He blew a kiss into the backseat and turned around.

Mrs. Collins passed the envelope back, and Claire shoved it into her skating bag. Probably more scholarship paperwork or something.

"When are you two competing next?" Claire asked.

"Probably not until regionals unless Coach decides we need practice in front of judges before then," Luke said.

"That's in October." Abby pulled two bottled waters from the cooler. "Want one?"

"Thanks." Claire's water bottle was still on the kitchen counter next to the jam.

Luke twisted in his seat to look at her. "Are you doing your same routine at regionals, or will you work up something new? Do you know yet?"

Claire shook her head. "I'm done at the end of August. Scholarship, remember?"

Abby looked at Luke and frowned. "Won't they extend it since she placed last weekend?"

"I sure hope so," Luke said, "And then if you do really well at regionals, you can usually find a sponsor to help with—"

"Whoa!" Claire held up her hand. "I never planned on all the competitions. I'm ready to be done soon."

"Okay." Luke turned back around in his seat. "I was just trying to help. There are probably opportunities if you want to keep skating."

"I know, but I'm good. It's been a great opportunity already."

There was that word again. *Opportunity.* It was supposed

to be a good thing, a choice. So how come if you said "No thanks" to one, you felt so awful?

Claire wrapped her second piece of toast in the napkin and tucked it into a side pocket of her bag. She wasn't hungry anymore.

"Bye, Mrs. Collins. Thanks!" A cool breeze ruffled Claire's hair as she climbed the hill to the Olympic Center. That was one good thing about training here in the summer. Even off the ice, Lake Placid was always cooler.

"Come on." Luke bumped Claire with his shoulder and swept his arm out as they looked down over Main Street. "How can you say good-bye to this?"

Claire grinned. She did love driving the curvy road into town, out of the woods and hills and into the white-trimmed buildings with their steep roofs. Lake Placid looked like somebody from Switzerland or Austria had gotten homesick and tried to make a little village for themselves here in the middle of the mountains. "I'm not saying I won't miss the hot chocolate and strudel," she said. "But I'll be okay when it's over."

"Will you miss me?"

"Well, of course, but you're just in Plattsburgh. I mean, we can still see each other." Oh no, that sounded wrong, like she thought they'd be seeing each other, like dating-seeing-each-other. "I mean, like, maybe if we both go to a regional MATH-COUNTS competition. And I'll probably see you at the mall sometimes because we go to the mall in Plattsburgh. . . ."

She looked up to see if she had saved herself from complete embarrassment. Luke was striking a skater pose, one leg extended high behind him in a spiral, his arms flailing wildly out to each side, head tipped, eyes crossed. "How could you not miss seeing this face every day?"

Abby shoved him and he tipped over into the grass. "Doofus. You're probably making Claire wish she could be done *now*."

Claire laughed and held the door for them, grateful that she hadn't had to blabber on any more about the mall.

"Claire!" Groshev's voice echoed down the hallway as she turned toward the locker room. "Get dressed quickly. You're on the ice first." He walked up to her and held out his hand. "I believe your father sent something for me?" Claire pulled the envelope out of her bag, handed it to him, and headed in to pull on her skates.

"Nothing like a relaxing start to the day," Claire grumbled, tightening her laces.

"Groshev's after-competition workouts are legendary," Abby said. "When you get out there, he's going to tell you what you did well. Then whatever you messed up, you're going to do until you get it right at least a dozen times."

"Guess I'll need these today." Claire opened a new package of hip pads and slid one into each side of her tights. Falling still hurt, but the bruises wouldn't be quite as bad with a little cushioning. She took a deep breath and headed out to the ice.

"Guards off." Groshev looked up to the sound booth. "All set, Bella! Give her a few laps to warm up and then start it." He flicked his hand toward the rink. "Take five minutes. Then the routine. Go."

Claire started stroking, arms out, chin up, but she couldn't enjoy the cool breeze in her face as usual. Would he make her do the whole routine over and over until she got it perfect?

On just her fourth lap around—she hadn't even tried any

spins or jumps yet—Groshev waved her back to the boards. "Ready?"

"Yep." Claire skated to the center of the rink and took her position, waiting for Vivaldi.

But the strings that drifted down from the speakers weren't the light, airy notes of "Autumn." They were strong, low notes.

Bella must have put in the wrong CD. Claire looked up at the box.

But Groshev's voice boomed out. "Do not look up there. Skate!"

"To this?" Trumpets blared from the speakers. She knew this song! It was—

"Let's go! Skate!"

"You want me to just . . . make something up?"

"Yes, make it up. Or let the music make it up. Let's go!" Groshev clapped his hands sharply in time with the music. "Skate! Skate the music. Skate the story you hear."

Claire listened.

Bum-ba-dum-bum, bum-ba-dah . . . Raiders of the Lost Ark! It was the theme song. The one Jake and Christopher hummed on all their treasure hunts in the woods.

Seriously? He wanted her to skate the story? She could skate this one, all right.

As the music got louder, she skated faster, launching into a double toe loop. She landed it perfectly, so she wouldn't fall into the trip-wired vines. One of those big explosions would make her fall for sure.

She couldn't help laughing, and when the music picked up its pace, she let her skates play with the notes, crossing over and back and over each other across the ice.

She felt the wind blowing her hair forward—this was the coldest ancient jungle ever—as she turned and skated into a double salchow right before the music slowed and the strings started playing a lyrical, gentle part of the piece.

She let the slower music lift her, let it guide her through her spiral, her sit spin, a single axel, a death drop into a sit spin, before the crescendo.

As the tempo picked up again, she let the rhythm of the percussion move her feet, faster and faster into another double toe loop, and then a double flip.

The only element from her program she hadn't done yet was the single axel. She did a series of quick turns and built up her speed. She remembered Harrison Ford, running from those evil guys in the jungle, swinging on a vine, and felt as if she were flying, too. The brass seemed to pump her full of power, and in the last second leading up to her final jump, she made a decision.

She'd only landed one double axel in her life, ages ago at the end of her best session ever with Mary Kate, and she hadn't even tried it in months. But what the heck.

Indiana Jones would never settle for a single.

She took off high, making one—two and a half revolutions over the ice before her left foot landed, solid and clean, chin up, arms strong. It was the kind of double axel you read about in skating manuals.

She slid into a final pose, a lunge with her arms held high.

Still breathing hard, she stood, brushed the ice shavings off her knee, and looked around. She waited for more music, or something, someone to tell her to start over, but the rink was absolutely silent.

A cooler engine clicked on and started humming. Claire looked over at Groshev. He leaned toward her on the boards, his gloved hands clasped in front of him, staring as if he couldn't quite recognize her.

"Come here." He waved her over and looked at her from under those thick eyebrows. "Where did that come from?"

"The double axel?"

"That and all of the rest." He waved his arm out over the ice, tracing the path of the impromptu routine she'd just skated. "The music of that skating, the rhythm, the passion, the height of the jumps, all of it. Where did you get that?"

"I guess, I just . . ." Where had she gotten it? She had just skated. And imagined that she was . . . "Indiana Jones, I guess."

"Indiana Jones?"

"You know, from the movie? The song is from a movie called—"

"Yes, yes, yes." He waved his hands as if brushing away her words. "I know about the movie. Your father told me that it is one of your favorites, and I was looking for some music, something to . . . ah . . . inspire you. Take you to the next level." He looked at her again. "So you find all this, the jumps, the spins, the . . . the skating . . . in your Indiana Jones?"

Claire shrugged. It sounded dumb, but that's what happened. She hadn't just been skating; she'd been playing out there. Like in the woods with Jake and Christopher. It had been fun. That was it, she decided, what she'd meant to say. "I had fun."

"Bella! Would you bring the CD back down, please?" Groshev hollered and then nodded at Claire. "Here is what we do.

We keep working on the doubles. The axel especially. We look at some new music—maybe this one, maybe another one you like—and we bring your Indiana Jones with us when you go to regionals in Buffalo."

"But I'm done at the end of August. My scholarship was only for—"

"Your scholarship has been extended," Groshev said, as if it were final. Extended whether she wanted it to be or not.

"But—"

Bella walked up and handed Groshev the CD. "Raiders Theme" was written on it in familiar handwriting. Groshev slid the CD into a big envelope—the one that Claire's father had sent in this afternoon—and put it in his bag.

Claire stared at the corner of the envelope poking out. Groshev had asked her dad for music to keep her going. That was it, wasn't it? He'd asked for music that would make her strong enough to keep training. And Dad had found it.

"Your scholarship has been extended," Groshev said again. "We have fifteen minutes more. Let us get to work."

She skated back out and let the *Raiders* theme play in her head, even though the rink was quiet except for the scratch of skates. Luke, Abby, Tasanee, Meghan, Alexis, and Stevie had started skating when she finished her first routine, so she claimed the corner closest to Groshev to practice jumps.

She landed the singles, no problem.

The first time she tried the double axel, she didn't get high enough and couldn't make it all the way around.

"Okay, stop." Groshev waved her to the boards. "When you are in the process of the takeoff, your body is going in a direction, yes?"

"Right."

"But you are . . . what . . . stopping the action to make your position. You need to take off first. You make a very nice position in the air. . . ." He tucked in his arms to demonstrate. "But you are making it too soon, you see?"

Claire nodded. "I think so."

"Go. Again. You can do it." He flicked his hand out to her circle of ice, and somehow that motion that she had always thought felt so dismissive, so condescending, felt encouraging. "You are doing the right thing. That is good. But you need to do the right thing at the right moment."

When she tried again, the thing came together with the moment. She took off, higher than the last time, and waited until she was high above the ice to tuck her arms into the spin.

"Good! Good!" Groshev looked at his watch, nodded, and actually smiled a little. "I will see you on Wednesday."

෧෧

She landed it again on Wednesday.

And on Friday.

And all through the Saturday session.

At the end of practice, she saw her father leaning over the boards talking to Groshev.

"Nice job out there." He leaned in to hug her when she skated up. "Your coach tells me you have an opportunity to keep training through the fall."

She nodded.

"That something you want to do?"

She thought about it. A week ago, she'd been ready to go home. But now . . .

"If we can work out rides and everything, yeah. I do."

He looked at her the way he had when she was little and had fallen off her bike, trying to decide if she was okay. "Rides are fine if you're sure that's what you want to do. I know the schedule's been tough on you. We can talk later if you want to think on it some."

She felt the ice under her blades and swished them back and forth. She didn't need to think. She'd done well at the Champlain Valley Open, but she could do better. She knew it. "I'd like to keep going."

Groshev nodded. "Regionals are the second weekend in October. We will have a sponsor take care of lodging for your family if you decide to go. Or she can come with one of us."

"Oh, we're going," her father said, grinning. "That's too big to miss."

CHAPTER 20

After the Champlain Valley Open, everyone's attention turned to regionals in October, and training stopped for nothing, not even final exams. The locker room was like a library the last week of school, with everyone sprawled out on the floor studying, every bench covered with books in between ice sessions. Claire and Luke teamed up to offer math tutoring one day during the dinner break. Even Alexis took them up on it.

The last days of school passed in a blur; Claire did well on her finals but never had a chance to celebrate the usual way, going out for pizza after the last test, because training started right after school. Everything had to revolve around ice time. Usually, Claire arranged her whole Fourth of July weekend around the parade in Plattsburgh and the fireworks. This year, practice had run late that night, and she'd just barely caught the end of the finale out the car window on the way home.

Claire had hoped she'd be free for a girls' night on Natalie's birthday at the end of July, but the week before, she got an invitation in the mail. "You're invited . . ." it said, "to a hay ride and slumber party!" Since when did Nat send her an invitation for girls' night? Claire felt a stab of jealousy, knowing she wasn't the only one who got an invitation. She probably wasn't even at the top of the list anymore. And it turned out that she couldn't go, anyway—Groshev had called one of his famous early Saturday sessions, so Claire spent the night at Tasanee's house after Friday Flair.

She watched summer pass her by like the cars carrying kayaks and bike racks that whirred past her car window every afternoon. She didn't even have time to help Nat with the honey, one of their favorite end-of-summer traditions. It was the one bee job Claire could do without actually dealing with bees. She loved turning the handle on the machine that spun the frames to get the honey out.

The honey harvest usually happened right before Claire's birthday on September third, but that was another one of those "usuallys" that skating messed up.

Just let us get out on time this once, Claire thought. *Just this once.* She'd persuaded Natalie to give milk-shake night another try.

But for whatever reason, Groshev was in rare form and kept them late.

"Again!" he shouted out at Meghan, while Tasanee and Claire waited on the bench for their turn to run their programs.

Claire sighed, louder than she meant to.

"What's wrong?" Tasanee asked.

"Aw, nothing." Claire picked at a pull in her glove. A thread unraveled and left a hole near her thumb. "Nothing new, anyway. I had plans with my friend. That I'm going to have to cancel. Again."

"Can't you do it another day?"

"Probably. It's my birthday, though." Claire's eyes filled as she said it. She hadn't told anyone until now.

"Oh my gosh, Claire. I wish I'd known." Tasanee gave her a quick hug. "Well, happy birthday, even if you're not spending it the way you planned."

When Claire called Natalie an hour later, she didn't even sound mad. "That's okay. Keene said he'd take Lucy and me to the movies if you ended up not being able to make it."

Natalie already had a backup plan. Just perfect.

"Claire, out to the ice! We run it from the beginning this time." Groshev kept her out there alone for twenty minutes, then ran a whole group session that lasted until almost seven.

"Your jumps looked great today," Claire said as she headed for the locker room with Tasanee. She was too tired to be sad about her birthday anymore.

"Thanks, you too. I can't wait for tomorrow." Tasanee stopped halfway down the hallway. "Oh, wait. I think I forgot my music. Will you go back with me? I'm afraid if I go alone, Groshev will corner me to talk about my flying camel again."

"Sure." Claire followed Tasanee back to the rink. It didn't matter at this point. Mrs. Collins had called to say she'd be a few minutes late, anyway, since she was picking up sandwiches for the way home. Birthday dinner. Just perfect.

"Thanks," Tasanee said, coming down from the sound booth with her CD in her hand. The hallway was empty as they headed back toward the locker room. "I'm so glad I remembered. One time two years ago, I got all the way to Buffalo and realized I didn't have my music and my mom had to drive out and find a store that sold blank CDs and then find someone with a laptop and then download it from iTunes and burn it to the CD, like, two minutes before I had to go on the ice."

"Wow," Claire said, pulling open the locker room door. "I can't imagine—"

"SURPRISE!!!!"

The chorus bounced off the locker room walls and almost knocked Claire right back into the hallway she was so surprised. Abby pulled her into the room, and Meghan handed her a shiny purple and silver balloon with "Happy Birthday" on the front in loopy writing. Mrs. Collins picked up a pile of paper plates next to a big pizza box and held them up. "We know it's not the birthday celebration you planned, but we wanted to make sure you had a memorable dinner. There's nothing like locker-room pizza."

Luke stepped forward holding a cake—chocolate with chocolate frosting—with thirteen candles burning on top. "You know, if you'd told me it was your birthday, I woulda made you a CD or something. Anyway . . . make a wish."

Claire smiled her first real smile since she'd walked into the locker room that morning, took a deep breath, and blew. They all went out.

"What'd you wish for?" Abby grinned.

"Can't tell," Claire said, "or it won't come true. Don't you know anything?"

"Hold on." Luke put down the cake and reached under the bench to pull out a plate, covered in foil. "I do have a gift for you, even though I just found out it was your big day. I was still able to create this masterpiece." He pulled off the aluminum foil to reveal a plate of tortilla chips with melted cheese, salsa, and sour cream. They must have come from the Mexican place up the street.

"Thanks." Claire reached for a chip, but Luke pulled the plate back.

"Whoa! This isn't just any birthday, you know. How old are you again?"

"Thirteen."

"Exactly. And these aren't just any chips. Take a minute to appreciate the presentation, please."

Claire looked at the chips again. They were arranged in tidy concentric circles, with five in the center ring, then eight, then thirteen, and twenty one, and— She started laughing before she got to thirty-four.

"Get it?" Luke looked so proud. "They're Fibo-nachos!"

"Best. Birthday. Present. Ever," Claire said. "Thank you."

Abby shook her head. "Do you really need to laugh at his jokes like that? You'll just encourage him."

Claire ate a few Fibo-nachos, accepted a slice of pizza from Mrs. Collins, and sat down on the bench next to Tasanee before she noticed that Groshev was there, too, leaning against the lockers with his arms crossed in front of him, but smiling.

"*Suh dnyem razh dayenia*," he said. "That's 'happy birthday' in Russian. And let us hope that your big present comes at the regional competition next month."

CHAPTER 21

On the first day of school, Claire saw Natalie for a minute before homeroom and then not again until fifth-period English.

"I can't stand eighth grade," Natalie grumbled, pulling out her schedule before the bell rang for class. "We don't have lunch until seventh period. I'm going to be starving by then." She peered over at Claire's schedule. "What do you have after lunch?"

"Math. I have Mrs. Cosgro again."

"Lucky. I got Mr. Nudderbaum." She reached up and rubbed the top of her head. Mr. Nudderbaum was famous for that move. Everyone said he used to have hair but he rubbed it all off worrying about the state math test. He was so obsessed with it that he gave practice tests as homework every day for three months leading up to it. Two hours a night.

"At least we have English together. I hear Mr. Smythe is good."

Natalie nodded. "But tough. You're going to be writing a lot of essays in the truck."

It was the first thing Natalie had said about Claire's decision to keep going with the scholarship. Claire really had thought she'd be happy to have her old schedule back when school started, but she just didn't feel finished in Lake Placid. If she left before she skated the way she knew she could, it would be like . . . like leaving buckets of sap all over the place just because you were tired of staying up late to get it boiled down to syrup. She just felt like she needed to finish. Like she needed to give herself the chance to do this right at regionals, and then she'd be done.

୶

When math class rolled around, Claire knew Mrs. Cosgro would want to know about MATHCOUNTS, and sure enough, it was the first thing out of her mouth after she asked about Claire's summer. "And how's your schedule looking this fall?"

"It's . . . the same." Claire stared at Mrs. Cosgro's scarf. It was electric blue, with the Pythagorean theorem printed over and over in bright yellow. "I made it to regionals, so they extended my scholarship through October."

"And then?"

"Then I'm done." She didn't need to worry about making it to nationals. Not with people competing from all over the state.

"Well, we don't have our regional MATHCOUNTS meet until February. And I'd really love to have you, so if you think you might still be interested, I could give you some practice problems to do on your own if you had to miss our first few team meetings."

"That would be great. Thanks." Claire wasn't as worried about balancing skating and homework this year. She'd gotten better at finding little bits of time, and she was getting better at writing in the truck. Plus with summer ending, she

thought the training sessions would be a little lighter . . .
more like they were when she was starting out last spring.

∾

She was wrong about that one. If anything, they grew more
intense.

"No, no, no. I need more. More height. Just more. You
need to keep playing that . . . ah . . ." Groshev waved his hand
around next to his ear. "The movie in your mind. Of the
jumping—the perfect jumping. So then you see it and you do
it that way."

She watched the movie in her head, over and over and
over. And by the end of September, her body could pull off a
double axel that matched the one in her mind. Her bruises
were starting to fade, but her feet were killing her after every
practice.

Groshev caught her wincing as she loosened her laces on
the bench one afternoon. "You are having trouble with your
skates?"

"No." She tried to tie them quickly, but her cold fingers
fumbled.

"Take the skate off. Let me see."

He held it up, bent the leather of the boot in his big
hands, then set it down and picked up her foot.

"Hey!" She almost slid off the bench.

"How long have you been skating in these?"

"I don't know . . . two years maybe?"

"Hmph." He let her foot go. "Get changed. You are done
for today. I will talk with your father about new skates."

"No!" Claire tugged at the tongue of the boot and started

to push her foot back in. Her parents had just spent almost a hundred dollars on her binders and stuff for school. "These are okay. I can have them punched out. They'll be fine."

Groshev held up his hand. "We will talk later. You are done for now."

Claire pulled on her wind pants. She couldn't let Dad talk to Groshev right now. There was no way they could buy the kind of skates he'd recommend, but even as the thought passed through Claire's mind, she knew her parents would find a way to get them for her if they knew she needed them.

She looked down at her old skates, gray and cracked. They'd already looked tired when Charlotte passed them down to her two years ago, but they'd worked out just fine until now.

Wait . . . Charlotte was back from London. And Charlotte had written about getting new skates last spring. Maybe her old ones would fit. Claire hurried out of the Olympic Center early to wait outside so her father wouldn't have a reason to go in. She needed to get in touch with Charlotte before Groshev got in touch with her dad.

෴

"Are you sure you don't want to room with Alexis and me for regionals?" Meghan pulled a purple-sequined skating dress from the rack at the Olympic Center shop and held it up. "It'd be so much more fun than being with your parents. We always bring movies and then we do our hair and makeup together in the morning before we go to the rink." She held the dress up toward Claire. "This one would look good on you. With your light skin."

Claire glanced at the price tag. $290. "It's pretty, but I'm all set. I'm wearing that one from my cousin I showed you last week." An urgent e-mail to Charlotte had resulted in a big package arriving via UPS with not only hand-me-down skates the next size up, but three more of Charlotte's old competition dresses. Claire had struggled to choose between the one with the brown skirt and sparkly gold top or the red one with the sequins on top and layers of flowing red and orange scarves as a skirt. She'd gone with that one, finally, because it reminded her of sugar maples' leaves in the fall—bright and full of energy.

"Well, you really ought to have a new one for regionals." Meghan handed her a green one. "This would look good with your eyes."

"I'm all set, Meghan. Thanks." Claire tucked the dress back onto the rack. "And thanks for the invitation to room with you, but my mom would have a fit if I didn't stay with the family." She didn't mention that rooming with Alexis would feel like sleeping in a hornets' nest.

Meghan pulled a fleece from the rack. "I'm getting this. My old one is all pilly."

Claire walked with her to the counter, and Bob-O rang up the fleece. No show to announce today, so he was apparently stuck in the shop.

"There you go." He handed Meghan her bag. "And Claire, hold on. I'm pretty sure your new skates came in."

Claire shook her head. "I didn't order skates."

"Your coach did. Hold on, I'll be right back." He ducked through the door to a back room and returned with two boxes. "Here we go. You're going to love these."

Claire stared into the first box. The blades were Paramount— the ones Meghan had talked about. The ones with the thousand-dollar price tag. "This is a mistake. I didn't order these, and I can't—"

"I said your coach ordered them. And don't worry." He followed her eyes to the price sticker. "They're billed to the scholarship fund."

Meghan's eyes were huge.

"But I have skates. My cousin sent me—"

"Look," said Bob-O, leaning over the counter with a grin. "You can refuse these skates and get both of us in trouble with your coach, or you can smile and get them fitted and thank him when you see him later on. Either way, you're going to end up skating in these because your coach . . . how can I say this delicately? Your coach wants things done his way." He held up the first boot and nodded toward the bench. "All right?"

The skates were beautiful. And they fit perfectly.

"Let me get these together for you. Can you wait?"

Claire nodded as he disappeared into the back again. She turned to Meghan, who had been quiet through the whole fitting. "I can't believe he did this."

"Believe it." Meghan started flipping through the dresses again. "And enjoy it while it lasts. You never know when somebody else will show up and jump higher than you." She pulled the purple and green dresses from the rack. "I'm getting these, too."

∞

"Ready?" Groshev waved up at the sound box on the Wednesday before regionals. "Last time, Bella!" He turned to Claire. "This is it until you get onto the ice for practice in Buffalo."

"All set." Claire believed it, too. She had been landing the doubles, even the double axel—no, especially the double axel—consistently for weeks.

Breaking in the new skates had taken two weeks and a whole box of Band-Aids to cover her blisters, but now they felt like old friends. She skated to the center and struck her opening pose.

It was funny, she thought, listening for the first notes, how her dad had known just which song to pass on to Groshev. She had listened to what felt like a hundred music samples, trying to decide on new music for regionals, but nothing came close to the Indiana Jones theme.

When it started, Claire made the turns and spins, took off into the jumps that were as much a part of her life as eating and sleeping now. She didn't even have to think "arms up" or "hold the landing" anymore; it just happened.

The new skates were perfect. They made her feel like she had in kindergarten when she had brand-new sneakers and thought she could run faster than Superman.

She slid into the lunge at the end and heard applause from the boards.

It was Meghan and Tasanee. Alexis was skating toward Groshev, but he raised a hand so she'd wait. "Claire. Good. Very good. You have the information packet for your father and will arrive in Buffalo Friday afternoon, correct?"

Claire nodded. "Thanks." Groshev turned his attention to Alexis, and Claire skated over to Tasanee and Meghan. "You guys all set?"

"Definitely." Tasanee grinned. She'd had a fantastic run the past few weeks, too, and she had added a double axel to her program, combined with a double flip combination that was awesome. She had a real chance at placing.

"As ready as I'll ever be." Meghan tugged at her braid. "My mother's booking extra ice for me tomorrow so I can make sure I'm really solid." She had been landing her double axel on and off, too. "And Coach said I could have Stevie's lesson slot since she's taking a break." Stevie hadn't done well enough to earn a spot at regionals, and no one—least of all Stevie—seemed upset. In fact, Claire had seen Stevie hanging around outside the high school next to the Olympic Center with some ninth-grade boys after school, and she looked more animated than she ever had at skating. Claire had expected the other Ice Queens to be disappointed—she was their friend, after all—but even Meghan seemed more interested in the extra ice time than in Stevie.

"I'm going to run and pick up some tights before the shop closes," Tasanee said. "You guys want to come?"

"Nah, I got a whole bunch of stuff a couple weeks ago." Meghan didn't say anything about Claire's new skates. Claire hadn't mentioned them to anyone, either, even when Tasanee complimented her on them. She'd just said, "Thanks." Not because she was embarrassed about getting them as part of the scholarship; everybody knew she was training for free. But because she still felt as if this whole thing, going to regionals, landing the double axel, the new skates . . . as if it were just a dream that might melt away like cotton candy when you put it in your mouth. She still carried Charlotte's hand-me-down skates around in her bag, as if she'd need them for when she woke up from the dream. But she finally felt as if she might be able to do it this time—skate one of those perfect shows at a real competition.

"You know," Meghan said, holding open the locker room door, "you're so lucky you have Kalina on your side."

"I know," Claire said, plopping down on the bench to unlace her skates. She hadn't seen much of Kalina lately—she hadn't needed to, really—but she'd had a last session with her this week to talk about strategies for dealing with nerves at regionals. "She's been awesome."

"She is. And I still can't believe she talked Groshev into all this."

"Into all what?"

"Well, your scholarship extension. And those." She nodded toward the new skates Claire had just tucked into her bag. "I'd be awfully surprised if it was Groshev who wanted to extend the scholarship. He has no patience with somebody popping all their jumps like you were." Meghan zipped up her skating bag and turned to Claire. "I'm glad you're still here. I mean, I never thought you'd be able to work through that rough patch you had. I really thought when Hannah freaked out and left because of all the stress, you'd be next. I mean, why do you need to put up with this?"

Meghan zipped the bag, and the noise made Claire want to scream. *Because I know I can do this! No matter what Groshev thinks about me popping jumps and no matter what Alexis says. Because I skate better than anyone here, including you with your three-hundred-dollar dresses!*

No. There was no way she was quitting now.

Whether she'd asked to come here at first or not, she belonged here. She was landing her doubles more consistently than anybody. Maybe Groshev had given up on the idea of her being his next big thing. Maybe he didn't even care about keeping her around anymore. But what if she could do it? What if she skated that program perfectly at regionals?

Claire wanted to shout it—all of it—but only Meghan was there to hear, and none of this was her fault.

She took a deep breath. "I guess I just want to see if I can do it. And you know what? I really think I can." Claire stood and slung her bag over her shoulder. "Plus I couldn't quit even if I wanted to. My brothers can't wait to see where the Sabres play. They'd never forgive me if I backed out now."

CHAPTER 22

Dude, did you see that humungous picture of the French Connection in the hallway? Jeezum!" Jake reached across the bed for a second slice of pizza. He was obsessed with the French Connection, that line of three French-Canadian hockey forwards who played together for the Buffalo Sabres back in the seventies. "Those guys were awesome. Especially Rick Martin."

"Nah, it was all René Robert." Christopher swiped Jake's chips and tipped half the bag out onto his paper plate before Jake noticed.

"Gimme those, doofus!" He lunged across the bed but lost his balance and his elbow landed in what was left of the pizza.

"C'mon, boys." Dad didn't raise his voice, but he used the no-more-nonsense tone. "Your mom's going to be back soon with the soda. Knock it off."

"Make him gimme back those chips."

Dad didn't say anything, but his eyes delivered the message. Christopher tipped his plate and dumped the chips back into the bag. "Baby."

"Loser. And René Robert was a loser, too. Everybody knows

it was Rick Martin who made that line." Jake reached for another slice of pizza, the one without his elbow print on it.

"You get to eat yet, Claire?" Dad asked.

She hadn't. She sat at the hotel desk, flipping through the program for tomorrow, reading the bios of all the skaters.

"You nervous?" Dad looked over her shoulder at the page of skaters in the program.

"You know, it's weird, but not really." Claire tipped her head up and smiled at him. "It's like I'm so far out of my league now there's nothing left to be nervous about."

He mussed up her hair. "Nothing is out of your league, and don't you forget it." He slid the last slice of pizza onto a plate and set it in front of her, next to the hotel stationery. "Better claim that before they inhale it."

There was a knock at the door, and when Claire jumped to answer it, she found Meghan, wearing a pair of pink flannel pajamas. "Want to come watch a movie with us?"

"No thanks, I'm just about to eat. We brought the portable DVD player from home, and I promised my brothers I'd watch a movie with them. I haven't been around much."

Meghan glanced over Claire's shoulder into the room just as Christopher dove from one bed to the other. "Geronimo!"

Meghan laughed a little. "Well, come with me to the ice machine then, okay? I want to talk to you."

"I'll be right back, okay, Dad? I'm going with Meghan to get ice."

"Get us some, too, would you?" He handed her the plastic bucket from the bathroom.

"So," Claire said, swinging the bucket back and forth as they walked down the dim hallway. "What's up?"

"I just wanted to see how you're doing. You must be so nervous."

Claire shook her head. "Nope. I'm actually okay. I feel like I'm going to have a good show."

Meghan gave a little smile and pushed the button on the ice machine. A wave of ice cubes tumbled into the bucket. "I wish I could say the same. I'm terrified to skate here again."

"How come?"

"You haven't heard? Ugh. The ice here is the worst; there are always imperfections. Most people pull back at least a little on their jumps here to be safe. It's insane they chose this for regionals."

Perfect, Claire thought. *Just perfect.* She finally figured out how to land her double axel and now she'd have to worry about bad ice. "Ah well." She was just plain tired of being upset. "I guess it can't be any worse than the cow pond, huh?" She stepped up and pushed the button to fill her bucket.

Meghan raised her voice over the falling ice. "Well, you know, I just wanted to tell you. It's a tough rink when you've never skated it before. I thought you might want to rethink some of those doubles."

"You know what?" Claire pulled back her ice bucket, and the last cubes spilled into the machine's tray. She had worked her tail off to land those doubles. She had the blisters and bruises to prove it, and she wasn't pulling back, no matter what the ice was like. "I'm jumping tomorrow. I don't care."

"Well . . . good." Meghan fidgeted with the handle of her ice bucket. "I mean, I *hope* you do great. It's just so not fair for your first regional competition to be *here.* I can't imagine skating under so much pressure."

Claire popped an ice cube into her mouth. She didn't exactly feel awesome, but she didn't feel horrible, either. Maybe she'd be nervous again tomorrow, like she was at the other competitions, but she didn't think so. She felt ... different. Changed. Like somebody who would be able to skate without a stomachache, no matter what the ice was like.

"I'll be fine," she said again and turned to head back down the hallway. Three girls were walking the opposite way, heading toward the ice machine. One had a familiar bounce in her step.

"Hannah!" Claire ran to hug her. But then she remembered Hannah leaving the locker room in tears and squirmed a little. She felt like she should apologize for still skating.

Hannah took care of that with her quick laugh. It was back. "Oh my gosh! Did you both make regionals?"

Meghan nodded.

"That's so awesome!"

"And you too?" Claire asked. "Where are you skating now?"

"In Plattsburgh. I joined the synchronized team there. My mom brings me up once a week for practice, and we do a few competitions. We just did really well at this show in Connecticut, so here we are!" Hannah threw her arms around the girls on either side of her and nodded toward the tall black girl on her right. "This is Jamie, and this is Marina." The girl on her left, petite with short blond hair, smiled.

"It's nice to meet you," Meghan said.

"Well, that's ... awesome!" Claire couldn't help staring. Hannah looked so different. So happy, compared to the last time she'd seen her. Maybe they had both changed.

"We need to get back because the team's going to

dinner," Hannah said, "but it was great seeing you. Good luck tomorrow!"

"You too!" Claire said, and walked with Meghan back down the hallway.

"You sure you don't want to come hang out with us?"

"I'm sure." Claire stopped at her family's room and reached into her back pocket for the key card. "Thanks, though. See you in the morning."

When she opened the door, a pepperoni flew out.

"Hey! You're back. Dad says we can watch a movie." Jake ducked past her out the door, picked up the pepperoni, and popped it into his mouth.

"Which one?"

"Whaddaya think?" Christopher held up the DVD, grinning. Harrison Ford's piercing eyes stared out from the cover. "*Raiders of the Lost Ark.*"

❀

Claire figured she'd be nervous in the morning, but even when they arrived at the arena, she felt calm. Ready. Today was it.

As soon as the door opened, Jake and Christopher took off down a long hallway, probably searching for more posters of hockey stars.

"Shoot," Mom said. "I need to catch them. Do you know where you're going?"

"I think so," Claire said. She didn't know, actually, but she knew that she could just follow the river of sparkly costumes. "I'll see you after I'm done, okay?"

Mom nodded, glanced down the hall after the boys, then apparently decided they didn't have too much of a head start because she turned back to hug Claire. "You have worked so hard, and I'm so, so proud of you. Have fun, okay?"

"Yep." Claire nodded. She would. Bad ice or not, she was going to skate the way she knew she could.

It seemed like every time she turned a corner in this arena, there was another sign that pointed her around the next corner. She stopped for a drink of water at a fountain and heard her name in a voice she'd know anywhere.

"Claire! There you are." Groshev tapped his watch. "I have been looking for you. Practice ice begins in five minutes. Today . . . it is a big day for you."

"I know." Claire stood and wiped water from her chin. "How's the ice?"

"It is fine. Why?"

"It is? I heard it was bad here sometimes." She looked out at the rink. No one seemed to be having trouble, but she was still surprised Groshev hadn't warned her ahead of time if the rink had a reputation for crummy ice. Maybe he didn't want to make her any more nervous, but it made her a little mad. She ought to at least have all the information. Then she could make her own decisions about how to skate.

"Let's go." He tapped his watch again.

"Fine," she said and turned quickly down the hall. It didn't matter. She knew what she needed to know about the ice, and it wasn't going to change how she skated. She wouldn't be in the top three—not in this group—but she'd feel the wind in her hair, and her parents would get to see her skate, and they'd tell Grandpa about it, and they'd probably have chili for dinner tomorrow night.

She'd skate the way she knew how.

When she found the locker room, Alexis was just leaving. With Stevie sitting out regionals, she was alone, for once.

Claire stepped aside to move out of her way, but Alexis paused. "Have you seen Coach?"

Claire nodded. "He's down the hall."

Alexis nodded but didn't leave. She shook out her hands. "I can't seem to get focused. I don't know why." She looked at Claire. "Are you nervous today?"

Claire shook her head. She wasn't nervous about skating, although the fact that Alexis was being so friendly was starting to creep her out a little. Maybe she was just missing Stevie.

Alexis took a deep breath. "I need to find Groshev and get ready. I know I'll be fine when I get out there." She sounded like she was trying to convince herself. "I have a terrific routine, and this is a great venue. I loved skating here last time."

Claire stared. Was she trying to make Claire feel over-confident so the imperfections in the ice would trip her up? Before Claire could sort out her thoughts, Alexis was gone.

No, she thought, and reached for her skating bag. She wasn't going to let it happen.

Not today.

Maybe if she just kept moving along that positive current she felt this morning, the nerves wouldn't catch up with her. She hurried into her skates, tossed her bag into one of the available lockers, snapped the lock shut, twirled the wheel, and rushed out to the rink for warm-up.

Groshev was waiting. "All right," he said. "Warm up, and then let us see the double axel—to be sure it is perfect for today." Claire took a deep breath and headed out to the ice.

She skated around a few times and did a few spins. The ice seemed okay. She tried the double salchow and the double-single combination before she looked up at Groshev, waving his hands at her, motioning for her to try the axel.

She wasn't ready yet, though, and she was still a little mad he hadn't just told her about the ice. She did a double flip instead.

Groshev turned to Alexis, who had been practicing her single-double combination. "Very nice," he said. "Very nice."

It wasn't that nice. She didn't get much height. She was probably too worried about the bad ice she pretended not to know about. Claire sped up and skated faster, launching into her own single-double combination right in front of Groshev. It was perfect, high and beautiful, but instead of telling her so, he motioned for her to come in to the boards.

"That element is not in your program."

"I know."

"Come now. Focus. Work on what you will do for the judges today. The double axel."

Alexis skated past again, turned, and did a double toe loop. Again, it was solid, but not that high.

"Good!" Groshev called. He looked at Claire, still standing there. "What is it you are waiting for? Go skate."

Why all the compliments for Alexis's mediocre skating? Hadn't Claire finally proved herself, too? She started out again but couldn't help herself from keeping an eye on Alexis, who tripped coming out of her next spin; she seemed to be having trouble with the ice now. Served her right.

Claire sped up, leading into a double salchow, but she

stumbled on the landing and slammed to the ice onto her hip, skidding into Tasanee's path. "Sorry."

She stood, brushed herself off, and started skating again gingerly. She'd landed hard and her hip throbbed. Her skate must have caught one of those glitches in the ice. And it would probably only get worse as the day went on.

Claire took a deep breath and tried a sit spin, but she caught another edge and stumbled even coming out of that. A stupid sit spin. Tears spilled from her eyes, from hot to cold as the breeze dried them on her cheeks.

And then the cold found its way inside. She was going to screw up; she could feel it in her sinking stomach. She'd been so excited to skate the way she knew how, but she didn't have a chance on this ice. This was going to be just like last year and just like Saratoga Springs. Why couldn't things go right for her *once*?

"Claire!"

The sharpness of his voice pushed her over the edge. She skated right up to the boards and slid into a hockey stop, throwing snow as high as his waist and practically shouted at him, "What?"

His face darkened. "What? How is it you ask 'what' when I have told you to do the double axel and you are skating everything except the double axel? What is the matter with you?"

"What's the matter with me?" Her voice was so high she didn't even recognize it. "I'll tell you what's the matter with me. I've been coming here—coming to Lake Placid, I mean—for six months. Six months when I could have been skating at home and hanging out with my family and having a *summer*!"

The words fought through her sobs as six months of insecurities came pouring out. "And the whole time, *the whole time*, you've been throwing compliments at Alexis and just waiting for me to screw up so you could send me back home and find somebody better."

"What is this?" Groshev looked at his watch. "You have fifteen minutes of practice, and then we must be off the ice. There is no time for this nonsense."

"It's *not* nonsense—it's my life! You didn't even bother to warn me about the ice here, and I know you're not the one who wanted to extend my scholarship. And you ask what's *wrong* with me?" Hot tears spilled down her cheeks. She swiped at them with her glove. "What's wrong with *you*?"

Groshev stared. "Why would I warn you about the ice?"

Claire flung her hand out toward the skaters. "Everybody knows this rink has a reputation for crummy ice. Everyone backs off their jumps so they don't make fools of themselves, and you weren't even going to tell me that?"

Groshev squinted. "The ice is fine. I don't see—"

"It's not fine, and you should have told me! Didn't you see how I was just skating?"

His eyes darkened. "That is not about the ice. It is about you. And you will not speak to me in this manner. You are being ridiculous. This rink is state-of-the-art. It has a more sophisticated resurfacing system than anywhere you will ever skate."

Claire knew she was risking his temper, but she couldn't stop the words from pouring out. "Well, what about the scholarship? You don't even want me here anymore, do you?

You just want to make sure you don't look bad. I heard you talking to Mr. Van Syke and you said I was a waste of time and money. You *did*."

Groshev drew in a deep breath. "This is not . . . how do I say it . . . not any of your business. But if you must know, I was talking to him about his daughter. She does not try hard enough. Stevie's focus is on her social life and it shows. She is not here."

Claire was so upset she barely heard him. "Well, what about the ice then? And the scholarship. You never wanted—"

"Stop." He held her shoulders so she couldn't turn away. "Just stop. You are about to compete in your first major competition. You are going to skate on a near-perfect surface. And you will skate beautifully. I not only want you here; I called a special meeting of the scholarship committee to make sure I could keep you. You are my star, Claire. You show promise I have not seen in years. Those are the facts. Now *who* is telling you otherwise?"

"Meghan," she said. "She told me about the ice, and how you were all frustrated with my jumps and probably trying to get rid of me." She looked down at her skates.

He shook his head. "Claire," he said. "This is . . . no. This is not true."

Claire lifted her head. He looked her straight in the eyes.

"What you have been told . . . no. There is nothing wrong with the ice. Nothing. Are you hearing me?" He kept his hands on her shoulders, and his eyes searched her face. "It is false. *All* of it. You have gotten . . . how do you say it . . . ."

"Bad information," Claire whispered. And finally, she understood.

She thought of Meghan's reaction at orientation, when Groshev had asked her to loan Claire her music, Meghan's face when Claire got her new skates, her voice . . . *You never know when somebody else will show up and jump higher than you.*

Claire understood perfectly. *She* was the somebody else.

"Yes, bad information. That is it." Groshev reached out with a rough glove and tipped up her chin. "We can talk more later, but you need to warm up now. You will skate beautifully, no?"

Claire nodded. "Yes. I will."

"Good. Go use your last three minutes of ice."

Claire tried a few jumps, including the double axel. She landed it out of habit more than concentration. She couldn't stop replaying all her conversations with Meghan. The almost-tears. The concern in her voice. Meghan was better at acting than skating.

What would Claire's other two competitions this season have been like if she hadn't been all a mess because of girls like Meghan and Alexis? Saratoga might have been different. No, it would have been awful, anyway, because of that rip that turned up in her tights. And the Champlain Valley show had ended with Alexis's cheese-puff-and-ketchup display on her dress. And Meghan had seemed so concerned both times. She'd been right there when it happened.

Oh my gosh, Claire thought.

Meghan had been right there.

Every time.

For a girl who was so good at seeing patterns, she'd been awfully slow to catch on.

Alexis might be so protective of her scholarship that she was downright mean sometimes, but she hadn't lied about the ice here. Meghan had.

The whistle blew, and Claire moved in autopilot. She stepped off the ice and slid her guards calmly onto her skates. But in her mind, the connections exploded.

Meghan.

It had been Meghan who had rushed into the locker room to get something she'd forgotten, right before Claire found her tights ripped.

Meghan, who was there on the locker room floor with the cheese puffs and ketchup packets when Claire left to eat with her family outside.

Meghan.

"Hey! You didn't warm up much. Everything okay?" And here she was, smiling like always.

Claire stared at her, with her perfect braid, and her eyes that always went from supercheerful to full of hurt, to empty, and she knew.

But there was no way to prove it.

"Yeah, I'm fine. I'm just going to take some time to myself before we go on, you know? Nerves." She shook out her hands, and Meghan smiled.

All this time I thanked her for being my friend. And she's been my worst enemy.

But what could she do about it? She was madder than Grandpa when he found those tiny green bugs—aphids, he called them—eating up his maples.

What had Grandpa done? Let the aphids' natural enemies destroy them, he said. He brought in a whole bunch of ladybugs to eat them. She tried to imagine a giant ladybug swallowing Meghan. Who was Meghan's natural enemy?

Meghan still stood there, smiling. "Well, break a leg." She gave Claire a quick hug, and it was all Claire could do not to pull away. "I'll be thinking about you when you're out there!"

I bet you will, thought Claire. *I bet you will.*

Her head was still spinning when she found her mom and the boys up in the stands. Jake and Christopher had unfurled big newsprint banners for her and taped them up along the top of the stands. One said, GO, CLAIRE! The other said, INDIANA JONES RULES!

"Do good, okay?" Christopher held up their father's new video camera. It was a tiny thing—nothing like their old one that weighed about ten pounds. "I'm taping so Grandpa can see when we get home." He pressed a button and the red light came on, pointed right at Claire. "Well? How do you feel, as you prepare for competition?" She stared. "Come on . . . Say something, at least."

She did.

"I need to borrow that camera."

She knew who Meghan's natural enemy was. The person Meghan couldn't control. The person who would make sure Meghan got what she deserved. It was Meghan herself. She just needed a little help.

CHAPTER 23

Claire hurried, and the locker room was still empty. She had everything ready before the door opened and Tasanee stepped in.

"I am scared to death," Tasanee announced, plopping down on a bench. She was reading her favorite killer fairy book again and had fidgeted with the cover so much it was all dog-eared. "If I don't place today, there goes my last chance at junior nationals."

"What about next year?" Claire tried to concentrate on the conversation, though her heart was pounding while she waited.

"Next year I'll be too old for juvenile, and I won't stand a chance in intermediate yet. I gotta pull it off this year."

"You will," Claire told her. "You will."

"Hey!" Alexis and Meghan came through the door, followed by Abby. "Coach says it's time for us to get out there."

"Oh, shoot!" Claire gasped. "I never turned in my music. I think my mom still has it." She looked at her watch. "I'm not on right away. I'm going to throw on my sneakers and run up to find her. I'll have time to get my skates back on after." She tugged the laces loose, pulled off her skates, and pushed her feet into her sneakers. She dropped the skates into her locker and left the metal door open.

"We'll see you in the staging area then, okay?" Meghan looked over her shoulder at Claire.

"Yep, I'll be there in . . . I don't know . . . probably fifteen minutes. They're sitting way over on the other side, and I'll have to run the music up. It's fine, though, I've got time."

Claire followed them out the door and turned to shout back at Tasanee. "Hey! Good luck! You're going to be great."

Claire waved and ducked around the corner toward the seating area.

Then she stopped.

She counted to five slowly and peered back around the corner. If she was right, she'd know pretty quickly.

Sure enough, she saw the group of skaters stop halfway down the hall, saw Meghan's hands flying through the air. Claire imagined her telling some dramatic story about forgetting her own music back in her skating bag or breaking her hair tie. She turned, flew back to the locker room, and disappeared inside.

Claire's heart pounded as she walked back toward the locker room. She waited outside, listening to the quiet, as the hallway grew emptier. She heard the first words from the announcer inside the arena, introducing the number one skater, a girl named Carlotta Alexandra. She was skating to *Carmen*, which Claire loved, but she forced herself to listen to the emptiness inside the locker room instead.

Finally, she heard what she was waiting for. The sound of sharp metal on metal. It started as quiet clinking and then grew louder, until it sounded like Meghan had ripped the lockers loose from the walls and was throwing them around. The clanging echoed down the empty hallway.

Claire pulled open the locker room door.

Meghan teetered on one of the benches, balanced on her skate guards, clinging to the edge of the lockers with one hand while she slammed the blade of Claire's new skate into the top metal edge with the other.

She didn't hear Claire come in.

Claire stood frozen, watching.

Meghan looked like someone else. Not like the girl who wore sparkly dresses and twirled so her skirt flared out. She still wore her dress, but her hair had pulled loose from her braid in angry, damp strands that stuck to her face, and her eyes. . . . Her eyes were fixed on the skate hitting the locker as if she were furious with it.

No, not furious.

She looked . . . terrified of it.

The locker room door thumped shut, and Meghan turned with a jerk. Her eyes looked wild when she saw Claire. Then she stared down at the skate in her hand, as if she hadn't known it was there.

"It's been you." Claire stepped forward. Meghan dropped the skate onto the floor. "All this time, I thought it was Alexis, and it was you."

"What are you doing here?" Meghan's voice shook. "I thought you went to get your music!"

"What are *you* doing here? Did you tell them you needed a hair tie? Or an extra pair of skate guards? Or were you going to borrow these?" Claire picked up her other skate off the bench.

The thousand-dollar blade was destroyed, full of so many nicks and broken edges that anyone who tried skating on it would be on their face with the first stroke.

"*Why?*" She stared hard at Meghan. "Tell me why."

Meghan stepped down from the bench, stumbled into a locker, and slumped down against it. "Because you showed up here and took away everything I had. With your 'look-I-can-do-a-double-toe-loop already' moves and your stupid perfect spins and . . . these." She picked up the skate she'd been destroying from the floor and held it up, chipped blade and all. "Only the best for Claire."

"That's not fair. I never did anything to you. I—"

"You *did*. Last year at this time, *I* was the person Groshev was pinning his hopes on. *I* was the one who got the extra lesson time and the choice of all the best music. *I* was the one who was going to be his star. And then Alexis did so well at regionals, and then *you* showed up and everybody forgot I even existed."

Claire shook her head. "I didn't—"

"Meghan!" Alexis tore open the locker room door, frantically waving her hand. "That girl from downstate who was supposed to be right before you didn't show up. Come on! You're up next."

Meghan stood frozen with the skate still in her hands.

Alexis looked from Meghan to Claire. Then her eyes fell on the ruined skate in Meghan's hand, and she sucked in her breath.

"You better go, Meghan," Claire said quietly. "You're on."

Meghan put down the skate, smoothed her skirt, pulled out what was left of her braid, corralled her hair back into a ponytail, took a deep breath, and walked past Alexis out the door.

Claire watched her walk away until the door swung all the way shut. Meghan never looked back.

Alexis stayed behind. "Did . . . Did she just—" Her eyes were huge as if she couldn't believe tiny Meghan could do so much damage. Claire had a hard time believing *anybody* could. But she nodded.

"What size are you?" Alexis asked quietly. "I have an extra pair."

Claire shook her head. "I'm all set." She tried to even her breathing. Her heart was beating so fast it felt like it would go flying out of her chest and right down the hallway any minute. She pulled her skating bag from the top shelf of her locker and took out Charlotte's old skates.

"Are you . . . sure you're okay?" Alexis stood, still holding the door open. "I . . . have to go because I'm on soon and I know you are, too, but I just . . . Look, I'm . . . sorry. You know I've always wanted to beat you. Just . . . not like this."

"I know. And I'm okay." Claire took a deep breath, steadier this time. "And for what it's worth, I want to beat you, too. I need to get ready now." She paused. "Good luck."

"Good luck." Alexis left, and Claire sat down on the bench. Her hands shook as she loosened the laces on Charlotte's hand-me-down skates and slid them on. The other ones had slicker blades, she knew, but somehow, these felt better on her feet.

She was taller with the skates on, and when she climbed up onto the bench, it was easy to reach up on top of the lockers across from hers. She pulled down the video camera, red light still shining, and pressed the black button.

Stop.

Claire packed up her ruined skates, zipped the camera into her bag, and went out to meet Groshev.

She got there in time to see the very end of Meghan's program—her last two jumps. She fell twice and skated off the ice without finishing. She didn't look at Groshev, didn't look at Claire. She walked past, out the door, and down the long hallway.

Groshev ran a hand through his hair and let out a loud breath. He turned to Claire and looked down at her feet. "Where are your new skates? You cannot skate in these. Not today of all days!"

"I am skating in these."

"But you cannot—"

"I *can*. And I have to." She held up her hand, and he didn't say anything else. "Here." Claire pulled the video camera from her bag and handed it to Groshev. "Would you please pass this to my family so they can record my routine? And later on there's something on there you need to see. It will explain a lot."

ⵥ

Claire pulled off her skate guards and leaned against the boards. Usually she didn't like to watch the person skating before her, but this was Tasanee.

Land that first double, she thought, willing Tasanee to keep her arms up and land strong.

She did, and Claire clapped louder than anybody.

The rest of Tasanee's program was close to perfect, though she backed off the double axel at the very end and landed a clean single instead.

"Great job!" Claire gave Tasanee a quick hug before Groshev tugged her away.

"Focus," he said. "You can do this. I do not know your story with the skates, but it does not matter. You can do this. In any skates. I believe that."

"I know," she said. "I believe it, too."

"And now," the announcer boomed, "our next competitor in the Juvenile Ladies Free Skate is Claire Boucher from the Northern Lights Skating Club of Mojimuk Falls, New York."

Claire struck her opening pose, with one of Charlotte's skates crossed in front of the other.

The music started.

The last thing she saw before she took off was the sign. Jake and Christopher had pulled it down and were waving it over their heads. INDIANA JONES RULES!

He sure does, Claire thought.

Then it all melted away except the music. And the blades. And the ice.

And she skated.

∽

She had to stay on the ice an extra minute to pick up the stuffed animals thrown from her family in the stands. A couple of teddy bears. A honeybee with a soft striped middle and a pointy little leather stinger. Natalie must have sent that one along. Claire smiled. There was a chipmunk, courtesy of Keene, no doubt. And a stuffed butterfly with floppy, bright blue wings—that had to be Grandpa's.

"Hey!" Luke met her at the boards. "Got room in those arms for one more present?" She nodded, and he produced a bouquet of black-eyed Susans from behind his back.

"Thanks!"

"Are you going to count the petals?"

"Don't need to." She smiled. "I already know."

Luke walked her over to Groshev, where it felt like she had to wait forever for her score. Finally, the announcer came on; his voice echoed around the rink, and out to the hockey players hanging in posters in the hallways.

"The score for Claire Boucher is a 46.2."

Her personal best by far.

"That's probably going to be good enough for first place!" Tasanee squealed. She'd scored a 43, which put her in second place at the moment. "Or at least silver or bronze if those last two girls are really hot stuff. Oh, Claire, that's awesome! And the top three qualify for junior nationals, so if you're first or second and I'm second or third that means we both go to nationals in December and they're right in Lake Placid this year, so everybody can come!"

She heard Tasanee, and she smiled and nodded as they found seats to watch the last two skaters. But mostly, Claire breathed in the cold, clean air of the rink and fingered the butterfly's soft wings. It was funny. After all this time training, she still felt more like a honeybee than a butterfly, happier as part of a big swarm than out there shining alone.

But she had done it. It didn't matter where the score placed her. In her hand-me-down dress and Charlotte's old skates. She had done it.

She had skated. The way she'd imagined it all those times.

"Ladies!" Groshev called up to them. "I need to go get some paperwork, but I will be seeing you both when it is time for the awards. You are top four—that is certain—and we will soon know the color of the medals, yes?"

"Woo-hoo!" Tasanee hooted, and she and Claire high-fived each other.

Groshev actually smiled. "Yes, you enjoy the woo-hoo tonight. Monday afternoon, we start training again. You were . . . how do you say it . . . hot stuff . . . today. But nationals are a whole new level. We will be stepping it up, yes?"

"Yes!" Tasanee shouted and gave Groshev a wave as he disappeared into the hallway to find his paperwork.

Claire waved, too, but didn't say anything. She needed to have a long conversation with Groshev on Monday—one in which she actually did her share of the talking.

She wasn't the same girl who sat holding her hot chocolate in silence at the Northern Lights rink. She knew what she wanted now and could imagine herself telling Groshev, loud and clear. She could hear it over the clamor of the packed hallways, the swell of the music, the clang of skate blades on metal, the rush of the cheering crowd.

She had made a decision.

CHAPTER 24

The Christmas lights on the big spruce tree by the door twinkled when Claire stepped outside. It was only December fifth, but she'd begged her father to put them up early this year. She wanted to soak up every minute of Christmas. She felt like she had missed so much of the summer and fall.

"Watch out!" A snowball whizzed by her right ear and splatted against the door. "Sorry," Jake said. "I was aiming for Christopher."

"You throw like Mom!" Christopher shouted from behind the spruce.

"Hey—I heard that!" Mom stepped out the door and tugged at the pom-pom on Claire's hat. "You almost ready to head to Lake Placid?"

Claire couldn't believe nationals had come so soon. It seemed like just last week she was on the podium in Buffalo, having that silver medal put around her neck. A girl from Long Island had taken the gold, and one from Albany had come in third. Tasanee had been disappointed she didn't place in the top three to qualify for nationals, but she'd still earned a platinum medal like the one Claire got in Burlington.

Alexis had landed all her jumps but stumbled during a

spin and fell. She'd recovered with a beautiful, high double axel at the end, though, and still came in fifth. Meghan had scored a personal worst, if there is such a thing. The judges had given her a 27, which was probably a gift, anyway, but it put her dead last, even before she was disqualified for what happened on the video. She and her mother moved back to New York City two weeks later. Claire heard her mother had gotten a new TV reporting job, and Meghan was going to start spending weekends with her father and Monica so she'd get to see him more often.

The drive to Lake Placid was longer this afternoon but prettier, too. Even though it wasn't yet dinnertime, the sky had darkened to a deep gray blue, and Christmas lights twinkled outside every house. Claire wondered if they had some sort of Christmas law here; it seemed like not a single house was without them, and the little family hotels had millions of the tiny white lights she loved best.

"Does it feel funny to be here as a spectator?" her mother asked as they walked through the Olympic Center door.

"A little." She hadn't been back here since the Monday after regionals, when she'd arrived at the training session without her skates, thanked Groshev for extending her scholarship again, and explained to him why she was turning it down.

"But you have so much . . . how do you say it . . . so much potential. And you have come such a long way. Are you sure I cannot persuade you to continue?" He looked down at her with those sharp dark eyes, and she looked right back. "You are a more confident skater. So much stronger than you were when you first came."

Claire smiled a little. "I know." She was stronger. And she'd choose her own dreams from now on. She had a bunch of them to get started on. "Thank you for everything."

She walked down the long hallway, out the athletes' entrance door, and right up into her dad's truck. "All set."

❧

Today they'd come in the big front doors with everyone else. Claire clutched a shopping bag with a plush fairy doll to toss to Tasanee after her routine, a frog for Abby, and something special for Luke. The hallways were lined with booths again, more than ever, since this was nationals.

"No second thoughts?" Her father looked out toward the ice, where the first skaters were warming up.

"Nope." Claire stopped at the snack booth. "Two large popcorns, please, and a cotton candy."

She turned and spotted Tasanee coming down the hall in her skate guards. "Oh, here!" She handed her mother the popcorn and gave Jake the cotton candy. "Don't eat it all. I'll be right back."

She ran so fast she almost knocked Tasanee right off her skates. "We're here! When do you skate?"

"I'm fifth," she said. "I just can't . . . I can't believe I'm actually here."

"You're going to do great." Claire smiled at her and looked down at the book in her hand. "Let me guess . . . raging mermaids?"

Tasanee laughed and held it up so Claire could see the cover, a teenaged girl in an old-fashioned dress looking up at the sky. "No, actually, this one's about a girl who makes her own homestead claim out west. I decided to try something new."

"Does she have a cow pond?" Claire grinned. "Maybe I would like that one."

"Listen, Claire, I have to get going, but I just . . . I can't thank you enough."

Claire shook her head. "I stepped down from nationals because it wasn't what I wanted, no matter what Groshev said. The fact that it opened up a spot for you was just a nice little bonus."

"Well, thanks for the bonus then." Tasanee wrapped her in a tight quick hug. "And don't worry about Groshev. He'll forgive you soon enough. He just signed up some ten-year-old he spotted at a show in Vermont. I have to go. Fingers crossed, okay?"

"Fingers and toes, but you won't need luck." Claire waved to her and headed down the hallway to find her family.

"Hey, fellow Fibo-nerd." She turned and saw Luke, dressed in a tuxedo outfit. He and Abby had qualified for the pairs competition. They were doing their Phantom routine again. His mask was up on top of his head, and he held out his arms.

"Hey, Phantom!" She stepped in and gave him a quick hug. He was still warm from practicing, and it made her face warm, too. She pulled back. "Good luck tonight. I'll be watching."

"When are you coming back?" He grinned.

She shook her head and smiled. "Not anytime soon, as much as I miss you and Abby and the granola bars. I joined the MATHCOUNTS team. We're competing in Plattsburgh this winter. And I'm junior coaching at home, and I have my first competition with my new synchro team in February. I'm where I want to be for right now."

"Yes, but can anyone on your synchro team do a perfect golden spiral?"

"Pretty much all of them." Claire grinned. "And there are twenty-one of us, too. Take that, Mr. Fibonacci."

"Well, sure, but can any of them do this?" His eyes twinkled as he struck the goofy, wobbly spiral pose. "You must miss me terribly."

"I'll see you at the mall, remember?"

He put his foot down and raised his eyebrows at her. "Promise?"

Her heart jumped. "Promise."

"Luke, come *on!*" Abby hustled down the hallway and saw Claire. "Oh, I should have known. You're the only thing that would hold him up tonight. Let's go, loverboy."

His face flushed, and Claire felt hers burning, too. "Here." He pulled a CD out of his skating bag and handed it to her. "I brought it hoping you'd be here. I think you'll like it." He waved and rushed to catch up with Abby.

Claire looked down at the CD. He had scribbled "Rockin' the Cow Pond" on it in blue marker. She laughed and headed for her seat, trying to guess what he'd put on the CD. Probably some Journey. And Springsteen. Maybe that Fleetwood Mac song "Don't Stop Thinking About Tomorrow." And that one about the Constitution. That would be totally Luke. Her mother waved to her as she started climbing. "Look who we found!"

"Hannah, you made it!" Claire took the steps two at a time. "Did you recover from practice this morning? She worked us hard. I thought I was going to collapse."

Hannah laughed. "It was worth it, though. That last part of our routine is awesome. I'm so glad you and Natalie joined." She looked around. "How come she's not here tonight?"

"Keene's birthday." Claire had been invited to the party, but she'd promised Tasanee she'd be here, and Natalie understood. Claire reclaimed her popcorn from Jake and sat down next to Hannah just as the rink grew quiet. "Oh, good, they're starting!"

"And now . . ." Bob-O's voice rang out through the arena. Having nationals here must have made that guy's whole life.

She reached in for a handful of popcorn as the first skater's music started. It was from the opera *Carmen*, the same song that girl had skated to at regionals. Claire watched and listened as the music picked up and the girl's feet moved faster into a cool footwork sequence.

Claire would have to try that one on the pond soon. Normally her mother wouldn't let her out skating until January, but it had been so cold the first week in December the ice had to be seven or eight inches thick already.

Next weekend, Charlotte would be home for Christmas break, and Claire would finally get to show off the routine she'd skated in Buffalo. She couldn't wait to show Charlotte the double axel, but more than that, she couldn't wait to skate with her again.

Claire dug to the bottom of the popcorn box, tossed a few partly popped kernels into her mouth, and let her eyes close. The notes from *Carmen* swept her over the ice in her mind. She liked this one.

It would be perfect for the spring Maple Show.

Claire opened her eyes, licked the butter from her fingers, and leaned back against her father's knees.

Just perfect.

༄

"Your friend Tasanee was great. She must have been so excited," Mom said on the ride home. Claire was sitting between the two boys in back so they wouldn't fight, but they'd both drifted off to sleep.

"She was. And tenth place is amazing, given how many girls were competing."

"And Luke and Abby were something to see, too," Dad said.

"Yep." They'd come in eighth in the pairs competition, out of fifteen. Claire had climbed down to meet them when they came off the ice. Luke was already smiling the biggest smile she'd ever seen, but somehow it had grown even bigger when she handed him the pineapple in keeping with their Fibo-nerd tradition.

When they pulled into the driveway, the Christmas lights outside the sugarhouse twinkled, and it was just starting to snow. Big, perfect, fluffy flakes. Claire stepped out of the car and caught one on her tongue. She looked over toward the pond. The snow hadn't accumulated yet, and the surface was perfect.

"Come on, boys." Mom managed to wake Christopher and guide him toward the porch, but Dad had to hoist Jake over his shoulder to carry him up the walkway and into the house. Halfway through the screen door, Claire stopped. She breathed in the cold air, and it filled her up. A snowflake landed on her nose. She wasn't quite ready for tonight to end.

"Go ahead." Mom stepped back onto the porch, holding up Claire's skating bag. She smiled. "I know you've been waiting. Go on. It's thick enough."

She didn't need to be told more than once. Claire took the bag and ran, boots crunching over the frozen leaves, to the splintery bench by the pond. She put on her skates, tightened the laces, and looked up to catch another snowflake. But the snow had stopped. The moon was starting to drift out from behind the clouds, and she could see better than before. The smooth black surface of the ice. The fir trees standing guard on the other bank. The black brown skeletons of maples behind them.

Had it really been less than nine months ago she'd come home from the Maple Show to share the news about her scholarship? So much had changed. But not everything.

She stepped over the frozen reeds at the edge of the pond and glided out. The ice groaned its familiar groan underneath her skates. Ice made strange sounds. The first time she'd skated out here as a little girl, the noises scared her, and she'd gone flying back to the bench in tears. But Grandpa had told her that all those unearthly noises—the pops and hisses and low grumbles that sounded like timpani drums—were just the pond talking to her, saying welcome to winter.

She was lucky the ice had formed so well so soon this year. Sometimes it froze and then broke up and froze again in big lumpy chunks and you couldn't skate at all. But tonight, it was just right.

Claire skated around a few times, found an extra smooth

space, and tried a spin. Charlotte would be so excited when she got home and found the pond frozen. There was so much to look forward to—Christmas and MATHCOUNTS and her synchro competition coming up and maybe even meeting up with Luke at the mall. But tonight, she was just thankful Mom let her out. Thankful to have the time and the cow pond and the trees.

Tonight, she skated under the moon and listened to the music of the ice.

Welcome to winter, it said. Welcome home.

ACKNOWLEDGMENTS

I started writing *Sugar and Ice* by accident in the summer of 2008, when my daughter signed up for a basic skills skating camp at the Olympic Center in Lake Placid. I had plans to hang out in the coffee shop across the street, revising a different book while she skated, but somehow I missed the fine print about the parent education program that went along with the skating camp. I found myself in a room next to the rink, listening to a parade of experts talk about everything from blades to blisters and costumes to coaches. After a few moments of panic over the book-that-would-have-to-be-revised-another-time, I settled in and started taking notes on what turned out to be an education indeed. I'm thankful to Lake Placid Skating for the inspiration, and especially to Dr. Mara Smith, who talked with me about sports psychology and the drama that can sometimes surround competitive skating.

Other friends in the world of figure skating taught me the difference between a salchow and a toe loop. Thanks to Sarah and Alexa Cosgro, the West family, and everyone from the Skating Club of the Adirondacks. Gilberto Viadana from the Lake Placid Skating School was kind enough to let me sit in on his coaching sessions and to read this manuscript for accuracy.

Figure-skating readers Meghan Weeden, Kianna Giroux, and Sabine Gang helped out by reviewing the early manuscript as well. Any errors that may have slipped by in spite of their efforts are entirely my own.

Thanks to math teachers Gale Carroll and Teresa Niles for consulting with me on Claire's Fibonacci project, to the folks at Sanger's Sugar House and the Parker Family Maple Farm for putting on delicious pancake breakfasts every spring and providing much of the inspiration for the setting of *Sugar and Ice*, and to Dave Greenwood, who taught me about honeybees and loaned me a beekeeper's suit so that I could experience what Claire experienced in the orchard with Natalie.

Writer friends Loree Griffin Burns, Eric Luper, Liza Martz, Ammi-Joan Paquette, Marjorie Light, Stephanie Gorin, Julie Berry, and Linda Urban offered feedback and encouragement along the way. The great librarians at the Plattsburgh Public Library were always there when I needed to do research or just find a quiet place to write, and my colleagues and students at Stafford Middle School inspire me every day.

An editor is a lot like a coach, and Mary Kate Castellani at Walker is the smartest, most supportive coach an author could wish for. Many thanks to her, along with the rest of the amazing team at Walker Books for Young Readers: Emily Easton, Beth Eller, Katie Fee, Deb Shapiro, Anna Dalziel, Nicole Gastonguay, and Susan Hom. Many thanks as well to Joe Cepeda, whose stunning art has graced the covers for two of my novels now.

My agent, Jennifer Laughran, is simply the best. Thanks, Jenn, for all that you do, and for cheering when I told you I was writing a book about mean girls on ice.

Like Claire, I am blessed to have a loving and supportive family. My parents, Tom and Gail Schirmer, always encouraged me to follow my dreams, even when those dreams changed along the way. I'm grateful to them, to the real Aunt Maureen and Uncle George, and to all of the Schirmers, Messners, Rupperts, Lahues, and Alois. Most of all, thanks to Tom, Jake, and Ella, who come along on research trips, skate with me on the frozen lake, and make everything more fun.